CONTENTS

The Way
We Lived Then –

The *English Story* in the 1940s

Introduction by Woodrow Wyatt

8 Grafton Street, London WI
1989

William Collins Sons & Co. Ltd
London · Glasgow · Sydney · Auckland
Toronto · Johannesburg

English Story first published 1941–50 in ten
volumes by William Collins Sons & Co. Ltd

Copyright all stories Woodrow Wyatt

This selection first published 1989

BRITISH LIBRARY CATALOGUING IN PUBLICATION DATA

Wyatt, Woodrow
The Way We Lived Then –
[English story. Selections] The Way We Lived Then:
The English Story in the 1940s.
I. Title
I. Short stories in English, 1900 – Anthologies
823′.01′08

ISBN 0-00-223539-0

Set in Linotron Ehrhardt by
Rowland Phototypesetting Ltd
Bury St Edmunds, Suffolk
Printed and bound in Great Britain by
William Collins Sons & Co. Ltd, Glasgow

INTRODUCTION

It was Edward J. O'Brien, an American living in England, who fired me with enthusiasm for the short story. Yearly he published in book form his selection of the best short stories, English and American. He included one I wrote in an undergraduate magazine in his choice for 1940. At that time several magazines which used to publish well-written short stories had disappeared. Yet, paradoxically, there was a growing demand for short stories which could be read, in their off duty spells, by those serving in the Armed Forces, the Fire Service and similar organizations when there was not always the inclination or leisure to read and absorb full-length novels.

I went to see Edward J. O'Brien in his pretty house on the green at Gerrards Cross and talked to him about starting a new magazine containing previously unpublished short stories. I believed there were many good writers who, because of their war occupations, were unable to settle down to writing novels. Then paper rationing caused the. government to ban new magazines and the only alternative was to seek a publisher who would be willing to publish new short stories in book form. I found him in a little book and paper cluttered attic room in the building occupied at that time by Collins in St James's Place. F. T. Smith was the Managing Editor of Collins, who affected no literary airs, and seemed to me more like an elderly local bank manager than a man of letters. But he was a shrewd judge of what might sell and was amused by my youthful eagerness and conviction that the short story collections I proposed might add new authors to the Collins list which he managed so successfully. He agreed with avuncular kindness to give the project a try.

Initially Edward J. O'Brien supplied numerous names and addresses of likely contributors. I also wrote letters to weekly papers with literary pages asking for contributions. Short stories rolled in by the hundreds. Many of the writers were unknown, although there was a spattering from people like Sylvia Townsend Warner, a story by whom was published in the First Series and whose story, published in the Sixth Series, is included here.

I read all the stories submitted which seemed to have a spark of interest. They were sorted out and the possibles sent on to me, originally by my first wife, and later by friends, at the various places the Army posted me. I did the final editing for the First Series at Dover, during the 1940 Battle of Britain, where as a Second Lieutenant I was commanding a platoon shelled by the German long-range artillery from France and attacked by German aircraft from overhead. This was a different form of excitement from the thrill I got from handling the manuscripts from which the First Series of *English Story* was to be formed. For the rest of the war the manuscripts followed me and none was ever lost whether they were carted around in the back of a jeep in Normandy or received through the Army post in India.

To the pleasure of Mr Smith and myself the First Series sold 10,000 copies and was a success among the critics. Praise came from the *New Statesman*, the *Observer*, *The Sunday Times*, *The Times Literary Supplement*, the *Listener*, the *Scotsman* and others. All encouraged the venture. The critics supported us throughout; James Agate and Stevie Smith wrote appreciatively of later Series. Elizabeth Bowen, reviewing the Fifth Series, described *English Story* as an increasing success. John Betjeman called one Series 'magnificent' and writing of the Ninth Series said, 'Each previous book in this Series has been an equally valuable collection,' while Peter Quennell remarked of the Ninth Series that 'It is a book not to miss.' C. P. Snow called it 'much the best of the nine', and Pamela Hansford-Johnson made similar comments, so the high standards we began with were maintained throughout.

After the war, with the end of paper rationing for book and magazine publishers, and with a less frenetic life for readers, new short stories in book form began to lose their wartime popularity to full-length novels and other literary forms. The Tenth Series, published in 1950, although selling more than many novels do now, had so dropped in circulation that the publishers understandably thought that ten years had been a long enough run.

The times had their tragedies, their humour and their optimism. In this selection the moods of the war and just after are reflected. The young poet Alun Lewis writes of what befell a soldier returning on leave. The death of Alun Lewis, on active service in Burma in 1944, at the age of twenty-nine was a bitter loss of a life which promised so much for literature. He won for a story in another Series, the £10.00 prize we gave annually in memory of Edward J. O'Brien. £10.00 does not seem much now but its 1989 equivalent would be at least £250.00.

Charles Furbank, a Sergeant, who wrote 'Conversations in Ebury Street', was killed flying with the RAF in August 1942 when only twenty-four. He had not had time to write more than two short stories for the old *London Mercury* and one in the Second Series of *English Story*, but the possibility of imminent death did not cast a shadow over his enthusiasm for life. None of us thought we would be killed and looked forward cheerfully: it is a pity that not all of us were right.

Obviously my choice of stories was influenced by the background and the lives of the writers and myself. Although contemporary in spirit, I hope this selection shows that the stories were more than of transient interest and will repay reading indefinitely. Elizabeth Bowen, Angus Wilson, Sylvia Townsend Warner, J. Maclaren-Ross and Stephen Spender contributed stories, republished here, worthy of the best of their work. Stephen Spender's long story, almost a novella, *The Fool and the Princess* is a remarkable account of an impressionable young married Englishman, attracted by a beautiful Russian girl in a displaced persons' camp in occupied Germany where he was an official immediately after the war, and accurately and fascinatingly records the political attitudes of his generation.

All the writers included here, whether well-known or not, responded in some manner to the decade of war and its aftermath. It was a period of change, wonderment, fear and hope. It has a literature of its own which, jostled out of memory by the writing of subsequent decades, has largely been forgotten. Now interest is reviving in what the war-battered writers of almost fifty years ago had to say. I hope this volume makes a good introduction for a wider search into the literature of those unusual years.

WOODROW WYATT

Songs My Father Sang Me

ELIZABETH BOWEN

'What's the matter,' he asked, 'have I said something?'

Not troubling to get him quite into focus, she turned her head and said, 'No, why – did you say anything?'

'Or p'r'aps you don't like this place?'

'I don't mind it – why?' she said, looking round the night club, which was not quite as dark as a church, as though for the first time. At some tables you had to look twice, to see who was there; what lights there were were dissolved in a haze of smoke; the walls were rather vaultlike, with no mirrors; on the floor dancers drifted like pairs of vertical fish. He, meanwhile, studied her from across their table with neither anxiety nor acute interest, but with a dreamlike caricature of both. Then he raised the bottle between them and said, 'Mm-mm?' to which she replied by placing the flat of her hand mutely, mulishly, across the top of her glass. Not annoyed, he shrugged, filled up his own and continued, 'Then anything isn't really the matter, then?'

'This tune, this song, is the matter.'

'Oh – shall we dance?'

'No.' Behind her agelessly girlish face, sleekly framed by the cut of her fawn-blonde hair, there passed a wave of genuine trouble for which her features had no vocabulary. 'It's what they're playing – this tune.'

'It's pre-war,' he said knowledgeably.

'It's last war.'

'Well, last war's pre-war.'

'It's the tune my father remembered he used to dance to; it's the tune I remember him always trying to sing.'

'Why, is your father dead?'

'No, I don't suppose so. Why?'

'Sorry,' he said quickly. 'I mean, if . . .'

'Sorry, why are you sorry?' she said, raising her eyebrows. 'Didn't I ever tell you about my father? I always thought he made me rather a bore. Wasn't it you I was telling about my father?'

'No. I suppose it must have been someone else. One meets so many people.'

'Oh, what?' she said. 'Have I hurt your feelings? But you haven't got any feelings about me.'

'Only because you haven't got any feelings about me.'

'Haven't I?' she said, as though really wanting to know. 'Still, it hasn't seemed all the time as though we were quite a flop.'

'Look,' he said, 'don't be awkward. Tell me about your father.'

'He was twenty-six.'

'When?'

'How do you mean, "when"? Twenty-six was my father's age. He was tall and lean and leggy, with a casual sort of way of swinging himself about. He was fair, and the shape of his face was a rather long narrow square. Sometimes his eyes faded in until you could hardly see them; sometimes he seemed to be wearing a blank mask. You really only quite got the plan of his face when it was turned halfway between a light and a shadow – *then* his eyebrows and eyehollows, the dints just over his nostrils, the cut of his upper lip and the cleft in his chin, and the broken in-and-out outline down from his temple past his cheekbone into his jaw all came out at you, like a message you had to read in a single flash.'

She paused and lighted a cigarette. He said, 'You sound as though you had never got used to him.'

She went on, 'My father was one of the young men who were not killed in the last war. He was a man in the last war until that stopped; then I don't quite know what he was, and I don't think he ever quite knew either. He got his commission and first went out to France about 1915, I think he said. When he got leaves he got back to London and had good times, by which I mean something larky but quite romantic, in the course of one of which, I don't know which one, he fell in love with my mother and they used to go dancing, and got engaged in that leave and got married the next. My mother was a flapper, if you know about flappers? They were the pin-ups *de ces jours*, and at the same time inspired idealistic feeling. My mother was dark and fluffy and as slim as a wraith; a great *glacé* ribbon bow tied her hair back and stood out like a calyx behind her face, and her hair itself hung down in a plume so long that it tickled my father's hand while he held her while they were dancing and while she sometimes swam up at him with her violet eyes. Each time he had to go back to the front again she was miserable, and had to put her hair up, because her relations said it was high time. But sometimes when he got back again on leave she returned to being a flapper again, to please him. Between his leaves she had to go back to live with her mother and sisters in West Kensington; and her sisters had a whole pack of business friends who had somehow never had to go near the front, and all these combined in an effort to cheer her up, but, as she always wrote to my father, nothing did any good. I suppose everyone felt it was for the best when they knew there was going to be the patter of little feet. I wasn't actually *born* till the summer of 1918. If you remember, I told you my age last night.

'The first thing *I* remember, upon becoming conscious, was living in one of those bungalows on the flats near Staines. The river must have been somewhere, but I don't think I saw it. The only point about that region is that it has no point and that it goes on and on. I think there are floods there sometimes, there would be nothing to stop them; a forest fire would be what is needed really, but that would not be possible as there are no trees. It would have looked better, really, just left as primeval marsh, but someone had once said, "Let there be bungalows." If you ever motored anywhere near it you probably asked yourself who lives there, and why. Well, my father and mother and I did. And why? Because it was cheap, and there was no one to criticize how you were getting on. Our bungalow was tucked well away in the middle, got at by a sort of maze of, in those days, unmade roads. I'm glad to say I've forgotten which one it was. Most of our neighbours kept themselves to themselves for, probably, like ours, the best reasons, but most of them kept hens also; we didn't even do that. All round us, nature ran riot between corrugated iron, clothes-lines and creosoted lean-to sheds.

'I know that our bungalow had been taken furnished; the only things we seemed to have of our own were a number of satin cushions with satin fruits stitched on. In order to dislodge my biscuit crumbs from the satin apples my mother used to shake the cushions out of the window on to the lawn. Except for the prettiness of the dandelions, our lawn got to look and feel rather like a hearthrug; I mean, it got covered with threads and cinders and shreds; once when I was crawling on it I got a pin in my hand, another time I got sharp glass beads in my knee. The next-door hens used to slip through and pick about; never, apparently, quite in vain. At the far end, some Dorothy Perkins roses tried to climb up a pergola that was always falling down. I remember my father reaching up in his shirt-sleeves, trying to nail it up. Another thing he had to do in our home was apply the whole of his strength to the doors, french window and windows, which warped until they would not open nor shut. I used to come up behind him and push too.

'The war by now, of course, had been over for some years; my father was out of the British Army and was what was called taking his time and looking around. For how long he had been doing so I can't exactly tell you. He not only read all the "post vacant" advertisements every day but composed and succeeded in getting printed an advertisement of himself, which he read aloud to me: it said he was prepared to go anywhere and try anything. I said, "But what's an ex-officer?" and he said, "I am." Our dining-room table, which was for some reason, possibly me, sticky, was always spread with new newspapers he had just brought home, and he used to be leaning over them on his elbows, biting harder and harder on the stem of his pipe. I don't think I discovered for some years later that the principal reason for newspapers is news. My father never looked at them for that reason – just as he always lost interest in any book in which he had lost his place. Or perhaps he was not in the mood for world events. My mother had never cared much for them at the best of times. "To think of all we expected after the war," she used to say to my father, from day to day.

'My mother, by this time, had had her hair shingled – in fact, *I* never remember her any other way than with a dark shaved point tapered down the back of her neck. I don't know when she'd begun to be jealous of him and me. Every time he came back from an interview that he hadn't got to, or from an interview that hadn't come to anything, he used to bring me back something to cheer himself up, and the wheels off all the mechanical toys got mixed with the beads and the threads and the cinders into our lawn. What my mother was really most afraid of was that my father would bundle us all off into the great open spaces in order to start afresh somewhere and grow something. I imagine he knew several chaps who had, or were going to. After one or two starts on the subject he shut up, but I could see she could see he was nursing it. It frustrated her from nagging at him all out about not succeeding in getting a job in England; she was anxious not to provide an opening for him to say, "Well, there's always one thing we *could* do . . ." The hard glassy look her eyes got made them look like doll's eyes, which may partly have been what kept me from liking dolls. So they practically never talked about anything. I don't think she even knew he minded about her hair.

'You may be going to ask when my father sang. He often *began* to sing – when he hammered away at the pergola, when something he thought of suddenly struck him as good, when the heave he gave at the warped french window sent it flying open into the garden. He was constantly starting to sing, but he never got very far – you see, he had no place where he could sing unheard. The walls were thin and the lawn was tiny and the air round the bungalow was so silent and heavy that my mother was forced to listen to every note. The lordly way my father would burst out singing, like the lordly way he cocked his hat over one eye, had come to annoy her, in view of everything else. But the still more unfortunate thing was that my father only knew or else only liked, two tunes, which were two tunes out of the bygone years which made him think of the war and being in love. Yes, they were dance tunes; yes, we have just heard one; yes, they also reminded my mother of war and love. So when he had got to the fourth or fifth bar of either, she would call out to know if he wanted to drive her mad. He would stop and say, "Sorry," but if he was in the mood he'd be well away the next minute with the alternative tune, and she would be put to the trouble of stopping that.

'Mother did not know what to look like now she was not a flapper. Mostly she looked like nothing – I wonder whether she knew. Perhaps that was what she saw in the satin cushions: they looked like something – at least, to her. The day she and I so suddenly went to London to call on her sister's friend she did certainly manage, however, to look like something. My father, watching us down the garden path, ventured no comment on her or my appearance. However, which ought to have cheered me up, we created quite a furore in the train. We went sailing into the richly-appointed office of mother's sister's friend, who was one of those who, during the war, had felt mother should be cheered up. Can I, need I, describe him? The usual kind of business pudge, in a suit. He looked in a reluctant way at my mother, and reluctantly, slightly morbidly, at me. I don't know how I got the impression mother held all the cards. The conversation, of course, flowed over my head – I just cruised round and round the room, knocking objects over. But the outcome – as I gathered when we got home – was that mother's sister's friend said he'd give my father a job. He had said he could use an ex-officer, provided it was an ex-officer with charm. What my father would have to do was to interest housewives, not in himself but in vacuum cleaners. If it helped to interest some housewives in vacuum cleaners, he could interest them just a little bit in himself. Mother's sister's friend called this, using judgment of character.

'When my mother, that evening, put all this to my father, he did not say anything but simply stood and stared. *She* said, "Then I suppose you want us to starve?"

'So my father stopped being a problem and became a travelling salesman. The best part was that the firm allowed him a car.

'I must say for my mother that she did not ask my father how he was getting on. At least she had much less trouble about the singing; sometimes he'd be away for two or three days together; when he was home he simply sprawled in his chair, now and then asking when there'd be something to eat, as unmusical as a gramophone with the spring broken. When I came filtering in he sometimes opened one eye and said, "And what have you been doing?" – as though he'd just finished telling me what he'd been doing himself. He garaged the car some way down the next road, and in the mornings when he was starting off I used to walk with him to the garage. He used to get into the car, start up the engine, back out, then look round at me and say, "Like to come out on the job? – yes, I bet you would," then let the clutch in and whizz off. Something about this always made me feel sick.

'I don't of course clearly remember when this began, or how long it went on for, but I know when it stopped. The night before my seventh birthday was a June night, because my birthdays are in June. The people who lived all round us were sitting out, on the verandahs or on their lawns, but my mother had sent me to bed early because she was having a party for me next day and did not want to get me over-excited. My birth-cake which had arrived from the shop was on the dining-room sideboard, with a teacloth over it to keep the flies off, and my father and mother were in the lounge with the french window shut, because she had several things to say to him that she did not want the people all round to hear. The heat travelled through the roof into all the rooms, so that I could not sleep; also, my bed was against the wall of my room, and the lounge was the other side of the wall. My mother went on like someone who has been saving up – just some touch, I suppose, had been needed to set her off. She said she would like to know why there was not more money – my father's job, I suppose now, was on a commission basis. Or, she said, was he keeping another woman – a thing she had heard that most travelling salesmen did. She said she really felt quite ashamed of having foisted my father on to her sister's friend, and that she only wondered how long the firm would stand for it. She said her sisters pitied her, though she had tried to conceal from them that her life was hell. My father, who had as usual got home late and as usual had not yet had any supper, could not be heard saying anything. My mother then said she wished she knew why she had married him, and would like still more to know why he had married her.

'My father said, "You were so lovely – you've no idea."

'Next morning there was a heat-haze over everything. I bustled into the dining room to see if there was anything on my plate. I forget what my mother had given me, but her richest sister had sent me a manicure case in a purple box; all the objects had purple handles and lay in grooves on white velvet. While I was taking them out and putting them back again, my father suddenly looked up from his coffee and said *his* present for me was in the car, and that I'd have to come out and fetch it. My mother could hardly say no to this, though of course I saw her opening her mouth. So out we set, I gripping the manicure case. I don't think my father seemed odder than usual, though he was on the point of doing an unexpected thing – when he had got the car started and backed out he suddenly held open the other door and said, "Come on, nip in, look sharp; my present to you is a day trip." So then I nipped in and we drove off, as though this were the most natural thing in the world.

'The car was a two-seater, with a let down hood . . . No, of course I cannot remember what make it was. That morning, the hood was down. Locked up in the dickie behind my father was the specimen vacuum cleaner he interested women in. He drove fast, and as we hit the bumps in the road I heard the parts of the cleaner clonking about. As we drove, the sun began to burn its way through the haze, making the roses in some of the grander gardens look almost impossibly large and bright. My bare knees began to grill on the leather cushion, and the crumples eased out of the front of my cotton frock.

'I had never been with my father when he was driving a car – it felt as though speed and power were streaming out of him, and as if he and I were devouring everything that we passed. I sat slumped round with my cheek against the hot cushion and sometimes stared at his profile, sometimes stared at his wrists, till he squinted round and said, "Anything wrong with *me*?" Later on, he added, "Why not look at the scenery?" By that time there *was* some scenery, if that means grass and trees; in fact, these had been going on for some time, in a green band streaming behind my father's face. When I said, "Where are we going?" he said, "Well, where *are* we going?" At that point I saw quite a large hill, in fact a whole party of them, lapping into each other as though they would never stop, and never having seen anything of the kind before I could not help saying, "Oh, I say, look!"

'My father gave a nod, without stopping singing – I told you he had begun to sing? He had not only started but gone on; when he came to the end of his first tune he said, "Pom-*pom*," like a drum, then started through it again; after that he worked around to the second, which he sang two or three times, with me joining in. We both liked the second still better, and how right we were – and it's worn well, hasn't it? That's what this band's just played.'

'Oh, what they've just played?' he said, and looked narrowly at the band; while, reaching round for the bottle on the table between them, he lifted it to replenish her glass and his. This time she did not see or did not bother to stop him; she looked at her full glass vaguely, then vaguely drank. After a minute she went on.

'Ginger beer, sausage rolls, chocolate – that was what we

bought when we stopped at the village shop. Also my father bought a blue comb off a card of combs, with which he attempted to do my hair, which had blown into tags and ratstails over my eyes and face. He looked at me while he combed in a puzzled way, as though something about me that hadn't struck him became a problem to him for the first time. I said, "Aren't we going to sell any vacuum cleaners?" and he said, "We'll try and interest the Berkshire Downs." I thought that meant, meet a family; but all we did was turn out of the village and start up a rough track, to where there could not be any people at all. The car climbed with a slow but exciting roar; from the heat of the engine and the heat of the sun the chocolate in the paper bag in my hands was melting by the time we came to the top.

'From the top, where we lay on our stomachs in the shade of the car, we could see – oh well, can't you imagine, can't you? It was an outsize June day. The country below us looked all colours, and was washed over in the most reckless way with light; going on and on into the distance the clumps of trees and the roofs of villages and the church towers had quivering glimmers round them; but most of all there was space, sort of moulded space, and the blue of earth ran into the blue of sky.

'My father's face was turned away from me, propped up on his hand. I finally said to him, "What's that?"

'"What's what?" he said, startled.

'"What we're looking at."

'"England," he said, "that's England. I thought I'd like to see her again."

'"But don't we live in England?"

'He took no notice. "How I loved her," he said.

'"Oh, but don't you now?"

'"I've lost her," he said, "or she's lost me; I don't quite know which; I don't understand what's happened." He rolled round and looked at me and said, "But *you* like it, don't you? I thought I'd like you to see, if just once, what I once saw."

'I was well into the third of my sausage rolls: my mouth full, I could only stare at my father. He said, "And there's something else down there – see it?" I screwed my eyes up but still only saw the distance. "Peace," he said. "Look hard at it; don't forget it."

'"What's peace?" I said.

'"An idea you have when there's a war on, to make you fight well. An idea that gets lost when there isn't a war."

'I licked pastry-crumbs off my chin and began on chocolate. By this time my father lay on his back, with his fingers thatched together over his eyes; he talked, but more to the sky than me. None of the things he was saying now went anywhere near my brain – a child's brain, how could they? – his actual words are gone as though I had never heard them, but his meaning lodged itself in some part of my inside, and is still there and has grown up with me. He talked about war and how he had once felt, and about leaves and love and dancing and going back to the war, then the birth of me – "Seven years ago today," he said, "seven years; I remember how they brought me the telegram."

'Something else, on top of the sausage and heat and chocolate suddenly made me feel sick and begin to cry. "Oh please, oh please don't," I said, "it's my birthday."

'"Don't what?" he said. I, naturally, didn't know. My father again looked at me, with the same expression he had worn when attempting to comb my hair. Something about me – my age? – was a proposition. Then he shut his eyes, like – I saw later, not at the time – somebody finally banishing an idea. "No; it wouldn't work," he said. "It simply couldn't be done. You can wait for me if you want. I can't wait for you."

'Then he began acting like somebody very sleepy: he yawned and yawned at me till I yawned at him. I didn't feel sick any more, but the heat of the afternoon came down like a grey-blue blanket over my head. "What you and I want," my father said, watching me, "is a good sleep."

'I wish I could tell you at *which* moment I fell asleep, and stopped blurrily looking at him between my eyelids, because *that* was the moment when I last saw my father.

'When I woke, there was no more shadow on my side of

the car; the light had changed and everything looked bright yellow. I called to my father but he did not answer, for the adequate reason that he was not there. He was gone. For some reason I wasn't at all frightened; I thought he must have gone to look for something for us for tea. I remembered that I was not at my birthday party, and I must say I thought twice about that pink cake. I was more bored than anything, till I remembered my manicure case, which owing to the funniness of the day I had not been able to open a second time. I took the objects out of their velvet bedding and began to prod at my nails, as I'd seen my mother do. Then I got up and walked, once more, all the way round the car. It was then that I noticed what I had missed before: a piece of white paper twisted into the radiator. I couldn't read handwriting very well, but did at last make out what my father had put. *"The car and the vacuum cleaner are the property of Messrs X and X"* (the firm of my mother's sister's friend), *"the child is the property of Mrs So-and-so, of Such-and-such"* (I needn't bother to give you my mother's name and the name of our bungalow), *"the manicure case, the comb and anything still left in the paper bags are the property of the child. Signed ——"* It was signed with my father's name.

'The two dots I saw starting to zigzag up the side of the down turned out to be two sweating policemen. What happened when they came to where I was was interesting at the moment but is not interesting now. They checked up on the message on the front of the car, then told me my father had telephoned to the police station, and that I was to be a good girl and come with them. When they had checked up on the cleaner, we all drove down. I remember the constable's knobbly, sticky red hands looked queer on the wheel where my father's had lately been . . . At the police station, someone or other's wife made quite a fuss about me and gave me tea, then we piled into another car and drove on again. I was soon dead asleep; and I only woke when we stopped in the dark at the gate of the bungalow.

'Having tottered down the path, in the light from the front

door, my mother clawed me out of the car, sobbing. I noticed her breath smelt unusual. We and the policeman then trooped into the lounge, where the policeman kept nodding and jotting things on a pad. To cheer up my mother he said that England was very small – "And he's not, so far as you know, in possession of a passport?" I sucked blobs of chocolate off the front of my frock while my mother described my father to the policeman. "But no doubt," the policeman said, "he'll be thinking better of this. A man's home is a man's home, I always say."

'When my mother and I were left alone in the lounge, we stared at each other in the electric light. While she asked if I knew how unnatural my father was, she kept pouring out a little more from the bottle: she said she had to have medicine to settle her nerves, but it seemed to act on her nerves just the opposite way. That I wouldn't say what my father had said and done set her off fairly raving against my father. To put it mildly, she lost all kind of control. She finished up with: "And such a fool, too – a fool, a fool!"

'"He is not a fool," I said. "He's my father."

'"He is not your father," she screamed, "and he is a fool."

'That made me stare at her, and her stare at me.

'"How do you mean," I said, "my father is not my father?"

'My mother's reaction to this was exactly like as if someone had suddenly pitched a pail of cold water over her. She pulled herself up and something jumped in her eyes. She said she had not said anything of the sort, and that if I ever said she had I was a wicked girl. I said I hadn't said she had, but she had said so. She put on a worried look and put a hand on my forehead and said she could feel I'd got a touch of the sun. A touch of the sun, she said, would make me imagine things – and no wonder, after the day I'd had.

'All next day I was kept in bed; not as a punishment but as a kind of treat. My mother was ever so nice to me; she kept coming in to put a hand on my forehead. The one thing she did not do was get the doctor. And afterwards, when I was let get up, nothing was good enough for me; until really anyone would have thought that my mother felt she was in my power. Shortly after, her rich sister came down, and my mother then had a fine time, crying, talking and crying; the sister then took us back with her to London, where my mother talked and cried even more. Of course I asked my aunt about what my mother had said, but my aunt said that if I imagined such wicked things they would have to think there was something wrong with my brain. So I did not reopen the subject and am not doing so now. In the course of time my mother succeeded in divorcing my father for desertion; she was unable to marry her sister's friend because he was married and apparently always had been, but she did marry a friend of her sister's friend's, and was soon respectably settled in Bermuda, where as far as I know she still is.'

'But your father?' he said.

'Well, what about my father?'

'You don't mean you never heard anything more of him?'

'I never said so – he sent me two picture postcards. The last' – she counted back – 'arrived fourteen years ago. But there probably have been others that went astray. The way I've always lived, I'm not long at any address.'

He essayed, rashly, 'Been a bit of a waif?'

The look he got back for this, was halfway between glass and ice. 'A waif's the first thing I learned not to be. No, more likely my father decided, better leave it at that. People don't, on the whole, come back, and I've never blamed them. No, why should he be dead? Why should not he be – any place?'

'Here, for instance?'

'Tonight, you mean?'

'Why not?' he said. 'Why not – as you say?'

'Here?' She looked round the tables, as though she hardly knew where she was herself. She looked round the tables, over which smoke thickened, round which khaki melted into the khaki gloom. Then her eyes returned, to fix, with unsparing attention, on an addled trio of men round the fifty-five mark. 'Here?' she repeated, 'my father? – I hope not.'

'But I thought,' he said, watching her watching the old

buffers, 'I thought we were looking for someone of twenty-six?'

'Give me a cigarette,' she said, 'and, also, don't be cruel.'

'I wouldn't be,' he said, as he lighted the cigarette, 'if you had any feeling for me.'

The Hell of a Time

J. MACLAREN-ROSS

Do I remember that night? God, I should say I do. We had the hell of a bloody time. That was when the Simon Commission first came out to India, in 1929, or thereabouts, and there was a lot of ill-feeling against the Europeans. All the native shops in Madras were closed down, every damn one of 'em; a *hartal* they call it, a strike of shopkeepers, as a political protest.

There was no actual rioting, but all day long cars kept on pouring in for repair, some with their windscreens smashed or darn great holes in the doors where bricks had been thrown at them.

At that time I hadn't been out East very long; I was in the works, sweltering under corrugated iron in 105 degrees of damp heat. You can't imagine what that's like until you've been there. We used to knock off about six in the evening.

Well, the night I'm telling you about, we were at a loose end and old Sturgess, who was coach-works manager, said to me, 'Adams, old boy,' he said, 'what about going along to George Town tonight and seeing the fun? There's bound to be something doing out there.'

'All right,' I said. 'We might have a drink at Harrison's.'

George Town is the native quarter of Madras and Harrison's is a damned awful place, full of Eurasian tarts and so on, where no decent European would be seen dead in the normal course of events. Though I've been there a good few times, I don't mind telling you.

'That's an idea,' Sturgess said. 'We'll do that.'

He was the hell of a fellow, old Sturgess. Drink? God, fish wasn't in it with him. He was the hell of a lad. Yet he never

27

got the push – how he kept his job, God only knows. I don't. He's probably a director by now.

Well, we had a lot of whisky first, and I don't mind telling you we were pretty well stewed by the time we started off, about half-past seven. Sturgess had a new motorbike, an Enfield, a damn good machine too. I climbed in the sidecar and we got going.

Half-way along we heard a shout and blowed if it wasn't Fred Logan, an American fellow we knew pretty well. He was on a motorbike too, a bloody awful thing he'd had for donkey's years. I remember the exhaust pipe used to come off at times and he'd tie it on again with his handkerchief.

Logan had another chap in the sidecar, bloke called Brady, a reporter on the *Madras Mail*.

'Where you guys going?' Logan shouted to us.

'We're going to have a drink at Harrison's,' Sturgess shouted back. 'Coming?'

'Okay,' Logan said; he was ready for anything. 'How about you, Dan?' he asked Brady.

'I'm on,' Brady said.

'Okay,' Logan said. 'Let's go.'

It was when we got down to Broadway that the fun started. There they were, milling and shouting, Muslims and Hindus all mixed up together, some of 'em wearing Gandhi caps. The police were holding them back one side of the esplanade. When they saw us, four Europeans together, they raised the hell of a row. As I say, feeling was pretty rife at that time.

The inspector in charge came over to us. He was a European too. He said, 'And where do you think *you're* going?'

'We're off to have a drink at Harrison's,' Sturgess said.

'That's right,' Logan said.

Brady and I nodded.

'Now listen,' the inspector said. 'You're going right back the way you came.'

'Oh, no, we're not,' Sturgess said. 'You're quite mistaken, inspector.'

'I'll say you are,' Logan said.

'We're going down to George Town,' I said.

'I'm a journalist,' Brady said. 'I'm gonna write it up for the *Mail*.'

'After we've had a drink at Harrison's,' Sturgess said.

'That's right,' Logan said. 'We wanna see the fun.'

'You'll see all the bloody fun you want if you go down there tonight,' the inspector said. 'And a bit more.'

'That's all right with me,' Logan said.

The crowd was pretty het up by this time, yelling and bawling, with the police keeping them back. They were beginning to sound ugly.

'Don't be damn fools,' the inspector said. 'Go on home while you're still in one piece.'

'No bloody fear,' Sturgess said.

'Not a chance,' Logan said.

'All right,' the inspector said. 'Don't say I didn't warn you.'

'Okay, sarge,' Logan said. 'Come on, you guys. Let's get going.'

We started off down the esplanade. The mob yelled and booed at us, sounding fierce. Something whizzed through the air by my head. 'God,' Sturgess said. 'The swine. They're throwing bricks.'

He drove on full speed. Suddenly there was a shout from behind us from Logan. I looked back and saw that Brady had been hit. He was lying back in the sidecar with blood running down his face.

'Don't stop,' I shouted to Logan. 'For Christ's sake don't stop.'

I knew if he did, with that bloody old bus of his, he'd never get her started again and then we'd be for it. The crowd was getting out of hand; bricks flew thick and fast. The police were having a time – they weren't allowed to use their batons. I crouched down in the sidecar, dodging the bricks. Logan kept calling out behind us. We'd given up the idea of going to George Town by this time. We thought we'd get away along the Marina once we were clear of the crowd. I looked back and saw Brady slumped down in Logan's sidecar. He'd been knocked cold.

At the Marina a military picket picked us up.

'Where the hell are you going?' the officer in charge asked us.

Sturgess said, 'Along the Marina.'

'You're bloody well not,' the officer said. 'Why, God Almighty, you'd be killed. Go back the way you came.'

'We can't do that,' I said. 'They're throwing bricks. This bloke's been hit by one. We can't take him back there.'

Logan had stopped and we all had a look at Brady. He was out all right, with a whacking great gash in his forehead and blood all over him.

'By Christ,' the officer said. 'He's caught a packet he has.'

'What the hell we gonna do?' Logan said.

I was sweating like a bullock. We were all near sober by this time and I don't mind telling you I had the proper wind-up because I'd just remembered Brady was a delicate sort of chap, who had a weak heart and was likely to conk out any time.

'Best thing is to go down the harbour,' the officer said. 'If you went on the Marina they'd spill your guts for sure. We couldn't help either – before we could draw a bloody bayonet we'd have to get written permission from the Fort. We've no authority to use violence. I can't think what the devil you're doing down here at all.'

Sturgess said, 'We were going to have a drink at Harrison's.'

'Christ,' the officer said, 'you must be crazy.'

Well, we went down the harbour and it was quite calm down there. We went on board the first BI boat we saw and had the doctor look at Brady. The cut turned out to be nothing much after all. The doc brought him to and he had a few with us in the bar and felt fine again, except he was fed up because of the blood on his suit. He was always a natty sort of bloke, old Brady.

We came back along the Marina about eleven and it was all quiet, not a native to be seen for miles, but down by the iron bridge there were three cars piled up, pretty badly smashed. God knows what happened to the people in them.

I saw Brady next day and he felt none the worse; he had written a piece about it in the *Mail* and was feeling pretty bucked, all told. Matter of fact, though, he did die a few weeks later. He was out on a binge and his heart went back on him, poor bastard.

Yes, I remember that night quite well. We never got our drink at Harrison's, but, by God, we certainly had the hell of a time.

Conversations in Ebury Street

CHARLES FURBANK

'*Salud, camarada*,' I said.

'Ah, you speak Spanish!' said the waiter.

'No, only Hemingway,' I said.

'It's the next best thing,' he said, smiling at me.

'Why the happy smile?' I said. 'Is that the feeling you get from being a member of a working-class democracy?'

'No, it's the joke you just made. It's the first Hemingway joke I've ever heard in the flesh.'

'I didn't know there were such jokes.'

'Don't you ever read the American papers?' he said.

'No,' I said, 'I'm English.'

'What of it? I'm Spanish, and I read the American papers.'

'The Spanish are a very cultured people,' I said.

'Thank you,' said the waiter. 'What are you going to have to drink?'

'What d'you suggest?'

'I suggest beer,' said the waiter.

'Have you any draught?'

'No, only bottled,' he said, as if it was unreasonable to ask for draught.

'Oh, bottled will do just as well,' I said.

The waiter went out to get the beer. I looked round the café. It was a very large café and it was full of foreigners. There were a lot more Spaniards fighting around in Spain than you'd think from reading the papers. I'd been in Madrid for four hours and I hadn't seen anyone except Spaniards. No one at all, not even a Frenchman, and unless the Russians looked like the Spaniards I hadn't seen any of them either. I guessed the English and the Americans might be harder to

33

see, as most of them out there were famous, and famous people are always harder to see, but I'd at least expected to see some foreign-legion-looking Germans. No, it was just Spaniards all the time; not that I've got any antipathy towards Spaniards. I think they're a very cultured people, as I said to the waiter, but I could only speak a few words of their cultured language, so it didn't look like being much of an evening.

Just as I was thinking all this an American hospital nurse came into the café. I stood up and waved to her.

'Hallo, comrade hospital nurse,' I said. 'Come and have some beer.'

'How did you know I was a hospital nurse?' she said. She had on the sort of civilian clothes that American hospital nurses wear.

'By the can!' I said. 'That unmistakable internee's despair! Put it on the chair, sweetheart,' I said.

'You're fresh!'

'I should be, I only got into this town four hours ago.'

'What'd you come here for?'

'Maybe so I can get a battalion of the International Brigade called after me.'

'You poor white, you café joker!' she said. 'Maybe you're a reporter for the London *News Chronicle*? That's a paper that's greatly admired in America.'

'It's greatly admired in England as well,' I said. 'They had a letter from industrial Wales the other day, saying that many people in Wales believed the *News Chronicle* was the real fighting paper for the working class.'

'Is it?'

'As near as makes no difference.'

'And you,' she said. 'What are you?'

'Maybe I'm a maker of jungle movies,' I said.

'Then what are you doing in Washington – I mean Madrid?'

'What was General Howe doing in New York?'

'Rioting.'

'That's all right then,' I said.

34

'This is one way of spending an evening,' she said, looking round the café. 'Where's that beer you promised me?'

'It's coming right now,' I said, and sure enough a waiter came along with a couple of bottles just as I was speaking. It was a different waiter.

'You've been a hell of a while getting that beer! D'you make it on the premises?' I said.

But being a working-class democracy the waiter didn't have to answer a question like that, so he just swore at me under his breath.

'Where's the other waiter?' I said.

'He was shot by a member of the Fifth Column while crossing the square to get your beer,' he said.

'I don't believe it. I haven't heard any shots,' I said.

'He has gone off duty,' said the other waiter and went away.

'Now, again,' said the American nurse, 'please tell me why you're here?'

'I've always wanted to enjoy being at a public school, so here I am,' I said.

'A public school!' she said. 'An English public school!'

'Or a Scottish one,' I said. 'I've always thought a public school would be great if you could believe in it, and now here's a public-school atmosphere you can believe in. You know, work hard and play hard for the sake of the school, and not yourself, or for coloured caps, or for any other cheap allurements. Just for the Commissar's hand on your shoulder and international justice. It's a fine ideal,' I said.

'You distinguished English author, you damn' bloody fool, you anti-joker,' she said, 'to hell with your fun!'

'Hey, keep it up, Ada! Remember the Hippocratean oath,' I said. 'I'm entirely pro. You completely mistake me; I'm pro all the time, I wouldn't be anti for anything. It's just that I like a joke occasionally.'

'You look anti,' she said. 'You look just how a member of the Fifth Column looks.'

'Please, don't say that, you make me feel terrible,' I said. 'I execrate the Fifth Column. I'm all for energetic action against them.'

'Then why don't you join in the songs they're singing over there, instead of just sitting over here and talking. Don't you ever do anything but talk?'

I looked over to where she was pointing, at some soldiers singing patriotic songs about three being the Comintern, and the Soviet land being so dear to every worker, set to old Irish melodies. At the edge of the group was a sailor who was trying to join in, but you could tell he didn't really know the words, and was having to hum most of them and fake the mouth movements to make it look natural. I felt sorry for the sailor. Republican sailors were having a rotten time in the war. Once, at a public meeting, I got up and asked a distinguished member of the International Brigade why the Republican Navy hadn't been able to play a more active part in the war, and he told me that the Republican fleet was unable to put to sea, as they couldn't get any spare parts for refitting, as the spare parts were of British manufacture. The audience thought well of the question, and many of them thought I was a sailor, some even said I was an Invergordon mutineer, though I hardly looked old enough for that. Anyway, I knew the Republican sailors were having a bad time, so I thought I'd ask him over to our table. I made a sign to the waiter.

'Ask the naval comrade to join us,' I said.

'Sailors are no-good bums, they'll drink all your beer,' he said.

'You're a pretty poor comrade to talk like that about the heroic defenders of your country. It's "Special train for Atkins when the trooper's on the tide" now,' I said, 'and you're still at the "Chuck him out, the brute" stage. You've got it all wrong,' I said. 'Go over and ask him nicely to join us.'

'All the same, sailors are no good,' said the second waiter.

'Good evening, comrades of both sexes,' said the sailor.

I poured out some beer for him.

'Not so good as "Le chant des matelots"?' I said, pointing at the soldiers.

'I don't know,' he said, 'we never sang where I came from.'

'Where d'you come from, sailor?' said the nurse.

'You never ask questions in wartime,' I said.

'I was a fisherman out of Barcelona,' he said.

'Why didn't you sing?' I said. 'That's not a personal question, that's an anthropological inquiry.'

'Because we didn't know any songs, I guess.'

'What did you do then, just stand about in a noble way like they do in citizen defence posters?' I said.

'There's an old Spanish proverb that says an Englishman's humour's as efficient as his automatic rifle!' said the sailor.

'He's a popular party sailor,' I said to the nurse. 'He knows all the latest Spanish proverbs. When I sat down at my automatic rifle they all laughed, but when I'd finished there wasn't a sound. Like the oysters!' I said. 'They were all dead. What a laugh! What a killer! Just a new twist to the piano ad. gag, and there you are,' I said. 'It's a gift!'

'Tell me what you do,' she said. 'Just tell me, you don't have to tell him anything; he knows it all from the magazines.'

'We talk,' he said.

'What do men like you talk about when you're alone together?' said the nurse.

'Three things,' said the sailor, 'football, anarchism, and film stars.'

'Greta Garbo, the Fourth International, and the Barcelona Hospital Cup – well, it's a great world,' I said.

'Not only Greta Garbo,' he said. 'We in Spain know of many talented actresses beside Greta Garbo. Women of equal talent and superior beauty!'

'Oh, I see, you're not a fan, I'm sorry,' I said.

'I wouldn't say that; it's just the imputation of the small range of subjects I don't like. If you keep abreast of current affairs there are any amount of things to talk about. Not just Greta Garbo and the Hospital Cup. Who cares about charity games anyway?'

'What about bullfighting?' said the nurse. 'That's a very

good sport also. I thought bullfighting was the national sport of Spain?'

'It's bullfighting that's got us where we are today. It's a terrible anachronism,' he said. 'Only antis are interested in bullfighting.'

'You must meet my friend,' said the nurse, pointing to me. 'He's a famous matador.'

'Are you really?' he said. 'Will you let me have your auto-graph?'

'No, I'm not really. It's just her way of saying she thinks I'm anti.'

'Are you?'

'No.'

'I'm glad to hear that,' he said. 'I didn't really think anyone could be anti after coming and seeing the facts for themselves.'

'Has he come to study the facts?' said the nurse. 'That's what I'd like to know. What has he come to study?'

'That's right, comrade, tell us what you came here for?'

'It's the only way to meet interesting people nowadays,' I said.

'Oh dear, comrade, you shouldn't say things like that,' said the sailor, 'you shouldn't really.'

'What the hell does it matter what he says?' she said. 'He's a nice boy, he reads the *News Chronicle*, he'll never come to any harm.'

'Let's talk about something uncontroversial. Let's talk about anarchism,' I said.

'There you have me,' he said. 'Come on, call me a Trotskyist wrecker, strike home, don't spare me!'

'I'm an anarchist too,' said the nurse, 'though politics seem unimportant when you do the work I do!'

'Turn out your lamp, Florence Nightingale!' I said. 'So am I! Now we've a common interest to base our friendship on, I'll get some more beer.'

I called the waiter over, and ordered three more bottles. When I gave the order he looked over towards the sailor, as if to say, 'I told you he'd soon drink your beer!'

'I don't like that waiter,' said the sailor, 'he looks like a liberal democrat.'

'Waiters are all radicals, they believe in a single tax,' said the nurse. 'They're very nice people when you get to know them.'

'I'm sick of just sitting here; let's go and Trotsky wreck something!' I said.

'Thank you!' she said. 'That was sweet of you; we just had a chance to be friendly, and you have to say something smart.'

'The more I go through life, the more I find the necessity of friendship,' said the sailor. 'Anarchists are friendly people. You won't find truer friends in the whole of Spain. I wish more people would be friendly and try and understand our point of view.'

'He wants to start a beautiful friendship with you,' I said to the nurse. 'You could write a book on your experiences in a few years' time. "Lived with an Anarchist on Eight Dollars a Week; what we lacked in money we made up in mutual friendship!"'

'That's rather good, you're a funny fellow,' said the sailor.

'Oh, you like him too! Here's someone else that appreciates the new style of humour the *News Chronicle* is popularizing,' she said.

'D'you write for the London *News Chronicle?*' he said.

'No, I don't do any of the things she says I do. She's just making things up to amuse us. She's a nice hospital nurse; she keeps everyone's spirits up.'

'Ah, you're a nurse!' he said.

'Well, what of it?' she said.

'They all know you're a nurse,' I said. 'It's that comforting can that gives you away.'

'D'you hoard foodstuffs?' he asked her indignantly.

'We've got him on the idiom at last,' I said. 'I'm not talking about tins, I'm talking about her happy-go-lucky hindquarters.'

'Ah, I see, the young lady's behind!'

'Do you, by God,' she said. 'Another one like that, you

merry marine, and I'll see you in the sailor's hospital! How did you learn to speak so smart anyway?' she said.

'It's like in the movies: the minor characters speak Spanish, the part players, like waiters, speak with an accent, and the important characters, like myself, speak English.'

'That's very convenient!' she said.

'I'll get some more beer,' I said. 'Here's to educated anarchy!'

'Skin off your bum!' he said, winking at the nurse.

'I'm warning you boys,' she said. 'One *News Chronicle* reader's enough.'

'Tell us about anarchy from the inside and how the movement's going,' I said.

'Badly,' he said, 'badly. Whatever happens, we get it. The only thing we can hope for is peace, and you never get anarchy in peace-time. It's terrible having to make up your mind you're going to be shot next year, but you've got to. Every political party in Spain, no matter what it is, always has it down on its agenda to shoot the anarchists next year. Sometimes you can get an extension for a year, but you've always got to be ready to be shot next year. It's worrying,' he said, 'you can't marry a nice girl and settle down, when you've got it hanging over you all the time. But I wouldn't be anything but an anarchist for all that; it's a great family tradition with us. My grandfather planted the first time bomb in Catalonia. If it had gone off an hour earlier we might have been living in the United States of Europe now.'

'Why?' I said.

'I don't know, but that's what they told me at home. He was a great old man, my grandfather. He believed in direct action. If he hadn't got anything else, he'd pick up a stone and throw it! He didn't believe in tyranny of any sort.'

'But surely they wouldn't shoot a nice boy like you?' said the nurse.

'You don't know, they'd shoot anybody now. It's awful the way they've started to shoot each other now. It's worse than ever before.'

'You poor boy, you make me feel quite melancholy,' she said.

'Thank you, thank you so much,' he said. 'I'd rather have your sympathy than anyone's in the whole world. I've often dreamt of a woman like you. Not just a silly girl, but some really beautiful woman. Someone intelligent. Someone you can really talk to; and an anarchist like myself. You're my dream come true!' he said.

'You've got quite a line, you fisherman out of Barcelona,' she said. 'You speak like a fisher of men!'

'Ah, Bible references, that favourite American sport,' he said. 'You've got every right to be happy, you're so young and beautiful. Often when we're afloat I can't sleep for imagining someone like you. Now you've materialized. I raise up my glass and drink to you,' he said. 'I drink to you, Goldenhair, my desire, my American beauty!'

'Be quiet, you bloody sailor!' I said. 'She's my hospital nurse, I found her first.'

'You don't count now. It's just between us. It's quite simple now – just the man and the woman. Lady, I want you, I've wanted you ever since I reached manhood,' he said. 'I want you just as I want anarchy, as an all-enveloping belief.'

'Don't forget that you're going to be shot next year! I'm just an anarchist that's not going to be shot next year; that's very inferior,' I said.

'She already knows that,' he said. 'I'm sorry to have to be like this, but this is something out beyond us. Come with me now,' he said to the nurse. 'Come with me, anywhere. This is our hour, this is our time together on earth. I love you, I desire you, I want you more than anything else in the world!'

'You jolly jack tar; first you drink my beer, and now you want to take my girl. You wouldn't like to borrow my pocket comb as well, would you?'

'Why, is my hair untidy?'

'The waiter was right – you're no good, you're just a lousy tramp; go to hell!' I said.

'What did that waiter say about me?' he shouted. 'I knew

he said something. I could see it from his face, the sneaking lackey!'

'I'm sorry to disturb you boys,' she said, 'but I've got to be getting back now. I'm on duty again in half an hour's time.'

'No, you can't go now, you can't just walk out like this! A woman's only got one duty in wartime!'

'Listen to him!' I said to her. 'You'll be an unmarried mother before you can say knife.'

'To be an unmarried mother is to be something very honourable now,' he said. 'Good parents are proud that their daughters should be the mothers of the fallen heroes of the revolution.'

'I'm sorry. It was a nice evening though. Thanks for the beer,' she said.

Just as she got up from the table, the original waiter returned and came up to our table.

'Good evening, Miss Belasco,' he said. 'I hope these boys haven't been annoying you?'

'Oh no, they've been very nice to me,' she said. 'They're a pair of anarchists from out of town.'

'You oughtn't to mix with such anti-social types, Miss Belasco,' he said.

'What d'ye mean, anti-social?' I said. 'You're too damn' fresh for a waiter, even if this is a working-class democracy.'

'Good night, boys,' she said to us. 'Don't be annoyed with them,' she said to the waiter.

'Just go to hell, will you!' I said.

'That's exactly where I am going,' she said. 'That's where I work, right in hell.'

'Go to hell, you bitch!' I said, 'and don't be so goddamn pleased about your profession.'

'You shouldn't speak to any lady like that,' said the sailor.

'That was no lady,' I said. 'That was my wife!'

'I think she ought to have been my wife as well. I'd very much like an American wife, they've got the nicest appearances,' he said, 'and nobody'd shoot me if I had an American wife.'

'Have another beer?'

'Well, I ought really to be rejoining my ship now.'

'Why, have you got it parked out in the Gran Via?'

'That's good,' he said. 'I liked the place name.'

'Here's to American wives,' I said. 'Bottoms up!'

'Here's to Eventual Anarchy,' he said.

'As if that's ever likely to happen!'

'Yes, as if that's ever likely to happen,' he said. 'Good night, comrade, and thank you for everything.'

'Good night. Wear plenty of hymn books over your heart, and don't let them pass you any wooden nickels,' I said.

He smiled at me and walked out, leaving me alone.

It suddenly occurred to me I'd been just sitting there and talking all the evening, nothing had happened to me at all. Absolutely nothing. It made me feel very angry. Here was I in a besieged city in the middle of a revolution and still everyone just talked.

'Well,' I shouted, 'isn't there going to be any action at all? Don't any of you happy flint-locks ever fight? Isn't there ever going to be any civil commotion? For Christ's sake start something! Anything, acts of foreign enemy, hostilities (whether war be declared or not), any bloody thing you like. Resurrection, conception, insurrection, military or usurped power, making man one with God, malicious persons acting for or on behalf of political organizations. Come on, use your ingenuity. Give me the elements of tragedy, then. Fill me with pity and terror! Purge me, please, for Christ's sake purge me!' I shouted. 'Give me some action, and some healthy exercise, I want to sleep tonight. It's essential I should sleep tonight! For God's sake give me some action, anything, as long as it's action, for pity's sake give me some action!' I shouted.

They just sat there, they didn't take any notice at all, they didn't even say anything consoling, like 'The mad Englishman!' they just sat there and said nothing. Maybe they thought I was trying to join in the patriotic songs the soldiers were still singing. The second waiter came over to me.

'How about going back to your hotel?' he said. 'The high altitude of the Meseta often makes people feel tired at first;

even I feel pretty tired. I wish I was going home,' he said.

'That's a nice thing to be able to say to drunks; it's even nicer than telling them you come from Los Angeles too. But I'm not drunk,' I said. 'You've got the wrong idea, I'm just bored.'

'I never said you were drunk, it's just the air, you'll feel better tomorrow. There's nothing much doing tonight, but tomorrow's our gala night. We've got a banjo band and a tap dancer coming. Be sure you come along tomorrow,' he said.

'OK, I think I will go back now,' I said.

'That's right,' he said, 'and mind out for the Fifth Column shooting you out of windows.'

'It just needed that,' I said. 'Look to the right and look to the left and you'll never, never be run over!'

'Safety first's a very good slogan,' he said.

'You're right,' I said. 'Good night.'

'Good night, comrade,' he said.

A Little Companion

—————— ✳ ——————

ANGUS WILSON

They say in the village that Miss Arkwright has never been the same since the war broke out, but she knows that it all began a long time before that – on 24 July 1936, to be exact, the day of her forty-seventh birthday.

She was in no way a remarkable person. Her appearance was not particularly distinguished, and yet she was without any feature that could actively displease. She had enough personal eccentricities to fit into the pattern of English village life, but none so absurd or anti-social that they could embarrass or even arouse gossip beyond what was pleasant to her neighbours. She accepted her position as an old maid with that cheerful good humour and occasional irony which are essential to English spinsters since the deification of Jane Austen, or more sacredly Miss Austen, by the upper-middle classes; and she attempted to counteract the inadequacy of the unmarried state by quiet, sensible, and tolerant social work in the local community. She was liked by nearly everyone, though she was not afraid of making enemies where she knew that her broad but deeply felt religious principles were being opposed. Any socially pretentious or undesirably extravagant conduct was liable to call forth from her an unexpectedly caustic and well-aimed snub. She was invited everywhere and always accepted the invitations. You could see her at every tea or cocktail party, occasionally drinking a third gin, but never more. Quietly but well dressed, with one or two very fine old pieces of jewellery that had come down to her from her grandmother, she would pass from one group to another, laughing or serious as the occasion demanded. She smoked continuously her own, rather expensive, brand of cigarettes.

'My one vice,' she used to say. 'The only thing that stands between me and secret drinking.' She listened with patience, but with a slight twinkle in the eye, to Mr Hodgson's endless stories of life in Dar-es-Salaam or Myra Hope's breathless accounts of her latest system of diet. John Hobday in his somewhat ostentatiously gentleman-farmer attire would describe his next novel about East Anglian life to her before even his beloved daughter had heard of it. Richard Trelawney, just down from Oxford, found that she had read and really knew Donne's sermons, yet she could swop detective stories with Colonel Wright by the hour, and was his main source for quotations when *The Times* crossword was in question. She it was who incorporated little Mrs Grantham into village life, when that rather under-bred, suburban woman came there as Colonel Grantham's second wife, checking her vulgar remarks about 'the lower classes' with kindly humour, but defending her against the formidable battery of Lady Vernon's antagonism. Yet she it was also who was first at Lady Vernon's when Sir Robert had his stroke, and her unobtrusive kindliness and real services gained her a singular position behind the grim reserve of the Vernon family. She could always banter the Vicar away from his hobby horse of the Greek rite when at parish meetings the agenda seemed to have been buried for ever beneath a welter of Euchologia and Menaia. She checked Sir Robert's anti-bolshevik phobia from victimizing the County Librarian for her Fabianism, but was fierce in her attack on the local council when she thought that class prejudice had prevented Commander Osborne's widow from getting a council house. She led, in fact, an active and useful existence, yet when anyone praised her she would only laugh. 'My dear,' she would say, 'hard work's the only excuse old maids like me have got for existing at all, and even then I don't know that they oughtn't to lethalize the lot of us.' As the danger of war grew nearer in the thirties her favourite remark was, 'Well, if they've got any sense this time they'll keep the young fellows at home and put us useless old maids in the trenches,' and she said it with real conviction.

With her good carriage, ample figure and large, deep-blue eyes, she even began to acquire a certain beauty as middle age approached. People speculated as to why she had never married. She had in fact refused a number of quite personable suitors. The truth was that from girlhood she had always felt a certain repulsion from physical contact. Not that she was in any way prudish: she was remarkable for a rather eighteenth-century turn of coarse phrase, indeed verbal freedom was the easier for her in that sexual activity was the more remote. Nor would psychoanalysts have found anything of particular interest in her; she had no abnormal desires, as a child she had never felt any wish to change her sex or observed any peculiarly violent or crude incident that could have resulted in what is called a psychic trauma. She just wasn't interested and was perhaps as a result a little over-given to talking of 'all this fuss and nonsense that's made over sex'. She would, however, have liked to have had a child. She recognized this as a common phenomenon among childless women and accepted it, though she could never bring herself to admit it openly or laugh about it in the common-sensical way in which she treated her position as an old maid. As the middle years approached she found a sudden interest and even sometimes a sudden jealousy over other people's babies and children growing upon her, attacking her unexpectedly and with apparent irrelevancy to time or place. She was equally wide-awake to the dangers of the late forties and resolutely resisted such foolish fancies, though she became as a result a little snappish and over-gruff with the very young. 'Now, my dear,' she told herself, 'you *must* deal with this nonsense or you'll start getting odd.' *How* very odd she could not guess!

The Granthams always gave a little party for her on her birthdays. 'Awful nonsense at my age,' she had been saying now for many years, 'but I never say no to a drink.' Her forty-seventh birthday party was a particular success; Mary Hatton was staying with the Granthams and like Miss Arkwright she was an ardent Janeite so they'd been able to talk Mr Collins and Mrs Elton and the Elliots to their hearts' content, then Colonel Grantham had given her some tips about growing meconopsis, and finally Mrs Osborne had been over to see the new rector at Longhurst, so they had a good-natured but thoroughly enjoyable 'cat' about the state of the rectory there. She was just paying dutiful attention to her hostess's long complaint about the grocery deliveries, preparatory to saying goodbye, when suddenly a thin, whining, but remarkably clear, child's voice said loudly in her ear, 'Race you home, Mummy.' She looked around her in surprise, then decided that her mind must have wandered from the boring details of Mrs Grantham's saga, but almost immediately the voice sounded again. 'Come on, Mummy, you are a slow-coach. I said "Race you home."' This time Miss Arkwright was seriously disturbed. She wondered if Colonel Grantham's famous high spirits had got the better of him, but it could hardly have been so, she thought, as she saw his face earnest in conversation: 'The point is, Vicar, not so much whether we want to intervene as whether we've got to.' She began to feel most uncomfortable, and as soon as politeness allowed she made her way home.

The village street seemed particularly hot and dusty, the sunlight on the whitewashed cottages peculiarly glaring, as she walked along. 'One too many on a hot day, that's your trouble, my dear,' she said to herself, and felt comforted by so material an explanation. The familiar trimness of her own little house and the cool shade of the walnut tree on the front lawn further calmed her nerves. She stopped for a moment to pick up a basket of lettuces that old Pyecroft had left at the door, and then walked in. After the sunlight outside, the hall seemed so dark that she could hardly discern even the shape of the grandfather clock. Out of this shadowy blackness came the child's voice loudly and clearly, but if anything more nasal than before. 'Beat you to it this time,' it said. Miss Arkwright's heart stopped for a moment and her lungs seemed to contract, and then almost instantaneously she had seen it – a little white-faced boy, thin, with matchstick arms and legs growing out of shrunken clothes, with red-rimmed eyes and an adenoidal open-mouthed expression. Instantaneously, because the next moment he was not there, almost like a flickering image against the eye's retina. Miss Arkwright straightened her back and took a deep breath, then she went upstairs, took off her shoes and lay down on her bed.

It was many weeks before anything fresh occurred and she felt happily able to put the whole incident down to cocktails and the heat, indeed she began to remember that she had woken next morning with a severe headache. 'You're much too old to start suffering from hangovers,' she told herself. But the next experience was really more alarming. She had been up to London to buy a wedding present at Harrods and, arriving somewhat late for the returning train, found herself sitting in a stuffy and over-packed carriage. She felt therefore particularly pleased to see the familiar slate quarries that heralded the approach of Brankston station, when suddenly a sharp dig drove the bones of her stays into her ribs. She looked with annoyance at the woman next to her – a blowsy creature with feathers in her hat – when she saw to her surprise that the woman was quietly asleep, her arms folded in front of her. Then in her ears there sounded, 'Chuff. Chuff. Chuff. Chuff,' followed by a little snort and a giggle, and then quite unmistakably the whining voice saying, 'Rotten old train.' After that it seemed to her as though for a few moments pandemonium had broken loose in the carriage – shouts and cries and a monotonous thumping against the woodwork as though someone were beating an impatient rhythm with his foot – yet no other occupant seemed in the slightest degree disturbed. They were for Miss Arkwright moments of choking and agonizing fears. She dreaded that at any minute the noise would grow so loud that the others would notice, for she felt an inescapable responsibility for the incident; yet had the whole carriage risen and flung her from the window as a witch it would in some degree have been a release from the terrible sense of personal obsession, it would have given objective reality to what now seemed an uncontrollable expansion of her own consciousness into space, it would at the least have shown that others were mad beside herself. But no slightest ripple broke the drowsy torpor of the hot carriage in the August sun. She was deeply relieved when the train at last drew into Brankston and the impatience of her invisible attendant was assuaged, but no sooner had she set foot on the platform than she heard once more the almost puling whine, the too familiar, 'Race you home, Mummy.' She knew then that whatever it was it had come to stay, that her homecomings would no longer be to the familiar comfort of her house and servants, but that there would always be a childish voice, a childish face to greet her for one moment as she crossed the threshold.

And so it proved. Gradually at first, at more than weekly intervals, and then increasingly, so that even a short spell in the vegetable garden or with the rock plants would mean impatient whining, wanton scattering of precious flowers, overturning of baskets – and then that momentary vision, lengthened now sometimes to five minutes' duration, that sickly, cretinous face. The very squalor of the child's appearance was revolting to Miss Arkwright, for whom cheerful good health was the first of human qualities. Sometimes the sickliness of the features would be the thick, flaccid, pasty appearance that suggested rich feeding and late hours, and then the creature would be dressed in a velvet suit and Fauntleroy collar that might have clothed an over-indulged French bourgeois child; at other times the appearance was more cretinous, adenoidal and emaciated, and then it would wear the shrunken uniform and thick black boots of an institution idiot. In either case it was a child quite out of keeping with the home it sought to possess – a home of quiet beauty, unostentatious comfort and restrained good taste. Of course, Miss Arkwright argued, it was an emanation from the sick side of herself so that it was bound to be diseased, but this realization did not compensate for dribble marks on her best dresses or for sticky fingermarks on her tweed skirts.

At first she tried to ignore the obsession with her deep reserve of stoic patience, but as it continued, she felt the need of the Church. She became a daily communicant and delighted the more 'spikey' of her neighbours. She prayed ceaselessly for release or resignation. A lurking sense of sin was roused in her and she wondered if small frivolities and pleasures were the cause of her visitation; she remembered that after all it had first begun when she was drinking gin. Her religion had always been of the 'brisk' and 'sensible' variety, but now she began to fear that she had been over-suspicious of 'enthusiasm' or 'pietism'. She gave up all but the most frugal meals, distributed a lot of her clothes to the poor, slept on a board and rose at one in the morning to say a special Anglican office from a little book she had once been given by a rather despised High Church cousin. The only result seemed to be to cause scandal to her comfortable, old-fashioned parlourmaid and cook. She mentioned her state of sin in general terms to the Vicar and he lent her Neale's translations of the Coptic and Nestorian rites, but they proved of little comfort. At Christmas she rather shamefacedly and secretively placed a little bed with a richly-filled stocking in the corner of her bedroom, but the child was not to be blackmailed. Throughout the day she could hear a faint but unsavoury sound of uncontrolled and slovenly guzzling, like the distant sound of pigs feeding, and when evening came she was pursued by ever louder retching and the disturbing smell of vomit.

On Boxing Day she visited her old and sensible friend the Bishop, and told him the whole story. He looked at her very steadily with the large, dramatic brown eyes that were so telling in the pulpit, and for a long time he remained silent. Miss Arkwright hoped that he would advise her quickly, for she could feel a growing tugging at her skirt. It was obvious that this quiet, spacious library was no place for a child, and she could not have borne to see these wonderful, old books disturbed even if she was the sole observer of the sacrilege. At last the Bishop spoke. 'You say that the child appears ill and depraved. Has this evil appearance been more marked in the last weeks?' Miss Arkwright was forced to admit that it had. 'My dear old friend,' said the Bishop, and he put his hand on hers. 'It is your sick self that you are seeing, and all this foolish abstinence, this extravagant martyrdom are making you more sick.' The Bishop was a great Broad Churchman of the old school. 'Go out into the world and take in its beauty and its colour. Enjoy what is yours and thank God for it.' And without more ado, he persuaded Miss Arkwright to go to London for a few weeks.

Established at Berners, she set out to have a good time. She was always fond of expensive meals, but her first attempt to indulge at Claridge's proved an appalling failure, for with every course the voice grew louder and louder in her ears. 'Coo! What rotten stuff,' it kept repeating. 'I want an ice.' Henceforth her meals were taken almost exclusively on Self-ridge's roof or in ice cream parlours, an unsatisfying and indigestible diet. Visits to the theatre were at first a greater success, she saw the new adaptation of *The Mill on the Floss*, and a version of *Lear* modelled on the original Kean pro-duction. The child had clearly never seen a play before and was held entranced by the mere spectacle. But soon it began to grow restless, a performance of *Hedda Gabler* was entirely ruined by rustlings, kicks, whispers, giggles and a severe bout of hiccoughs. For a time it was kept quiet by musical comedies and farces, but in the end Miss Arkwright found herself attending only *Where the Rainbow Ends*, *Mother Goose*, and *Buckie's Bears* – it was not a sophisticated child. As the run of Christmas plays drew near their end she became desperate, and one afternoon she left a particularly dusty performance at the circus and visited her old friend Madge Cleaver – once again to tell all.

'Poor Bessie,' said Madge Cleaver, and she smiled so spiritually. 'How real Error can seem.' For Madge was a Christian Scientist. 'But it's so *un*real, dear, if we can only have the courage to see the Truth. Truth denies Animal Magnetism, Spiritualism and all other false manifestations.' She lent Miss Arkwright *Science and Health*, and promised that she would give her 'absent treatment'.

At first Miss Arkwright felt most comforted. Mrs Eddy's

denial of the reality of most common phenomena and in particular of those that are evil seemed to offer a way out. Unfortunately, the child seemed quite unconvinced of its own non-existence. One afternoon Miss Arkwright thought with horror that by adopting a theology that denied the existence of Matter and gave reality only to Spirit she might well be gradually removing herself from the scene, whilst leaving the child in possession. After all, her own considerable bulk was testimony enough to her material nature, whilst the child might well in some repulsive way be accounted spirit. Terrified by the prospect before her, she speedily renounced Christian Science.

She returned to her home and by reaction decided to treat the whole phenomenon on the most material basis possible. She submitted her body to every old-fashioned purgative, she even indulged in a little amateur blood-letting, for might not the creature be some ill humour or sickly emanation of the body itself? But this antiquarian leechcraft only produced serious physical weakness and collapse. She was forced to call in Dr Kent, who at once terminated the purgatives and put her on to port wine and beef steak.

Failure of material remedies forced Miss Arkwright at last to a conviction which she had feared from the start. The thing, she decided, must be a genuine psychic phenomenon. It cost her much to admit this for she had always been very contemptuous of spiritualism, and regarded it as socially undesirable where it was not consciously fraudulent. But she was by now very desperate and willing to waive the deepest prejudices to free herself from the vulgar and querulous apparition. For a month or more she attended seances in London, but though she received 'happy' communications from enough small Indian or Red Indian children to have started a nursery school, no medium or clairvoyant could tell her anything that threw light on her little companion. At one of the seances, however, she met a thin, red-haired, Pre-Raphaelite sort of lady in a long grey garment and sandals, who asked her to attend the Circle of the Seventh Pentacle in the Earl's Court Road. The people she found there did not attract Miss Arkwright; she decided that the servants of the Devil were either common frauds or of exceedingly doubtful morals, but the little group was enthusiastic when she told her story. How could she hope to fight such Black Powers, they asked, unless she was prepared to invoke the White Art? Although she resisted their arguments at first, she finally found herself agreeing to a celebration of the Satanic Mass in her own home. She sent cook and Annie away for a week and prepared to receive the Circle. Their arrival in the village caused a great stir, partly because of their peculiar clothes, partly because of their retinue of goats and rabbits. It had been decided that Miss Arkwright should celebrate the Mass herself; an altar had been set up in the drawing room, she had bought an immense white maternity gown from Debenhams and had been busy all the week learning her words, but at the last minute something within her rebelled, she could not bring herself to say the Lord's Prayer backwards, and the Mass had to be called off. In the morning the devotees of the Pentacle left with many recriminations. The only result seemed to be that valuable ornaments were missing from the bedrooms occupied by the less reputable, whilst about those rooms in which the Devil's true servants had slept there hung an odour of goat that no fumigation could remove.

Miss Arkwright had long since given up visiting her neighbours, though they had not ceased to speculate about her. A chance remark that she had 'two now to provide for' had led them to think that she believed herself pregnant! After this last scandalous episode Lady Vernon decided that the time had come to act. She visited Miss Arkwright early one morning, and seeing the maternity gown which was still lying in the sitting room, she was confirmed in her suspicions. 'Bessie, dear,' she said. 'You've got to realize that you're seriously ill, mentally ill.' And she packed Miss Arkwright off to a brain specialist in Welbeck Street. This doctor, finding nothing physically wrong, sent her to a psychoanalyst. Poor Miss Arkwright! She was so convinced of her own insanity, that

she could think of no argument if they should wish to shut
her up. But the analyst, a smart, grey-haired Jew, laughed
when she murmured 'madness'. 'We don't talk in those terms
any more, Miss Arkwright. You're a century out of date. It's
true there are certain disturbingly psychotic features in what
you tell me, but nothing, I don't think, that won't yield to
deep analysis.' And deep analysis she underwent for eight
months or more, busily writing down dreams at night and
lying on a couch 'freely associating' by day. At the end of that
time the analyst began to form a few conclusions. 'The child
itself,' he said, 'is unimportant; the fact that you still see it,
even less so. What is important is that you now surround
yourself with vulgarity and whining. You have clearly a need
for these things which you have inhibited too long in an
atmosphere of refinement.' It was decided that Miss Arkwright
should sublimate this need by learning the saxophone.
Solemnly each day the poor lady sat in the drawing room –
that room which had once resounded with Bach and Mozart
– and practised the altosax. At last one day when she got so far
as to be able to play the opening bars of 'Alligator Stomp',
her sense of the ridiculous rebelled and she would play no
more, though her little companion showed great restlessness
at the disappearance of noises which accorded all too closely
with its vulgar taste.

I shall treat myself, she decided; and after long thought she
came to the conclusion that the most salient feature of the
business lay in the child's constant reiteration of the challenge,
'Race you home, Mummy'; with this it had started and with
this it had continued. If, thought Miss Arkwright, I were to
leave home completely, not only this house, but also England,
then perhaps it would withdraw its challenge and depart.

In January 1938, then, she set out on her travels. All across
Europe, in museums and cafés and opera houses, it continued
to throw down the gauntlet – 'Race you home, Mummy,' and
there it would be in her hotel bedroom. It seemed, however,
anxious to take on local colour and would appear in a diversity
of national costumes, often reviving for the purpose peasant

dresses seen only at folk-dance festivals or when worn by beggars in order to attract tourists. For Miss Arkwright this rather vulgar and commercial World's Fair aspect of her life was particularly distressing. The child also attempted to alter its own colour: pale brown it achieved in India, in China a faint tinge of lemon, and in America, by some misunderstanding of the term Red Indian, it emerged bright scarlet. She was especially horrified by the purple swelling with which it attempted to emulate the black of the African natives. But whatever its colour, it was always there.

At last the menace of war in September found Miss Arkwright in Morocco, and along with thousands of other British travellers she hurried home, carrying, she felt, her greatest menace with her. It was only really after Munich that she became reconciled to its continued presence, learning gradually to incorporate its noises, its appearance, its whole personality into her daily life. She went out again among her neighbours and soon everyone had forgotten that she had ever been ill. It was true that she was forced to address her companion occasionally with a word of conciliation, or to administer a slap in its direction when it was particularly provoking, but she managed to disguise these peculiarities beneath her normal gestures.

One Saturday evening in September 1939, she was returning home from the rectory, worried by the threat of approaching war and wondering how she could best use her dual personality to serve her country, when she was suddenly disturbed to hear a clattering of hoofs and a thunderous bellow behind her. She turned to see at some yards' distance a furious bull charging down the village street. She began immediately to run for her home, the little voice whining in her ear, 'Race you home, Mummy.' But the bull seemed to gain upon her, and in her terror she redoubled her speed, running as she had not run since she was a girl. She heard, it is true, a faint sighing in her ears as of dying breath, but she was too frightened to stop until she was safe at her own door. In she walked and, to her amazement, indeed, to her horror, look where she would, the little child was *not* there. She had taken up his challenge to a race and she had won.

She lay in bed that night depressed and lonely. She realized only too clearly that difficult as it was to get rid of him – now that the child was gone she found herself thinking of 'him' rather than 'it' – it would be wellnigh impossible to get him back. The sirens that declared war next morning seemed only a confirmation of her personal loss. She went into mourning and rarely emerged from the house. For a short while, it is true, her spirits were revived when the evacuee children came from the East End; some of the more cretinous and adenoidal seemed curiously like her lost one. But country air and food soon gave them rosy cheeks and sturdy legs, and she rapidly lost her interest. Before the year was out she was almost entirely dissociated from the external world, and those few friends who found time amid the cares of war to visit her in her bedroom, decided that there was little that could be done for one who showed so little response. The Vicar, who was busy translating St Gregory Nazianzen's prayers for victory, spoke what was felt to be the easiest and kindest verdict when he described her as 'just another war casualty'.

The Hard and the Human

————————— ❧ —————————

ELIZABETH BERRIDGE

The doctor watched the green charabanc emerge from among the yews flanking the drive and draw up in front of the wide stone porch.

They were late. From habit she glanced at her watch. That meant she would be late examining them. As she looked the door of the charabanc opened and the women dropped heavily, one by one, on to the snow-buried gravel. For a moment she was reminded of the blundering honey-bees of summer, over-weighted with pollen. But the image passed as they clustered together before the house, gazing about, their faces cold, movements distrustful. Swiftly she counted them. Two missing. That always happened: a husband or mother insisting on the child being born at home, raid or no raid. Turning from the window she caught a glimpse of a scarlet coat. Startled by the colour, she looked closer. She saw a girl standing apart, as in denial, and something about the arrogant head with its swathes of rich hair disturbed her. The others would be no trouble, but – with a definite feeling of unrest the doctor drew back into the room as Sister Matthews stepped out from the porch to welcome them.

The women looked hardly more at ease when they gathered for their examination. The doctor glanced swiftly at them as the nurse set up the screens at the far end of the room. They looked strange and pathetic, most of them in their early twenties, schoolgirl faces peaked with cold and the unaccustomed surroundings. They seemed unable to believe that the journey was over: the cold journey had started early that morning from among familiar streets, bombed buildings looking like half-destroyed snowcastles; the long journey during

59

which each had had time to realize that before she could return there would be pain and a new experience, to be borne alone. And at last the flat, frost-bitten country, which bewildered even the driver, had yielded them up to shelter – no, they could not quite believe it.

It seemed to the doctor that pregnancy had given back to each of them an innocence which sat hauntingly behind her eyes. It mixed with the flame of fear that gathered up and exposed each separate strand of emotion, weighting more finely the balance between reason and hysteria. She felt this fear reach out to claim her as she started the examinations, bending over each full-formed belly, placed so incongruously between a girl's face and slender legs, she felt the full flood of power take possession of her hands, giving out calmness and strength, guiding her to the living child. Confidence was the first essential. Something had to replace the loss of home, the cosseting of friends. Here one made the first move towards a successful delivery.

She was fully absorbed when the girl she had seen from the window walked round the screen. She recognized her thick hair and upright carriage. The doctor saw her eyes were large, the pupils dilated, dark, with green lights, as if she continually strained to focus attention away from her heavy body. She sat on the couch and drew away from the nurse's hands, pulling off her clothes. The doctor felt her shock of interest deepen and realized for the first time that Sister Matthews' actions were repellent – impersonal as a brothel-keeper's, partially undressing a girl for a client's appraisal. 'That will do, sister,' she said, and the tone of her voice made the nurse withdraw, hurt, to the table, where she made a show of checking names.

What lay behind those painfully wide eyes, wondered the doctor as she carried on the examination. 'Relax,' she said. 'Relax.' But the girl's muscles seemed locked. That would mean trouble later. 'Relax,' she said again. 'You must let yourself go loose. There's nothing to be afraid of. I won't hurt you.'

That touched something in the still face and a flare of colour covered the cheeks. 'I'm not afraid,' said the girl. 'This is just a process, like anything else . . .', but she relaxed and smiled slightly. The doctor nodded approval.

'That's better,' she said. What a voice the girl had. After the hesitancy of the others, their frayed enunciation, its clearness was astounding. It was like her own voice, decisive, entirely under control. Sister Matthews handed her a slip of paper, and she frowned slightly, motioning the girl to dress. 'We'll be keeping you in here for a few days,' she said, 'then we'll see about billeting you out.'

The girl sat up and pulled on her clothes. 'Oh!' she said, 'I expected that. My blood-pressure's always been erratic.' She laughed, as if here she was on the doctor's ground and could claim equality.

The doctor looked at her sharply. 'Then you'll know how to take care of yourself. No smoking, no alcohol.'

'Alcohol? In this wilderness?' the girl raised her eyebrows. 'All right to go now?' she asked.

'Lady touch-me-not,' murmured the sister as she re-adjusted the screens. She was angry and her eyes were unkind. 'She'll soon find her level here.'

In the days that followed, the doctor and each one of the staff saw Theresa Jenkins moving silently among the other women, accepting no mien of behaviour. Hers was a dark dress where the others wore flowered smocks, full, but not full enough to disguise the bouncing burdens which governed their every movement. She walked erect and lightly in contrast to the lurching tread of those around her. She did not knit or sew to patterns; she very seldom read. But every day she walked the two miles into the nearest market town and brought back silks or wools or books for the others.

It was here the doctor next encountered her; on a day of blizzard when the snow drove horizontally across the heath, lying flat as a footprint between the hall and Airton. She was leaning against the low wall on the bridge, the wind whipping the scarlet coat around her. Below, the waterfall was frozen.

She did not look round when the car drew up until the doctor's voice, sharp with command, came through the blinding flakes. The door was opened and she climbed in, shutting it behind her with dead fingers. 'A little exercise I said, not a cross-country run . . .' Firmly the doctor rubbed the windscreen and adjusted the wipers. They moved forward as a camouflaged army lorry passed them in a white cloud.

'Yes, it was a bit too much today,' said the girl; she was blue round the lips. 'But I'm well ballasted.'

'Well, I'm putting you and your ballast to bed when we get back, and you're staying there.'

Theresa looked coolly at the determined face beside her and shrugged. 'But not in one of those great communal bedrooms – there's no fire, and the beds are awful, filled with chicken food . . .'

They entered the drive. There was a tensed, sparring atmosphere between them. The doctor fell back on her power of position. She said, 'I'm putting you into solitary confinement. You're in for an attack of 'flu.'

As she drove the car round to the back of the house she thought: she upsets me, makes me feel – oh, I don't know.

In the nursery on the ground floor there was never complete silence. Nurse Griffith, standing by the weighing machine, looked with sudden exasperation along the rows of baskets. From nearly each one came a thin gasping cry or a long effortless wail. 'If they'd only stop. Just for a moment. All together,' she said aloud. But as if in defiance a quacking gurgle joined in. 'Well, you'll be gone tomorrow, glory be,' she observed, 'and I wish your mother joy of you.'

The door opened and two other nurses came in, carrying bundles under their arms, bundles done up in striped blankets and shaped like paper twists for sweets.

'Bullying them again, Griffith?' said one of them and, laying one of her burdens in a basket she sat down and unwrapped the other, revealing a tiny crumpled face and one red fist. She started to change its napkin.

'I was just telling Donald Duck how glad I shall be when he goes.'

'Poor little Donald, I shall miss him. Such an *individualist*,' said the other nurse. Her eyes were dark and moist. She looked as if she overflowed with love for each baby there.

Nurse Griffith grunted. She was Scottish and spared her emotion. 'Have you seen the doctor?' she inquired. 'I want her to look at young Rolly – he'll have to be circumcized, I think.'

'She's due any minute.' The dark-eyed nurse was frowning at the child she had unwrapped and who now lay screaming on the scales. She checked the weight, then whisked the child off. 'Not enough food. I thought her milk was going off. Come along, chicken.' She took up a bottle warming by the fire and settled herself in a chair. The child's face uncrumpled as its mouth found the teat. 'I can give a guess where she is, though. In Ward 12, and there's nothing wrong with Mrs Jenkins now.'

'Nothing apart from having a baby,' said Nurse Griffith. 'I said to her the other day, "Soon be over, Mrs Jenkins. Next week for you." And she gave me such a look. Sat up and said, "No doubt you're looking forward to it. Well, I'm not." So I said, "One baby more or less makes no difference to me, my girl. I've brought enough into the world."'

'Doctor seems to get on well with her, though,' said the other nurse.

'Get on well!' Nurse Griffith sniffed. 'There *was* an atmosphere when I went in this morning. Cut it with a knife, you could.' She broke off as the door opened and the doctor came in with the matron, who was in her outdoor clothes. She was frowning slightly, and Nurse Griffith looked keenly at her. It seemed that the wailing of the babies affected her more than usual this morning; her frown had deepened as they walked down the rows together. Carefully she asked questions and conducted examinations in her usual capable manner, but it seemed to the nurse that her eyes were preoccupied.

'You're quite right, nurse,' she said. 'Baby Rolly needs to

63

be circumcized. I'll see his mother.' Turning to the matron she said, 'I think I'll leave those vaccinations now, and do all three together later.' With a nod she left them and walked quickly from the nursery.

'Perhaps she's a little tired,' said the matron, 'she *does* work hard.'

But the doctor was not feeling tired as she walked across the cold stone hall and down the passage opposite to where the narrow wooden stairs ran up from just past the dining-room door. As she went slowly up to the next floor and passed along the narrow corridor of closed doors she thought, a little shakily: that was a strange thing for a patient to say to me. It's never happened before. She had passed through the width of the house and now stood on the first main landing. The huge polished space of floor with the broad and shining staircase curving down to the hall below and up to the labour ward on the next floor quietened her. As always its familiarity was startling; she might have been born here. The wide windows framed the winter and for a moment she stopped, undecided. She's no right to speak to me like that, she thought, and made to go to her own room, with the comforting china procession along the mantelpiece; ducks, elephants, donkeys – but the pricking unease forbade her the comfort of a fire or even the absorption of study. No right?

She had said, going into Ward 12 that morning, 'You'll be having your baby very soon, Mrs Jenkins. I like to tell the more intelligent mothers exactly what happens, it makes it easier . . .', but had been unable to go on, seeing the irony on the other's face. The girl sat there in bed, a little flushed, the eyes mocking her, openly mocking the whole procedure of birth, the diet, the routine, the urine tests.

'I expect I shall find out for myself, thanks,' she said. Her voice was casual as if she were turning away an itinerant salesman. The doctor went white, but forced herself to say, as if she had heard nothing, 'And if there's anything worrying you, preventing you from sleeping, you'll tell me, won't you? It's important not to have anything on your mind.' She turned from the bed and walked over to the fireplace as she spoke, and standing in the attitude of her father, with legs apart and hands clasped loosely, she felt some of his strength flow into her.

'Yes, people seem to hate you having anything on your mind,' came the voice from the bed. 'Calm motherhood, that's the idea, isn't it? The most beautiful time of a woman's life, preparing for the little stranger –' her whole face twisted suddenly, but whether with pain or disgust the doctor could not make out.

'That wasn't my idea at all,' she said. 'Some people think that way, others don't. Nurse Barnes tells me you're not sleeping. I want to know why.' She had accepted the challenge flung out by the mocking face, but immediately regretted it. For the girl had sent her a glance meaning: is it really your business? The door opened then and Nurse Griffith had come in.

Now, standing in the faint chilled sunlight, she thought: of course it's my business. Did the girl think that having a baby was as easy as that? Did she think that at such a time she could remain private and apart? Where would you be in medicine without method and routine? I won't let her bother me, she thought, and shrugging, turned to go up the stairs past the labour ward. I must see Mrs Rolly.

The visit to the quiet ward with its rows of docile women knitting or talking was curiously soothing. Here was her defence, among the soft-eyed women, soft as if milk flowed through every vein. No complications. No questioning of her authority and importance. They were gentle as cattle in good pasture. I must go back to Ireland, she thought as she left the ward in a small stir behind her. That's what's wrong. I need a holiday. Whenever things were too difficult – examinations near, her mind caught at the low green image of the land near her home.

She looked in at the dispensary on her way down.

'Oh, Nurse Barnes,' she said, 'give Mrs Jenkins a sleeping draught tonight.'

From below, distantly, came the ring of the telephone. 'I'll go,' she said. 'Matron's out.' But as she ran down the main staircase the bell stopped abruptly. Opening the door of the matron's sitting room she saw Theresa Jenkins at the desk, a blue dressing-gown clasped round her, and holding the receiver tightly to her ear.

The girl looked up.

'Long distance,' she said, her hand over the mouthpiece, 'for me.'

It was annoying how composed, how *right*, she looked, sitting there in the matron's room, at the matron's desk. The doctor let her feelings out in a sentence she knew with all her being would hurt. 'You know you women are not allowed in here,' she said, leaning deliberately against the door, eyebrows raised. She saw the deep flush spread over the girl's face, and knew she had scored. But next moment the girl was speaking into the phone. Her voice was hurried, a little shaken. 'Hallo, yes darling, it's me.' The doctor could hear nothing of the voice at the other end of the line, but it spoke at length and the girl listened, her colour ebbing to normal. Then, 'Of course,' she said.

The doctor walked towards the wide white fireplace where the matron's cat, grey as the ash falling from the logs, arched itself for a caress. What can I say to her, she thought, automatically smoothing the quick ears. The quiet of the pale walls, the cat's electric purring, the soft private answers of the girl at the telephone helped the doctor to define the feelings which had disturbed her since that first glimpse of the scarlet coat through the window. Odd how she had felt there would be trouble from her. She was always right in these things. She remembered the old man who had said he could see the power about her: 'You could heal by a touch, dear young lady,' and the sweat was ridged above his eyebrows, caught in the bushiness of them. He had died the next day. Shaking herself free of that Dublin slum she looked into the fire. The girl was different, outside her power. It was like being faced by a new and hostile world. She heard footsteps and laughter go past the door and felt again the tremendous difference between the girl at the desk and those others. They had accepted life in the hospital as a logical conclusion to the months of carrying the child; putting behind them their private lives. At this time everything was swamped in the expectation of birth; husbands were unreal, the newspapers not important. They were the childbearers.

The doctor pushed a log in place with her foot and watched the sudden sparks showering. The cat jumped a little. That attitude makes it much easier for us, she thought. Biological, impersonal. The nurses must feel the same.

The girl at the desk was speaking now, purposefully, with a hint of impatience.

She mightn't be having a child at all, thought the doctor with indignation. She goes on exactly as if she were at home, or on a visit. Perhaps her own life is too exciting. As this thought passed through her mind a sudden envy attacked her. It came as unexpectedly as the sound of the clock outside the door, striking with the ponderous hesitation of old age.

Snaking over the countryside went the wire connecting Theresa's life with Rowley Hall. Somewhere out in the snow, in a city, a man was sitting, or maybe standing, one leg up on a chair, watching his cigarette spiral in smoke as he spoke into the receiver. Other worlds, other relationships; the whole organization of Rowley Hall meaning nothing beside them. She, the doctor, of as little significance as an obliging bus conductor, a helpful policeman. She felt enclosed in this smooth-running house, its babies across the hall, its mothers above. Yet they all depend on me. The thought brought no pride, only a sense of suffocation and a sudden, I would give it all up for a telephone call from a city . . .

The receiver was hung up with a small metallic noise.

For a moment both women stared at it. The line was dead now: over snow wastes ran the slack wires.

'Come and get warm before you go upstairs,' said the doctor, and the girl moved slowly, heavily towards the fireplace. Her face was like stone.

'Cats are so magnificently selfish,' she said, staring down.

The doctor knew it was her moment; the girl looked drained, as if contact with the vital world outside had been too much for her. She was lost between the two existences; a word and she would be shattered. As a woman, cunning, before the fire, the doctor could spin a web of words – she could capture that world, suck it from the girl. But she said, 'I'll walk upstairs with you,' and put a hand on her elbow. 'You'd better get into bed and rest.' Without a word they left the room and went up the shallow stairs in silence. Something has happened, thought the doctor. I do hope . . . but her fear was a vague thing, scarcely yet known to her intuition.

As they turned in to Ward 12 the girl said, 'Matron knew I was expecting a call.' She sat on the bed and knocked off her blue slippers. As she settled against the pillows the doctor pulled the clothes round her. She felt at ease doing these things, her brain working. Does she need sal volatile, a cup of tea? A glance at her watch told her tea would be brought round within ten minutes. She sat down.

'Do you really want your baby?' she asked.

They looked at each other. The distance between them was so vast, so wearying, that it had to be accepted, could never be crossed.

'You'd like me to want it, wouldn't you?' said Theresa. Exhaustion seemed to edge her voice, and increase the hidden store of rancour. Or was it bitterness, torment, sorrow? 'You'd like to feel it meant everything to me, and I was relying on you to get me through.'

'What nonsense,' said the doctor. Despite her reason she felt suddenly malicious. 'You're just one patient, and I don't want any trouble. You're the sort of person to cause it . . .'

'Trouble?' Theresa laughed outright. 'No, you're not used to that, are you? The only people you can deal with are weaklings – the world's temporary throw-outs. The world's too sharp a place for you . . .'

The doctor was stung to anger. Almost with relief she let hatred take possession of her. 'And you,' she said, 'and you?

What do you do to face the world – what do you do for it?'

But the girl turned away; her face suddenly dulled.

'I?' she asked, and dropped her hand on the sheet. 'I?' Glancing at the doctor, still white and taut by the fire, she smiled, almost kindly. 'I am the pincushion you sit on by mistake, or perhaps a rash between the shoulder blades you cannot reach. A very special function. And very necessary. Look how I have roused you.'

The doctor turned away with a gesture. Lack of sleep, nerves. She didn't like it. Futile to waste the energy of anger on her.

The door opened and a nurse brought in the tea.

'Mrs Stimpson is up in the labour ward, doctor,' she said, placing the tray in front of the girl in bed, on to her flattened knees. 'Run it pretty close,' she moved over to the windows and hauled the black-out into position. 'Went into town this afternoon to have her hair set. What will they do next?'

'I'll go up,' said the doctor. As she went from the room she saw a letter lying on the tray. 'I was expecting this,' she heard Theresa say to the nurse, and as she walked away up the corridor it was as if some other world had brushed against her own, brushed past and was gone forever.

The next afternoon Mrs Stimpson lay in the smaller post-natal ward, which was on the ground floor next to the nursery. Centuries back it had been a refectory, built on to the side of the house with its own fine pointed roof, all timber. Later, as sunroom, the roof had been cut off and sheets of glass laid across, so that now, lying flat in bed and gazing up, it was as if the sky itself domed the room.

Red Cross nurses stood on chairs pulling the cords which operated a complicated system of black-out.

'Goodbye to the evening star,' said one of them as the black canvas was slowly manœuvred across the darkening sky. Mrs Stimpson glanced at the empty bed beside her.

'Still worrying, Stimmy?' said the woman in the bed opposite. 'She'll be all right, you'll see.' She broke off as one of the regular nurses entered the ward. 'Any news, nurse?'

'Doctor's still up there. She looks worn out.' The little nurse, trim and young, was concerned. 'Mrs Jenkins will be down sometime this evening . . .'

'Boy or girl?' asked the woman eagerly.

The nurse turned away. They would know later.

'She lost it. A boy,' she said, and to calm the sudden gasp quickly went on, 'Now, Sister will be round in a minute. What shall it be? Liquid paraffin or cascara?'

Mrs Stimpson lay still. She remembered the hurry and shock of the matron, brought at midnight to the labour ward; the quiet sobs of pain, the sudden high note in the doctor's voice. Then silence and they had quickly carried her down here.

There was another empty bed in the ward, and the occupant was moving uncertainly about. The other women watched her. The floor seemed ominous as a stage, an empty dance floor; too big, too shiny to cross. They had seen her dressing, shared the pleasure in pulling on the narrow elastic belt, the slim skirt. With the putting on of normal clothes she had stepped out of the circle of their small world; already she was apart from them. She had become once more the wife, the mother with a home of her own. In a day or two she would be gone, in a week forgotten: they would never meet again. She moved across to put more coal on the fire, then sat down, grave. Fancy losing your baby, she thought, shocked. Tomorrow at nine she was to bathe hers. In a month, in a week, it would be a common thing, but now it was terrifying. The experience upstairs would be forgotten too, forgotten as were all shattering things, the edge of them anybody's adventure.

The woman by the fire stirred, shivered a little, she must get back to bed.

Later, when the whole ward was settled into sleep, the firelight tossing darkness into corners, the door opened and a night-nurse pushed open the door. She wore a thick black cape against the chill of the stone corridors, and carried a storm lantern held high. Four figures came heavily into the room, bearing a stretcher. Silently they opened the bed next to Mrs Stimpson and slid their burden into it. After a careful survey they went out again, four shadows following them to the door. There was no sound from the bed.

Once outside the matron put her arm round the doctor's shoulders. 'You did all you could, my dear. You were wonderful,' she said. 'It was not your fault. Not in the least. The girl –' she let her hand fall. 'Hopeless, disgraceful.'

'It's the first baby I've lost,' said the doctor. 'It's never happened before. To lose a life –' she shook her head.

'*You* didn't lose it,' said the matron sharply. 'I can't understand it. Such a dreadful thing to do – we must ask her – so wicked – wicked.'

'No, she must sleep now,' said the doctor. 'Must give her time.' Time. She was dazed with the strain and shock. Her mind was empty and yet terribly clear. I couldn't have saved the child. She saw to that. Too late . . .

The matron opened her sitting-room door. 'A cup of tea,' she said, 'before you go to bed.'

They sat down before the fire and the matron made tea. The doctor carefully built up the dying fire. The exactitude soothed her hands, she felt steadied. She could bring her mind round to face the thought that had been tugging at her all day, ever since the bitter knowledge of what the girl had done was clear to her. Theresa had known what she was going to do – perhaps she had discussed it over the phone, with the doctor in the room. But that was too horrible. Perhaps it was the letter. Or, worst of all, she may have done it knowing what a shattering effect it would have on her. She said in defence against the evil she felt beating at the walls of her house, 'Every child we bring into the world is some sort of victory. We must always be against the destroyers.'

The matron poured milk into the cups and tested the tea. Her face, smooth as a nun's, looked towards the other woman, with her young blonde head and the blue ribbon threading her hair. How young she looks, she thought. Yet I suppose she's right. I suppose that's what a hospital is for. And yet was it? To her a hospital entailed lists of necessities, changing faces, great quietness and clean smells. When I was young, she thought. But years pass and peaks become plains; the war against disease and germs becomes a routine thing. You win and you lose and miracles sometimes happen. I am old, she thought. I fight in my own way.

She shook her head.

'The risk,' she said in awe. 'What a risk to take, and how wicked! Yes, wicked after all these months' – for an instant she knew grief at the thought of the flawless kicking child, a sound boy. Life in the shell – frail fingers and curled toes. To cut this life off, which was the world's life, belonged to the world – with – what, a hairpin? Wicked, wicked. Denying God a life. She shook this thought away, cast away too, the little cold curled body in the white wrappings. It would have to be buried.

'Your tea, my dear,' she said. 'I'll have to take you in hand, I can see. Can't have our doctor cracking up.'

In her own room later, the doctor remembered this phrase. Our doctor. It set the tempo of her dreams. Theresa, at the end of a narrow corridor, a naked child held high, always eluding her. Theresa laughing, big-bellied; calling in the soundless medium of a dream-shout: Doctor! Our doctor! And near dawn, a procession of women passing, herself in a cage, and each woman having a key to fasten the many locks. Our doctor, said their devoted faces. Dear doctor.

All the next day Theresa slept. She had a pale, burnt-out look to her, and her mouth lay defenceless and innocent. What sort of woman is she? thought the doctor, what sort of life has she? Is she really married? What will she do? The doctor stood over her, thinking, probing. But the sleeping face was closed to her.

As she left the ward, she saw the dark look in Nurse Griffith's eyes and on impulse took her aside and said what was in her own mind, said it as much in warning to herself. 'We are here to get people well, nurse. Their lives outside are not our concern; we are not judges. I don't want the other women to hear about this. She lost her baby, that is all. And she is to be treated exactly as they are.' Looking into the tightened face she knew the ways an unpopular patient could be treated. A rough shouldering whilst making the bed or changing dressings, delay with the bedpan, pillows set uncomfortably. A dozen small unkindnesses. 'Very well, doctor,' said the nurse stiffly.

It helped the doctor to give these instructions. It gave her ascendancy over that other world, sensed through a phone call, seen in a letter, but strangely missing from the relaxed face on the pillow. All that day she was at peace, she was taking no advantages, the two worlds lay quiescent.

The next morning she watched the girl wake up, turning on her back, the eyes suddenly wide and dark. Her arms were bent up from the elbows and the palms of her hands lay on the pillow either side of her face. 'Philip,' she said.

The doctor was moving forward to lay her hand on the girl's forehead, but the voice, so weak and certain, made her draw back sharply. Philip? Her husband? The action attracted the girl's gaze and in an instant she understood. 'Could I have something to drink?' she asked.

In the days that followed she gradually recovered. Silently she sat propped high and watched the other women as they knitted or talked or fed their children. At first they did these things almost furtively, feeling guilt in her quiet presence, but as the days passed they came to expect her silence and almost forgot her. If the peace of the room, with its six low oaken beds and warm mauve blankets flowed into her, she never showed it, although her face softened as her split body healed, and her eyes assumed an abiding sorrow, something indefinable which would never leave them.

One day, early on, at feeding time, the doctor was helping the woman in the next bed when Nurse Griffith dropped a glass and rubber instrument on to the girl's bed. 'You'll need this, Mrs Jenkins,' she said as she passed on. 'I'll come back and show you how to use it.'

The girl and the doctor looked at it together. 'It's a breast pump,' said the doctor, her hand on the other woman's shoulder. 'You *must* relax your shoulders,' she said.

Theresa stared at it, then round at the others, busy with their children, each sunk into a cocoon of warm flowing milk.

'Let me show you,' said Nurse Griffith. 'Over here. So. Then pump gently here. It's quite easy.'

She went away after a minute and the girl watched the needle sprays of milk jetting into the glass bulb. Glancing across at the doctor she gave a short laugh. The doctor's fingers trembled. She knew what it meant: the final gesture. But from somewhere deep in her mind echoed the calm voice, the beloved voice: *don't choose medicine unless you believe in it . . .* What did it say, what had he said, all those buried years ago? *People are lost, all of them. Lost in soul or body, mind or spirit, call it what you will. You can help them. You're a healer. I know it and you know. Help, heal . . .*

Help, who was to help whom? It was all lies, the voice from the past, your hand's cunning, lies to get you into a bright little, tight little hygienic cage, rubber-sprung – and still you helped nobody.

'Oh doctor,' said the woman beneath her hand. 'Oh doctor,' she said in pain.

The day Theresa Jenkins left Rowley Hall it was snowing again. Flakes hesitated in the still air, settling chill and furtive on windowsills, gravel and in the furrows of the ploughed field before the house. The doctor saw her as she came across from the stairs, holding a notice in her hand to pin to the board. Healed, departing, life in the ward behind her, the girl stood in the grey hall, thin and empty-armed. On impulse the doctor went up to her.

'Don't you want to see where your baby –?'

Theresa looked at her, moistening the lips she had reddened for the journey. 'No,' she said. 'Thank you for seeing to all that.'

A car came up the drive, churning through the snow. Theresa picked up her case and held out her hand.

'Goodbye,' she said, and the snow blew in as she opened the door.

As the car slowly turned and brushed its way past the overladen yews, the doctor ran on to the porch, leaning into the snow and fighting an almost uncontrollable urge to run after it. Suddenly she could not bear to see her go, knowing nothing. It was as if the girl was driving into a void, travelling always out from the place where the child lay, a cold body, never to uncurl. As if with her, she took the whole meaning of the doctor's life, her work. I can't stay here, she thought, moving back to the board in the hall. She tore down an old notice and crumpled it in one swift movement. Have to get another job. Go out into the world. Do something. But what? She looked at her hands; they had made her a doctor. Healer's hands. But what was a doctor? An attendant upon life only. Apart from the mainstream: receiving and sending forth, healing and bringing forth. But why? Where did they all go, the healed in body? Looking at her hands, she thought with panic: if I was asked to deliver a child now, what would I do? What *do* you do? The printed page of one of her textbooks was before her. She saw clearly the form of the printed page, the paragraphs, sub-headings, the diagrams, carefully coloured. But the meaning was lost to her, the type meaningless. A nurse crossed the hall and disappeared into the nursery, two babies tucked under her arms. She was smiling. The doctor thought, I must have some reason for staying here in the cold. Then she saw the notice she had to pin up: 'Permission must be obtained . . .' She smoothed it out, and pinned it in a good light. When it was done another surge of irritation ran through her. Nurses and wards, patients and deliveries, was there no end to them? What of the free, the open life outside where you could be a woman, nothing more? Theresa Jenkins had no struggle there – her only problem was to be a woman, how to get through that way. A doctor had one path before her; everything must be seen in that one clear light, no muddleheads, no sidetracks, no envy. After all, in medicine you knew too much, perhaps that kept you apart. The earth was teeming, all you did was to direct the flow. We're all the same, she thought; bus conductors, commission-aires, doctors. She laughed a little. But do they really trust us?

She shivered. She saw that the door was open again. How could that be?

She had not heard the charabanc churning up the drive, had missed the pull of brakes, and the women dropping heavy as honey bees to the white-felted ground. Sister Matthews had come through the hall and was gathering the women together, driving them in from the cold.

A touch, like a summons, fell on her arm.

'You're the doctor, aren't you?' said a small Cockney voice. The doctor looked round, saw the customary fear, the pinched mouth, hair damp with melting snow. 'My friend, Mrs Stimp-son, told me about you. She said to tell you the baby's doing well, thanks to you. She said you'd take care of me. It's my first –' the woman paused. Woman? She was little more than a girl. 'A child's a precious thing,' she said shyly.

The doctor was staring at her. 'Yes,' she said. 'Yes, I'm the doctor.' Although the world can turn up and around like the snowstorm in a glass ball, it will settle, and I am still the doctor: there is still humanity. She passed a hand over her eyes, as if to wipe away a lifetime's doubt, a six-week torment.

'Don't you worry at all,' she said. 'I'll see you through.' And walking along the hall with her, she knew she could.

They Came

ALUN LEWIS

The evening was slowly curdling the sky as the soldier trudged the last mile along the lane leading from the station to the Hampshire village where he was billeted. The hedgerows drew together in the dusk and the distance, bending their waving heads to each other as the fawn bird and the blackbird sang among the green hollies. The village lay merged in the soft seaward slope of the South Downs; the soldier shifted his rifle from left to right shoulder and rubbed his matted eyelashes with his knuckles. He was a young chap but, hampered by his heavy greatcoat and equipment, he dragged his legs like an old clerk going home late. He cleared his throat of all that the train journey, cigarettes and chocolate and tea and waiting had secreted in his mouth. He spat the thick saliva out. It hung on a twig.

Someone was following him. When he heard the footsteps first he had hurried, annoyed by the interfering sound. But his kit was too clumsy to hurry in and he was too tired. So he dawdled, giving his pursuer a chance to pass him. But the footsteps stayed behind, keeping a mocking interval. He couldn't stop himself listening to them, but he refused to look back. He became slowly angry with himself for letting them occupy his mind and possess his attention. After a while they seemed to come trotting out of the past in him, out of the Welsh mining village, the colliers gambling in the quarry, the county school where he learned of sex and of knowledge, and college where he had swotted and slacked in poverty, and boozed, and quarrelled in love. They were the footsteps of the heavy-jawed deacon of Zion, with his white grocer's apron, and his hairy nostrils sniffing out corruption.

But that was silly, he knew. Too tired to control his mind, that's what it was. These footsteps were natural and English, the postman's perhaps . . . But still they followed him, and the dark gods wrestling in him in the mining valley pricked their goaty ears at the sound of the pimping feet.

He turned the corner into the village and went down the narrow street past the post office and the smithy, turned the corner under the AA sign and crossed the cobbled yard of the hotel where the officers' and business men's cars were parked. A shaggy old dog came frisking out of its straw-filled barrel in the corner, jumping and barking. He spoke to it and at once it grovelled on its belly. He always played with the dog in the mornings, between parades. The unit did its squad drill in the hotel yard, kitchen maids watching flirtatiously through the windows, giggling, and the lavatory smelling either of disinfectant or urine.

He pushed open the little door in the big sliding doors of the garage which had been converted into a barrack room for the duration. The electric bulbs high in the cold roof dangled a weak light from the end of the twisted, wavering flex. Grey blankets folded over biscuits or straw palliasses down both sides of the room. Equipment hanging from nails on the whitewashed wall – in one corner a crucifix, over the thin, chaste, taciturn Irish boy's bed. He was the only one in the room, sitting on his bed in the cold dark corner writing in his diary. He looked up and smiled politely, self-effacingly, said, 'Hallo. Had a good leave?' and bent his narrow head again to read what he had written.

'Yes, thanks,' said the soldier, 'except for raids. The first night I was home he raided us for three hours, the sod,' he said, unbuckling his bayonet belt and slipping his whole kit off his shoulders.

Last time he returned from leave, four months back, he had sat down on his bed and written to his wife. They had married on the first day of that leave and slept together for six nights. This time he didn't ferret in his kitbag for notepaper and pencil. He went straight out.

The hotel management had set a room aside for the soldiers to booze in. It was a good class hotel, richly and vulgarly finished with plush and mirrors and dwarf palms in green boxes. The auctioneers and lawyers and city men, the fishermen and golfers and bank managers, most of whom had weekend cottages or villas of retirement in commanding positions at the local beauty spots, spent the evening in the saloon bar and lounge, soaking and joking. So the soldiers were given a bare little bar parlour at the back, with a fire and a dartboard and two sawdust spittoons. The soldiers were glad of it. It was their own. They invited some of their pals from the village to play darts with them – the cobbler, the old dad who lived by himself in the church cottage and never shaved or washed, the poacher who brought them a plucked pheasant under his old coat sometimes – all the ones the soldiers liked popped in for an evening. A few girls, too, before the dance in the church hall, on Tuesdays.

Fred Garstang from Portsmouth and Ben Bryant from Coventry, the two oldest soldiers in the unit – regulars who had never carried a stripe – were playing darts, two empty pint glasses on the mantelpiece by the chalk and duster.

'Owdee, Taffy?' they said in unison. ''Ave a good leave, lad?'

'Yes, thanks,' he said automatically, 'except for raids. The sod raided us for three hours the first night I was home.'

'Damn. Just the wrong side of it,' said Fred, examining the quivering dart. 'I deserve to lose this bloody game, Ben. I 'xpect you're same as me, Taff; glad to get back to a bit of peace and quiet and a good sleep. My seven days in Pompey's the worst I've ever spent in India, China, the Rhineland, Gallygurchy, or anywhere. But we're nice and cosy here, thank God. They can keep their leave. *I* don't want seven nights in an Anderson. I'd rather stay here, I would.'

Old Fred never stopped talking once he started. The soldier tapped the counter with a shilling and leaned over to see whether the barmaid was on the other side of the partition. He saw her silky legs and the flutter of her skirt. He hit the counter harder, then, while he waited, wondered at his impatience. His body wasn't thirsty; it was too damned tired to bother, too worn-out. It was something else in him that wanted to get drunk, dead, dead drunk.

The barmaid came along, smiling. She was natural with the soldiers. She smiled when she saw who it was and held her pretty clenched fist to him across the counter. He should have taken it and forced it gently open, of course. Instead, he just put his flat palm underneath it. She looked at him with a hurt-fawn reproach in her smiling eyes, and opening her hand let a toffee fall into his.

'One from the wood, Madge,' he said.

'I'll have to charge you for *that*,' she said.

'That's all right,' he replied. 'You always pay in this life.'

'Why don't you take the girl, Taffy?' said old Fred as he came and sat by them, their darts over. 'If I was your age . . .'

He had been in the army since he was fifteen. Now he was past soldiering, wandering in the head sometimes, doing odd jobs; in peace time he kept the lawns trimmed at the depot, now he was tin-man in the cooking-shed, cleaning with Vim the pots and pans Ben Bryant used for cooking. 'Vermicelli tastes all right,' he said. 'Better than anything you can pick up in the streets. Yellow or black, or white, German or Irish. I've never had a Russian though, never. It's not bad when you're young, like a new crane when the jib runs out nice and smooth; it's better than sitting in the trenches like an old monkey, scratching yourself and not knowing whose leg it is or whose arm it is, looking in his pockets to see if there's anything worth taking, and not knowing who'll win the race, the bullet with your number on it or the leaky rod you're nursing. But I like it here. It's nice and peaceful up here, in the cookhouse all day. We ought to try some vermicelli, Ben, one day.'

'Don't you get impatient now, Freddy,' Ben said with the calmness of a father of many children. 'We'll stuff your pillow full of it next Christmas and put a sprig of it on your chest. Don't you worry, boy.'

But old Fred went on talking like an old prophet in a volcanic world, about and about. 'There's no knowing when you've got to fight for your king and country,' he said. 'No matter who you are, Russian, or Frenchy, or Jerry – and the Yankee, too. He'll be in it, boy. I've seen him die. It's only natural, to my way of thinking. I wore a pair of gloves the Queen knitted herself, she did, last time. The Unknown Soldier I was, last time.'

None of us are ourselves now, the Welsh boy sat thinking: neither what we were, nor what we will be. He drained his pint glass and crossed to the counter, to Madge smiling there.

'You never looked round all the way up from the station,' she said, pulling her shoulder-straps up under her grey jumper and exposing the white rich flesh above her breasts.

'So it was you followed me, eh?' he said sardonically.

'Why didn't you turn round?' she asked. 'Did you know it was me? You knew someone was behind you, I could tell.'

'I didn't turn round because I didn't want to look *back*,' he said.

'And you mean to say you don't know how the Hebrew puts out the eyes of a goldfinch?' Freddy's aggrieved voice swirled up.

'Afraid of being homesick for your wife, eh?' she jeered.

He covered his eyes with his hand, tired out, and looked up at the vague sensual woman playing upon his instincts there like a gipsy on a zither.

'Not homesick,' he said drily. 'Deathsick.'

'What d'you mean?' she said.

'Well, she was killed in a raid,' he shouted.

He went up to the orderly room then, having forgotten to hand in his leave pass to the orderly corporal. The room was in the corner of an old warehouse. The building also housed the kitchen and the quartermaster's stores. About the high bare rooms with their rotten dry floors and musty walls, rats galloped in the darkness; in the morning their dirt lay fresh on the mildewed sacks and the unit's cat stretched her white paws and got a weak and lazy thrill from sniffing it.

The orderly corporal was dozing over a Western novelette from Woolworth's, hunched up in a pool of lamp- and firelight.

'Hallo, Taffy,' he said. 'Had a good leave?'

'Yes, thanks,' he replied. 'Except for raids. Am I on duty tomorrow?'

'You're on duty tonight, I'm afraid,' the orderly corporal replied with the unctuous mock-regret of one who enjoys detailing tired or refractory men for unexpected jobs.

'Dave Finley had a cold on his chest this morning and didn't get out of bed. So they fetched him out on a stretcher and the MO gave him pneumonia pills before Dave could stop him; so he's got pneumonia now. You'll go on guard at midnight and at six hours.'

'OK.'

He turned to go.

'Better get some sleep,' said the orderly corporal, yawning noisily. 'Hell! I'm browned off with this war.'

The soldier yawned too, and laughed, and returned to the barrack-room to lie down for a couple of hours. He rolled his blankets down on the floor and stretched out.

Old Ben and Fred were back, also, Ben fixing bachelor buttons into his best trousers and singing Nelly Dean comfortably to himself, Fred muttering by the stove. 'There's some mean and hungry lads in this room,' he said; 'very hungry and mean. It's an awful nature, that. They'll borrow off you all right, but they won't lend you the turd off their soles. And always swanking in the mirror, and talking all the time, saying, yes, they can do the job easy. The fools! Whip 'em! Whip 'em!'

Ben was toasting bread on the point of his bayonet and boiling water in his billy. A tin of pilchards left over from tea was for them all.

'Come on, Taffy. Have a bellyful while you can,' he said.

'No, thanks,' said the soldier, restless on his blankets. 'I don't feel like food tonight, Ben, thanks.'

'Ain't you never bin hungry?' Fred shouted, angrily. 'You don't know what food is, you youngsters don't.'

'I've been without food,' the soldier said, thinking of the '26 strike; and going without peas and chips in the chip shop by the town clock in college, when a new book must be bought. But not now, when everything is free but freedom, and the doctor and dentist and cobbler send you no bills. What survives I don't know, the soldier thought, rubbing his hot eyelids and shifting his legs on the spreadout blankets. What is it that survives?

He got up and buckled his battle order together, adjusting his straps, slipping the pull-through through his Enfield, polishing boots and buttons, tightening his helmet strap under his chin.

'There was a religious woman used to come to our house,' Ben was saying, 'and one day she said to me, sociable like, "You're a Guinness drinker, aren't you, Mr Bryant?" and I says, "I am, mum." And she says, "Well, can you tell me what's wrong with the ostrich on them advertisements?"'

The soldier went out to relieve the guard.

They were only twenty soldiers altogether, sent up here to guard a transmitting station hidden in the slopes of the Downs. A cushy job, safe as houses. There was a little stone shed, once used for sheep that were sick after lambing, in a chalky hollow on the forehead of the hill, which the guard used for sleeping in when they were off duty. Two hours on, four hours off, rain and sun and snow and stars. As the soldier toiled up the lane and across the high meadows to the shed, the milky moon came out from grey clouds and touched with lucid fingers the chopped branches piled in precise lengths at the foot of the wood. The pine trees moved softly as the moon touched their grey-green leaves, giving them a veil that looked like rainy snow, grey-white.

The lane running up through the wood shortened alarmingly in perspective. A star fell. So surprising, so swift and delicate, the sudden short curved fall and extinction of the tiny lit world. But over it the Plough still stayed, like something imperishable in man. He leant against the gate, dizzy and light-headed, waves of soft heat running into his head. He swallowed something warm and thick; spitting it out, he saw it was blood. He stayed there a little, resting, and then went on.

He went along the sandy lane, noticing as he always did the antique sculptures of sea and ice and rain, the smooth twisted flints, yellow and blue and mottled, lying in the white sand down which the water of winter scooped its way.

At the top of the lane was the lambing shed – guard room. He slipped quickly through the door to prevent any light escaping. There was gunfire and the sound of bombs along the coast.

The sergeant of the guard was lying on a palliasse in front of the stove. He got up slowly, groaning lazily. 'So you're back again, Taffy, are you?' he said, a grudge in his too hearty welcome. 'Relieving Dave Finley, eh? He's swinging the lead, Dave is. I've a good mind to report him to the OC. It's tough on you, going on night guard after a day's journey. Have a good leave, Taff?'

'Not bad,' the soldier replied, 'except for the raids. Raided us the first night I was home.'

'It's a sod, everybody's getting it,' the sergeant replied, yawning. 'They dropped two dozen incendiaries in our fields in Lincs last week.'

He was drinking a billy can of cocoa which he had boiled on the fire, but he didn't offer any. He had weak blue eyes, a receding chin, fresh features of characterless good-looks, wavy hair carefully combed and brilliantined. He was always on edge against Taffy, distrusting him, perhaps envying him. He lived in terror of losing a stripe and in constant hunger to gain another promotion. He sucked and scraped the officers for this, zealously carrying out their orders with the finicky short temper of a weak house-proud woman. He polished the barrack-room floor and black-leaded the stove himself because the boys refused to do more than give the place a regulation lick. And he leaped at the chance of putting a man on the peg, he was always waiting to catch somebody cutting a church parade or nipping out of camp to meet a girl when he should be on duty. Yet he was mortally afraid of a quarrel, of unpopularity, and he was always jovial, glassily jovial, even to the Welsh boy whom he knew he couldn't deceive.

'Who am I to relieve on guard?' the soldier asked.

'Nobby Sherraton. He's patrolling the ridge.'

'OK.' He slipped his rifle sling over his shoulder and put his helmet on. 'You marching me out? Or shall I just go and send Nobby in?'

For once laziness overcame discretion.

'There's nobody about. Just go yourself,' the sergeant said, smiling, posing now as the informal honest soldier. 'I'll be seeing yer.'

'Some day.'

He left the hut and crossed the dry dead-white grass to the ridge where Nobby was on guard.

Nobby was his mate.

He had only been in the unit about a month. Before that he had been stationed just outside London and had done a lot of demolition and rescue work. He was from Mile End, and had roughed it. His hands and face showed that, his rough blackened hands, cigarette-stained, his red blotchy face with the bulbous nose, and the good blue eyes under tiny lids, and short scraggy lashes and brows. His hair was mousy and thin. He had been on the dole most of the time. He had been an unsuccessful boxer; he cleared out of that game when his brother, also a boxer, became punch-drunk and blind. He had plenty of tales of the Mosley faction. He was sometimes paid five bob to break up their meetings. He always took his five bob, but he let the others do the breaking up. Who wants a black eye and a cut face for five bob? 'Tain't worth it. He rarely said anything about women. He didn't think much of lots of them; though like all Cockney youths he loved the 'old lady', his mother. He wasn't married. No, sir.

He was a conscript. Naturally. He didn't believe in volunteering. And he didn't like the Army, its drills and orders and its insistence on a smart appearance. Smartness he disliked. Appearances he distrusted. Orders he resented. He was 'wise' to things. No sucker.

Taffy felt a warm little feeling under his skin, relief more than anything else, to see Nobby again. He hadn't to pretend with Nobby. Fundamentally they shared the same humanity, the unspoken humanity of comradeship, of living together, sharing what they had, not afraid to borrow or talk or shut up. Or to leave each other and stroll off to satisfy the need for loneliness.

Nobby was surprised so much that he flung out his delight in a shout and a laugh and a wave of his arms.

'Taffy, lad!' he said. 'Back already, eh? Boy!' Then he became normal.

'Can't keep away from this bloody sannytorium for long, can we?' he grumbled.

Taffy stood looking at him, then at the ground, then he turned away and looked nowhere.

'What's wrong, kid?' Nobby said, his voice urgent and frightened, guessing. 'Anything bad? Caught a packet, did you?' He said the last two phrases slowly, his voice afraid to ask.

'*I* didn't,' Taffy said, his voice thin and unsteady. '*I* didn't. *I'm* all right. *I'm* healthy.'

Nobby put his hand on his shoulder and turned him round. He looked at the white sucked-in face and the eyes looking nowhere.

'Did *she* get it?' and he too turned his head a little and swallowed. 'She did,' he said, neither asking a question nor making a statement. Something absolute, the two words he said.

Taffy sat down, stretched out. The grass was dead; white, wispy long grass; Nobby sat down, too.

'They came over about eight o'clock the first night,' Taffy said. 'The town hadn't had a real one before. I've told you we've only got apartments, the top rooms in an old couple's house. The old ones got hysterics, see, Nobby. And then they

86

wouldn't do what I told them, get down the road to a shelter. They wouldn't go out into the street and they wouldn't stay where they were. "My chickens," the old man was bluttering all the time. He's got an allotment up on the voel, see. Gwyneth made them some tea. She was fine, she calmed them down. That was at the beginning, before the heavy stuff began. I went out the back to tackle the incendiaries. The boy next door was out there, too. He had a shovel and I fetched a saucepan. But it was freezing, and we couldn't dig the earth up quick enough. There were too many incendiaries. One fell on the roof and stuck in the troughing. The kid shinned up the pipe. It exploded in his face and he fell down. Twenty-odd feet. I picked him up and both his eyes were out, see?'

He had gone back to the sing-song rhythm and the broad accent of his home, the back lanes and the back gardens. He was shuddering a little, and sick-white, sallow. Nobby waited.

'I took him into his own house,' he said, controlling his voice now, almost reflective. 'I left him to his sister, poor kid. Then I went in to see if Gwyneth was all right. She was going to take the old couple down the road to the shelter. She had a mack on over her dressing gown. We'd intended going to bed early, see? So I said she was to stay in the shelter. But she wanted to come back. We could lie under the bed together.

'I wanted her back, too, somehow. Then some more incendiaries fell, so I said, "Do as you like," and went at them with a saucepan. I thought sure one would blow my eyes out. Well, she took them down. Carried their cat for them. Soon as she'd gone the heavy stuff came. Oh, Christ!'

Nobby let him go on; better let him go on.

'It knocked me flat, dazed me for a bit. Then I got up and another one flattened me. It was trying to stop me, see, Nobby. I crawled out of the garden, but it was dark as hell, and buildings all down, dust and piles of masonry. Then he dropped some more incendiaries and the fires started. I knew she must be somewhere, see? I knew she must be somewhere. I began pulling the masonry away with my hands, climbed on to the pile of it in the fire. I couldn't see with the smoke and I knew it wasn't any use, only I had to do it, see?

'Then suddenly the masonry fell downwards. The road was clear on the other side. I thought it was all right after all, then. I thought she'd have reached the shelter . . . But she hadn't . . . I found her about twenty yards down the road . . .

'She wasn't dead. Her clothes were gone. And her hands. She put them over her face, I reckon.

'She couldn't speak, but I know she knew it was me. I carried her back in my arms. Over the fallen house. The fire wasn't bad by then. Took her home, see, Nobby. Only the home was on fire. I wanted her to die all the time. I carried her over a mile through the streets. Fires and hoses and water. And she wouldn't die. When I got her to the clearing station I began to think she'd live. But they were only playing a game with me, see?'

He stood up, and made himself calm.

'Well, there it is.' He rubbed his face with the palm of his hand, wiping the cold sweat off.

'I knew she was going to die. When they told me she was – I didn't feel anything, Nobby . . . But she died while they were messing her body about with their hands, see? . . . And she never said anything. Never said anything to me. Not that it makes any difference, I suppose. We never did speak about those things much. Only, you know how it is, you want a word somehow. You want it to keep.'

'Sure, I know,' Nobby said.

'What's it all for, Nobby?' he said in a while. He looked so tired and beat. 'I used to know what it was all about, but I can't understand it now.'

'Aw, forget all about that,' Nobby said. 'You're here, aincher, now?'

He put his hands on his mate's shoulders and let him lean against him for a bit. 'I reckon you belong to each other for keeps, now,' Nobby said.

'You believe that, Nobby?' he asked, slow and puzzled, but with a gathering force as his uncertainty came together.

88

'Yes. For you and 'er, I do. It wouldn't be true for me, or the sergeant in there, but for you two it is.'

Taffy was still against his shoulder. Then slowly he straightened himself, moved back on to himself, and lifting his face he looked at the milky-white fields and the sentinel pines and the stars.

'I knew it was so, really,' he said. 'Only I was afraid I was fooling myself.'

He smiled, and moved his feet, pressing on them with his whole weight as if testing them after an illness.

'I'm all right, now, Nobby. Thank you, boy.'

'I'll go, then,' Nobby said. He slipped his rifle over his shoulder and as he moved off he hesitated, turned back, and touched his mate's arm lightly.

'Two's company, three's none,' he said, and stumped off slowly to the lambing shed through the dead strawgrass.

And the soldier was left alone on the flat upland ridge.

Below him the valleys widened into rich arable lakes on which the moonlight and the mist lay like the skeins which spiders spin round their eggs. Beyond the pools another chain of downland lay across the valleys, and beyond those hills the coast. Over him, over the valleys, over the pinewoods, blue fingers came out of the earth and moved slanting across their quarters as the bombers droned in the stars over his head and swung round to attack the coastal city from inland. The sky over the coast was inflamed and violent, a soft blood-red.

The soldier was thinking of the day he received his calling up papers, just a year ago. Sitting on the dry stone wall of his father's back garden with Gwyneth by him; his ragged little brother kneeling by the chicken-run, stuffing cabbage stumps through the netting for the hens to peck, and laughing and pulling the stumps out as the old hen made an angry jab; his father riddling the ashes and the ramshackle garden falling to bits, broken trellis and tottering fence; his mother washing her husband's flannel vest and drawers in the tub, white and vexed. He had taken Gwyneth's hand, and her hand had said, 'In coming and in going you are mine; now, and for a little while longer; and then for ever.'

But it was not her footsteps that followed him down the lane from the station.

Now over his head the darkness was in full leaf, drifted with the purity of pines, the calm and infinite darkness of an English night, with the stars moving in slow declension down the sky. And the warm scent of resin about him and of birds and of all small creatures moving in the loose mould in the ferns like fingers in velvet.

And the soldier stood under the pines, watching the night move down the valleys and lift itself seawards, hearing the sheep cough and farm dogs restlessly barking in the farms. And farther still the violence growing in the sky till the coast was a turbulent thunder of fire and sickening explosions, and there was no darkness there at all, no sleep.

'My life belongs to the world,' he said. 'I will do what I can.'

He moved along the spur and looked down at the snow-grey evergreen woods and the glinting roofs scattered over the rich land.

And down in the valleys the church bells began pealing, pealing, and he laughed like a lover, seeing his beloved.

Grass in Winter

———— ✳ ————

DENYS VAL BAKER

Grass in winter clings to the feet with the hungry grasp of the unloved, cold and lifeless to the touch. The grass is lean and coarsened by the winds, dulled by sunless rains. Bare to the frowning sky, it bends and sways tremulously across lonely landscapes, occasionally shuddering as if from some deep, unknown agony of frustration. Like a vast sea, empty of purpose, grass in winter is alone and friendless; its reality of warmth and colour drained deep into the sleeping earth.

In a field of thick dark grass the soldier from another country crouched while the early but hidden sun struggled to colour the clouds. He crouched low in the grass, forgetting where he had come from, losing his other world into the coarse unreality of his new world. Around him the grass arose disinterestedly, high enough to shelter him from curious eyes, high enough to wash his strange dull uniform with a cold green sea.

Hidden in the grass, the soldier breathed uncomfortably, constantly brushing the long stalks out of his face. He had taken off his helmet and strapped it to his haversack, to avoid any danger of light being reflected from its surface. Now his hair, wet and dank from the morning dew, hung matted across his forehead, shrouding his small, square-set face. He looked tired and sleepless . . . the darkness of his expression was emphasized by a straggly stubble of beard. Only the eyes bespoke life, darting from side to side nervously – wild green pin-points among the wild green grass. The eyes burned with anxious life, while his tongue ran thick and dry, and a spasmodic, taut, sick feeling caught at his stomach.

Cautiously, for the first time since the light had come, the soldier moved. Slowly he raised his dark, rain-soaked head until it floated silently among the thin tops of the grass, like a dead log drifting in a lake. His eyes peeped at the long bent rows of grass, watched the shallow blends of green disappearing down the hillside . . . saw, uneasily, the faraway hedges, the grey-blue tint of a farm cottage. Slanting sideways, as the dead log aimlessly slants, the soldier's eyes followed another slope of green, endless across desolate fields, burying on the horizon in the faint glint of a river. Turning, and looking behind, he saw again only the wide green of his own field, curving suddenly to meet the sky, falling into some eternity beyond his gaze.

The soldier shivered. He fingered nervously at the cold wet shaft of his rifle, stretched beside him in the grass. His mind flickered irritably, longed to flash away beyond the horizon. Only with difficulty could he bring himself to concentrate on the reality of this world of cold green grass to which he now belonged utterly. Except that he was lost, he knew nothing. He did not know whether the dull rumbles of guns on the horizon were made by the enemy or his own side – whether the roar of sudden battle that had swept him along on its tide the previous day had ebbed away into nothingness, or stormed on to new horizons . . . or merely sunk into the very fields, to bubble like a volcano awaiting the next spurt. He only knew he was alone, vastly alone; and lost, unreally lost. He was only aware, instinctively, of a scent of death in the passing wind, wafted from some hidden, unrealized centres of life among the innocent waves of grass that filled his view. And he hated the long, treacherous grass, hated its evil secretiveness, even as he knew that his safety depended on it . . . He remembered how, in summer, the grass at home would be thick and warm and soft, so that he could sink into its folds and float into dreams. Now the grass had no warmth, no softness: it was only unreal – strands of shadowy, dank unreality. He could feel the long stalks, but they were cold and dead, and when he sank among them they parted lifelessly.

Most of the night he had lain curled uncomfortably on the

hardened soil. Thick as his uniform was, he had felt the cold and the wetness gradually seeping through, until the clothes were damp and clogging, chilling into his skin, paining his bones. The breaths he took were heavy with wetness from the grass, and hurt his lungs. He was thankful when the grey light had come. He felt that if he had lain there much longer he would have frozen into the cold earth.

When the morning had fully risen, the soldier began to crawl slowly through the grass. He crawled on his belly, for in parts the grass fell short and he dared not take any risks of being seen. He crawled like a snake, wriggling slowly and stealthily through some green, overhanging undergrowth. It struck him, in fact, that the grass itself was composed of so many snakes – dying snakes that wound and coiled around him as he crawled. Viciously he smashed ahead of him with the butt of his rifle, breaking and tearing the surprised stalks. It gave him a sense of pleasure, almost of power, to do this. It relieved a strange buried fear within him.

After a time, the soldier came to the end of the field and climbed through a hedge into the next field. He was moving in the direction of the plains where he felt vaguely there was more chance of discovering his whereabouts. Soon he came to the outskirts of the small cottage he had seen. Here, the grass petered out into a muddy garden, and he was forced to remain some distance away, pressed deep into the grass for a desperate shield. He lay there for some time and was thankful for his caution as, with a thud at his heart, he saw a man emerge from the back of the cottage. He recognized the enemy uniform. For a moment his finger itched at the trigger of his gun; then he let go, frightenedly, hearing other voices from within the kitchen . . . Two other men came to the doorway.

The wave of fear that came over him tingled at his skin, shivering into his hair. He lay nerveless on the dead grass, conscious of the flimsiness of the stalks, fearful that a gust of wind would suddenly blow them aside. Only after what seemed an eternity, when the men had gone in again, did he stir. Then he began backing away into the deeper grass, making a wide circuit of the cottage as he passed on down the slope. But after he had disappeared, one of the men came out into the garden again and, looking casually out to the field, caught sight of the pathway forced through the grass. He hurried towards this, his look of curiosity fading into sudden alarm.

By the middle of the day the soldier had crawled down the slope and on to the plain, but still he found himself deep among seas of clinging grass. As he crawled from one field to another it seemed to him that he was lost, queerly and for ever, in the endless waves of grass. Looking around him, he could see nothing else, no other signs of life – of roads or habitation. Only here and there, startlingly, coming across half-hidden bodies of dead soldiers, was he reminded that death had passed this way before. Being reminded, he felt sickened again. He crouched lower in the grass, frightened of the oncoming clumps of green, suspicious of the faraway breezing grass-tops at which he aimed.

He became aware of hunger. It was more than twelve hours since he had eaten. With him he had only a water flask, already half-empty, and some biscuits. He ate these slowly, savouring the dry taste to the full. Then he lay on his back, gazing up at the colourless sky. Half-closing his eyes he could shut himself off from the one world, and the other world surged joyously into his thoughts. Drowning into sleep he was still faintly aware of the soft wind blowing across the field. He, felt, strangely, the harsh rub of the grass against his hands and under his head, and then he fell asleep.

When he awoke he was surprised to find a thin shaft of sunlight falling upon the green-sloped horizon. Fascinated, he followed it, watching it creep like a pointing finger across the waving grass. The sunlight crept towards him, wavered, then broke around him, flooding the field with whiteness. But even as he felt the unexpected warmness on his cheeks he sensed an intrinsic falsity about it. It was not the warmth he had felt at home in the summer fields; it was a false warmth, a false sun, giving out dead sunshine to the dead grass. He ran his fingers through the grass beside him: it was unchanged

– dank, cold, lifeless, unawakened by the sunshine. He tore up the unresisting stalks, throwing them away in sudden repulsion.

When next he moved, it was with a strange urgency. He was suddenly conscious – frighteningly conscious – of the endless evil lurking in the grassy, bland-faced fields. He shuddered at the thought of the shallowness, the bareness, the inadequacy of the grass. He longed to rise to his full height and take deep grateful gulps of sweet free air, free from the harsh smell of the soil, the damp odour of the grass. Yet even as the longing grew on him, tormenting him, tantalizing him – he felt the necessity to crouch even lower, to drag himself even more quickly through the slithering wet grass. His eyes ached from endless peering through the swaying tree-tops of grass. His cheeks smarted from the cuts of the coarse grass stalks. Sometimes a tuft of grass choked his nostrils, sticking to his mouth, leaving an unpleasant taste on his tongue as he spat it out.

He crawled on, across the longest and most torturous of all the fields. It seemed to stretch halfway across the plain. Looking sideways he could see, far away, the hill from where he had started, and the innocent blue tiles of the cottage. But his eyes blinked from the effort of looking, and he turned and went forward. He crawled on and on and on . . . and as he did it seemed to him that the grass deepened and grew thicker, rising higher and higher, engulfing him so that he could hardly breathe or open his mouth or his eyes. And with it he felt a terrible unknown fear burning within him, a sensation of wanting suddenly to hide from something, like the worm fearful of the hovering bird wings.

He pressed himself deeper into the grass, but as he did so it seemed to cling thicker and tighter to his body, winding around him, clutching at his throat, grasping at his thick boots, dragging him down into cold, empty arms. The wetness of the grass, the endless cold wet kiss of the grass on his skin sent tremors through his body . . . He felt like a drowning man, burrowing forward desperately into the thickening walls of grass – only to feel himself being overwhelmed, feeling the grass mounting round him like the sea waves. It seemed that the grass was holding him, dragging him down, wrapping one long tentacle after another around his limbs so that he was relentlessly borne down and halted. He felt himself drowning in the grass, felt his other warm, loving worlds slipping and fading away, while around him ominous menacing shadows fell across the cold sunlight . . .

Crying out in anguish, he suddenly scrambled to his feet. His eyes, round and fearful, stared desperately at some unseen horizon. He began running, stumbling awkwardly as the grass clung heavily to his feet.

He did not hear the shots that rang out bleakly. He twisted round and fell slowly and grotesquely, crumpling his out-stretched shape into the thick grass.

The enemy men who had trailed him from their outpost cottage came up to him and went methodically through his pockets. When they had finished they turned and began tramping back.

Later, the sky darkened and a lonely wind blew across the vast quiet field, blowing the cold grass in green waves, hiding the soldier for ever.

Arsace, Il Faut Partir

━━━━━ ✳ ━━━━━

SYLVIA TOWNSEND WARNER

Growing old, the body develops imperious idiosyncrasies, and for some years Odette de Boulay's body had obliged her to get up in the middle of the night and go to the orchard. The usual receptacle, said her brother Yves, would have sufficed any other woman. But not Odette. Odette must needs promenade herself like the Ankou, like a portent of death. At first there had been a show of pretexts, footsteps near the hen-house, the bull rattling his chain. But pretexts had been cast aside, the habit became a habit and nothing could alter it, not even the quartering of two occupying lieutenants.

'Now at least you will behave like a reasonable woman! You'll be arrested. You'll be shot.'

'On the contrary. I shall tell them I suffer from insomnia. They won't be able to say anything,' she added derisively. 'They are too correct.'

And indeed since they were under orders to behave as correctly as possible, and since Mademoiselle was the aunt of Clovis de Boulay, nothing was hinted or done to restrict the visits to the orchard. The two lieutenants, the captain who followed them, the chaplain who followed the captain, even the Todt personage who settled in as unobtrusively as a mildew, all correctly knew and correctly admired the regional novels of Clovis de Boulay, novels so expressive of the true, the traditional spirit of France.

Habit persists, subjugating the will that first abetted it, habit becomes a ghost stalking through the deserted manor of the body. In her seventy-third year Odette might think better of an indoor chamber pot; but habit clawed her into the orchard where the winter frosts (though in the Cotentin the frosts are

97

not so severe as those inland), were scarcely less chilling than the heavy dews of summer.

Now it was June. In another three months the apples would be falling. But many would fall before then, shrivelled and useless. It would be a bad apple year, the Ice Saints·had come at their sharpest, and now it was not possible to ward off the spring frosts with bonfires. However carefully one covered the fire it might burst into flame and become a signal to the English bombers. So there would be few apples this year. Meanwhile the weather was changing. A wind swung the boughs, there was rain in the air, the moon . . .

Inattentively, she glanced up to examine the moon. A cloud encompassed it. Only by force of habit interested in the moon she continued to stare at the cloud, which had a rim that recalled to her the ermine tippet she had worn in the first decade of the century. Laid aside in 1914 it had got the moth. Only out of the tail of her eye did she become aware of something in the reinette apple tree, a something, a bulk.

With half of her mind she thought, a clump of mistletoe. Mistletoe grew well in the orchard; before the war they had made quite a good sum of money sending mistletoe to England for the Christmas market. Naturally, that was now at an end.

With the other half of her mind she thought that Yves would not live to see another Christmas.

It was odd that she had not noticed so large a clump of mistletoe before. No! It was not so odd. The mistletoe was a man.

A man was entangled in the tree. And now this noise which she had taken to be in her head, for she was rheumatic and suffered considerably from head noises, was plainly the wind fidgeting in an extraordinary sort of drapery that depended from the tree.

That was it! He had come down by parachute and had entangled himself in the reinette. She had sometimes foreseen such a thing happening, and now it had happened. He might have chosen a better place. She walked up to the tree, treading on swathes of cold silk, waited a little, said, 'Well?'

There was no answer. She put up a hand and took hold of his foot and pulled at it experimentally. It yielded with the meekness of what is newly dead and still in the limbo between the validity of life, the rigidity of death.

She sighed – a sigh of relief. Presently she began to climb into the tree, hauling herself from bough to bough, carefully not touching the young man who reposed lopsidedly in the heart of the old reinette. At last, leaning along a bough, she was able to look down on his face. It was a young face, in no way remarkable until the moon, poking out of her ermine tippet, looked down too, and gave it a romantic intensity and delineated quite clearly the lappet of blood she had first supposed to be a lock of hair.

What a long way to come in order to lie dead in the old reinette! For he was an American.

They needn't have all this good silk, was her next thought. Yards and yards of silk, and that Herr Kummer sending it off to become chemises for his fat daughters in Saxony. A knife! Doubtless the young man would have a knife on him, and that would save her the trouble of going back for a knife from the kitchen. A knife was strapped to his leg ... a long killing knife. He had descended, not to escape death but to inflict it. A piece of metal had interposed between him and his intention. But the others, who had come with him? ... young men, so armed, coming down by parachute, do not come alone.

Here, beside her in the tree, was the invasion! She began to sidle backwards along the bough, making her way to the ground. Various impulses shook her: to run into hiding, to escape, to hide for her life; to run back to bed and pull the bedclothes over her ears; to run, not to her own bedside, but to that of Kummer's, the knife in her hand. But instead she fell on her knees, leaning her grey head against the lichened tree, clinging to its bole with all her force.

It had come, and she dared not receive it. It was too much for her, she was too old, too much disheartened. It had come too late. She could not readjust herself, now, in her seventy-third year and in the fourth year of dishonour. She could not readjust herself to liberty. It was too late, she had made her choice and could not unmake it. For one has to choose, and if one is a woman one cannot choose for oneself. There had been Yves, sickly, always dying, asking only to die in peace. There had been the property. There had been the Germans, inescapably victorious, inescapably correct, and appreciating Clo-Clo's talent as his own countrymen had never appreciated it. And there had been Clo-Clo.

'Not that I thought anything of his books,' she exclaimed, addressing the dead soldier's boot. 'All that nonsense about nature and the soil! If he had stayed on the place he'd have learned better. But apparently, it was all he could do.'

'And I brought him up; he was like my own child,' she said to the boot.

A child in his forties, still dependent, still needing pocket-money, still sending home his linen to be washed, his socks to be mended, his dialect passages to be corrected, becomes a burden; and even, it seems, becomes aware of becoming a burden. Clovis had drooped, had pined, had written of the heartlessness of Paris and the quiet of country cemeteries, describing himself wistfully brewing tisanes at midnight and thinking of home. Then, in the van of the forces of occupation, Clovis arrived: flushed, dimpled, annunciatory, a little breathless. 'Like a zephyr,' as Yves remarked. At last, he said, embracing her, at last he was in a position to show his gratitude. Henceforth she and Uncle Yves could depend on him.

'It will be difficult to transport Yves,' she had said. 'He went to England once, a town called Worthing, and disliked it.'

The zephyr stiffened. It was not, he explained, a question of flight, and above all not a question of England. The hour had struck for France to embrace her new career as a collaborator in the new Europe. His dear relations would continue to live quietly on their property, setting an example. Honour, comfort, revenue, would flow to them, and he himself would visit them whenever his duties allowed it. For he would be immensely occupied. But even when he could not visit them personally his voice would reach them on the radio.

'It seems you have everything arranged,' said Yves.

Clo-Clo flickered his hand.

'It is a little in the air. It would be better if you don't talk of it just yet. But the essentials are arranged.'

'I don't like it.' She had said that.

He turned pale, his lips trembled, his eyes became the eyes of a calf dragged to the butcher.

'My career . . .' His voice rose. 'After all these years of being slighted, of being kept down and reviewed in corners, my career opens. They appreciate me, I tell you. They know my work. They are going to re-issue me in a collected edition. Are you going to wreck me? Now?'

While she had hesitated, confused and in anguish, Yves, rearranging the rug over his legs, remarked that it would scarcely be worth it.

'And so . . . and so,' she murmured, staring at the boot.

So close above her head the boot was enormous. It seemed about to descend, to crush her. Birds flew in and out of the trees, the day was coming, every moment the drapery of the parachute grew paler and its folds more distinct, and she saw that some of it was charred with fire. Holding to the trunk of the old reinette she clambered stiffly to her feet. There was an apple-spray in her hand; for a long time she had been clutching it unconsciously. Now she became aware of it. It was crushed, sodden, done for. She opened her hand and let it fall. Clo-Clo's flourishing career, Clo-Clo himself, and Yves, and she, a flourish put out from an old tree, all done for in this early morning.

She looked at the dead man. He was distinct now, in an hour or so the flies would come buzzing about him. She gave – a courtesy – a thought to the woman who had reared him as she had reared Clovis. A convulsion of misery shook her, but she was scarcely aware of it for in the same moment the air was convulsed by the vibration of heavy gunfire. The parachute fluttered as if it were coming to life. Immature fruit pattered down. It was beginning! It was ending! From long ago, from Paris and her year at the finishing school and the visits in muslin to the Comédie Française, the words, the declamation, the attitude came back to her.

Arsace, il faut partir quand j'aurai vu la reine.

Her cracked voice rang out. She seemed to be standing on an enormous stage. Then, walking rigidly under the tumult of the naval bombardment, she went back to the house.

Haven of Despair

✠

ERIC RAE

Lying flat on his back on the rocks near the sea a young man lay gazing at the sun. It was an Egyptian sun, fiery, sweating hot, terrible in the intensity with which it beat down upon the wide deserts and small towns of this parched land. But the young man was accustomed to its glare: he had looked at it every day now for more than a week, at first for two or three moments, then for two or three minutes, then for ten. Now he could gaze almost for so long as he wished without discomfort. He was already half-blind.

The British Army provides a life eminently suitable for some people. There are men who, both as conscripts and as volunteers, fit easily into the discipline, the boredom, and the moronic companionship that life in the ranks has to offer. Some who do not quite fit in find, nevertheless, that the freedom from responsibility (of which they have had more than enough in civilian life) makes the parades, the fatigues, and the general dullness and uncreativeness of this existence tolerable. Some just do not fit in at all. One of these was Edwin Ralph.

He had joined the army of his own accord; so that if there was anyone at all to blame for his predicament when he found himself trying to live with people and to do work completely in opposition to everything in his own nature, it could only be himself. But he had been in the same predicament before. He did not fit in with any ordinary environment; and, as a boy of nineteen working in a labouring job in a country which could boast two million unemployed, a job which he could neither like nor exchange for another, he had little option. The army had been a haven of despair. That it had turned out to be as bad or worse than what he had left behind was simply unfortunate.

He had enlisted in 1939. Now it was 1944. That was five years. Five years, mostly at war; but against an enemy in whom he had no especial interest and whom he was never called upon to fight anyway. He had been told that in modern warfare there must be nine men behind the lines for every one actually in contact with the enemy. He was one of the nine. And so far as he was concerned the army at war was as dull as the army in peace.

That he had the sort of nature – acquired, he did not know where or when – which fitted in badly with the people among whom he had been born and educated, he had had reason to regret before. He was just beginning to realize how regrettable it was. He had written a little. He had tried to sketch. He had even tried to learn music. In 1941, when he was just twenty-one years of age, he had contributed a poem, gratis, to a magazine. Since then the editor had accepted more poetry and several short essays, also gratis. But this mild success only made him the more discontented. Life as he was expected to live it stood in the way of life as he wished to live it, more and more so as time went on. Finally, in 1941, the army authorities had capped the unpleasant with the impossible by sending him to sweat in Egypt, performing the same futile tasks and usually living where there were even fewer of the things which interested him – books, music, paintings – than he had been able to find in England. It had taken him two years to discover how to get out of it all.

What he was going to do when he did get out he was not certain. He thought he might write for a living. But he was not very concerned with events so far ahead.

The job he was doing at the moment, among the multitude of jobs that he had been put to and failed at during his army service, was that of telephonist. It was work, fortunately, in which he could function efficiently without good sight. He was not prepared yet to allow anyone to know what he was doing. He meant to take no chances. He would stare the sun out until he was almost completely blind, so that there would be no doubt at all whether the authorities would send him back to England with his discharge. And he wanted to run as little risk as possible that the effects would wear off to any very noticeable degree before he did receive his discharge.

He had been told that the effects would wear off. Perhaps not altogether; but they would wear off.

One day in the previous week he had first heard of sun-blindness; that with little damage to the eyes it was possible to stare the sun out and to acquire a temporary failure of the sight indistinguishable from that caused by a certain disease. What he had been told, by a drunken soldier just out of the line, was neither precise nor even very clear, not based upon the personal experience of the man who had told him, and perhaps not true. He had faced the worst, that it was not true, and had asked himself if he was prepared to risk complete blindness for life, whether he would do that or remain in the unending futility and blindness of what he was doing now. The answer had been that he had reached the end of his tether and could hardly be worse off. If he had to remain in Egypt he would go mad. And this, mixed with a sentimental feeling that if he *was* blind, he could still write, and that society would both have to look after him and leave him alone, the summit of his ambitions at the moment, had been more than enough to convince him which way he wanted to go. In his bitter despair and hatred of the unendingly useless life that he was leading now he had not required a great deal of convincing.

So he lay on his back and stared at the sun.

It is not necessary to go to Egypt to learn that for a person of normal sight to look directly at the sun is difficult. Even in England in the summer a glance is enough to bring on a sneezing attack. He had begun his experiment, therefore, very cautiously, looking first at the sky some little distance from the sun itself, snatching quick glances over to where the huge fiery eye stared at him, than hastily glancing back, sneezing.

It had cost him half an hour of patient effort to accustom his eyes to the direct merciless glare for so long as two or three seconds. Even then as he glanced away, first at the sky and then at the rocks about him, the sea at his side, the army tents and gun emplacements in the distance, the world had seemed to dance in a shimmering haze, reeling drunkenly; wherever he looked directly was distorted, awry, and he felt sick. It was some little while before he was able to bring himself to repeat the exchange of stares.

He lay there in a swimming costume, one arm across his brow. Very few soldiers came to the spot he had chosen, because so many jagged rocks stood out of the sea here as to make the little platform where he lay unsafe to dive from; since this was a military area no civilians ever came there. Probably in the course of several hours no one would come within twenty yards of him. But he meant to take no chances at all. He could not be surprised in what he was doing. To all appearances he was a sun-bather. Only if a second person were standing directly over him would it be possible for them to see that his arm did not actually shade his eyes at all. He thought that the likelihood of anyone's knowing what it was all about even if he were caught would be exceedingly small; but he could see no reason for leaving anything to chance.

It was possible to be absolutely sure of secrecy. He was certain of that.

Slight distortions in his direct vision were the first lasting symptoms he had observed. In a closed space, such as a tent or even in the large telephone room, a hall about twenty feet long, this was not noticeable. He could read normally. But in the open, gazing at an object perhaps thirty or forty yards from him, he saw in a peculiar way. The tent, the gun, the rock, whatever it was that he happened to be looking at, dissolved and altered shape a little, shimmering with a peculiar brightness. It was as if he saw it through a pane of glass, not placed near him but directly in front of the object itself, and that very intense sunlight was shining on both, so as to give a vivid, distorted account of violent light and impenetrable shade. By moving his direct gaze a very little here and there over the object, or, if it was small, slightly above and to either side, he could follow its shape, distinguish quite clearly what it was; but in the pin-point of direct vision it was a blur. As the blur became stronger and moved closer to him he found it correspondingly more easy to look into the sun.

He was careful to remember every safeguard against others noticing an oddness about himself or his conduct until he wished them to do so, and inspected his eyes closely in a mirror whenever he was alone in his tent. They appeared to be more or less normal. He continued to live as he had before, reading a little, taking a lorry into Alexandria occasionally, working at his telephone. And unless he was absolutely sure of being unobserved he did nothing at all to draw attention to his eyes. He had no friends, especially. There was no one whom he had to go out of his way to avoid.

The sessions on the rocks did not occur regularly. The telephones, passing messages from aircraft observation to the anti-aircraft guns, had to be manned twenty-four hours a day, and sometimes his duties made sun-bathing awkward. Unless going to the rocks should seem quite natural he did not go. On these days he merely glanced as often as he could in the sun's direction: when walking alone across a strip of desert, such as that which separated the telephone exchange from the guns and the camp, when hanging his washing on the line outside his tent, when waiting in the road for a lorry to take him into the town. Every little glance helped; and he was glad to feel that he was always playing safe.

The strange sensation of staring into a violent brightness was at first extremely unpleasant, then adventurous, then vaguely interesting. At first he sneezed, choked, and his eyes filled with tears, his head ached violently, he felt ill. After a while, however, the explosive viciousness of the sun's answering stare faded, and he could look without hard effort. The glare about the sun itself, making it shapeless to his normal vision, subsided, leaving it only an uncertain ball, violently orange, such as one may see in the Northern countries in the

beginning of winter, still appallingly bright but less antagon-
istic to his eyes. And in this period he felt more an affinity
with it. The heat did not only strike his body and his face and
eyeballs; it seeped into him through his eyes into his brain.
He felt that the sun was in his brain. And later, when a week
or ten days had passed, he felt quite friendly to the sun, almost
as if he lived in it and it in him. He was warm; it was warm.
It burned and so did he. He felt like a cinder, tossed in the
sun's gaseous flare, like a warm movement that swirled on the
rocks with the sun in its centre. Gradually the sun diminished
both in strength and in apparent size, until it was remote from
him, insignificant and not so meaningful. But here was still
an affinity. It was capable still of warming him, of lulling his
senses, of overcoming him.

He never at any time felt especially friendly towards the
sun. It was an abstract, something that he made use of;
and however powerful it may be, however violent, however
subservient to his wishes, he could not logically acquaint
himself with it. Yet if he had any interest of any kind now it
was connected with the sun. If he had any confidant, if there
was anything in the world that saw what he was doing, if
there was anything in his present environment of which he
thought with gratitude, it was the sun. He did not personify it
because he was not capable of the romance. But the link
between himself and this ball of flame was strong, and
if he felt it separated from him emotionally, playing the role
of a servant useful only for so long as it could serve, he was
nevertheless dependent upon it and grateful for what it
gave. If he had anything to say about himself at this particular time, or about his future plans, he told them only to the
sun.

He was not completely thoughtless about his future. He
could accept the fact that he might become permanently blind;
he would not invite it. He had decided before he began upon
a few seconds the first day, half a minute the next, two or
three minutes the next, and so on; and he was resolved never
to gaze into the sun for longer than half an hour in each

twenty-four. He had been told that this would be sufficient. He found from experience that it was. To check the time, since he had no watch, he could only guess; but this he did by reciting poetry under his breath. This also gave him something to think about while he waited to become blind. Tennyson's *Ulysses*, recited slowly, he thought would count about seven minutes. *Oenone*, he thought, would be fifteen. He was not particular about five minutes one way or the other, he simply planned not to overdo it very much.

He thought of many things as he lay there on the rocks, not always looking at the sun, but sometimes, when his time was up, sunning his back and sides, flicking the little rock-lice off his naked flesh, drawing the sweet salt air of the neighbouring ocean through his nose, seeing the broad expanse of it dancing in the sunlight out to infinity, the soft warm flails of the sun beating down upon his skin. He thought of England, of his home; of his mother, and of what he was going to do when he returned to live with her. But these were abstractions from life as it was now, vague and occasionally quite unreal hopes which he did not like to put much of himself into. He had not even seen his local medical officer yet, and he knew perfectly well that if he were to blind himself sufficiently to obtain his discharge he would have to face and outwit very many more than this one man. There would be hospitals, eye-specialists, medical boards. He concentrated all his efforts and all the thought he could upon these immediate obstacles. Their surmounting meant almost the difference between life and death to him.

What would happen if he were to be discovered after all in what he was doing, if a doctor who could see through the trick were to report him to the authorities, if he were trapped into a confession, he had no set idea. He thought, vaguely, that he might simulate insanity, or commit suicide. They would be half-prepared to believe him insane in any case. But this thought also was remote from him. He could plan only in the assumption that everything would go smoothly. If anyone were to put a spoke in his wheel he would have to face the consequent fall when it came. He thought he might be given a two-year sentence in an army jail. But he was playing for high stakes, and was not going to take his mind off the exact carrying out of what he had to do now to worry about what may happen if he were to fail.

It was five days after he had begun the experiment, when a definite failing of his sight was evident, that he mentioned, casually, to the NCO in charge of the particular job he was doing, that his sight was giving him trouble. The NCO questioned him without a great deal of interest and made as light of it as Edwin intended that he should. Two days later the young soldier mentioned his sight again, when the blur had become a distant but impenetrable mist, and his eyes wore an expression of slight daze obvious to a second person. The NCO suggested that he should report sick. He said that he would and did not.

It was interesting to watch this bright mist before his eyes grow, resolve itself into a definite entity. It was blindness. If it had been natural, a consequence of damage to his sight over which he had no control, it would probably have seemed horrible to him. But it was a thing of his own creation, a mist that he could roll back or forward as he wished. Once he abstained from gazing at the sun at all for a day and found that the mist (hardly a mist, he thought sometimes, but a curtain made of brightness) receded quickly; far too quickly, indeed, for his liking. He would very likely be shut up in a hospital when the condition of his sight was revealed, if he did not go to jail, without opportunity to keep it permanently close to him. He decided to go as far as he possibly could with the experiment before making it public.

Indoors, now, he also had difficulty in seeing somewhat distant objects. He noticed this especially with faces. At first, close to him, or reasonably close, say within ten or fifteen feet, he could distinguish features clearly. Farther away they were a little blurred. Across the length of the telephone room people became unrecognizable. There was no danger of discovery for him in this fact, because he was familiar enough with the other fifteen or twenty officers and men with whom he worked to be able to distinguish from their build and uniforms whom they were. He watched with interest as the faces became unrecognizable at shorter and shorter distances from him, as, gradually, it became a little difficult for him to read. He felt that when he could no longer see the numbers on his telephone board clearly the time would be ripe for him to complain officially. The telephone board was two feet away.

Two slight dangers of discovery began to crop up during the second week: the first, that when waiting in the road outside the camp to beg a lift in passing vehicles into the town, he was now no longer able to distinguish the type of lorry or car that was approaching until it was almost on top of him, an inconvenience which might have unpleasant consequences if he were to try and stop the car of a snappy staff officer, the second and somewhat more real danger that his eyes, when he studied them in the mirror, now had a definite squinted and glazed appearance. This was probably not very apparent, because no one had remarked upon it; but it was now a habit of mind with him to whittle every danger down to the slightest that he possibly could, and when speaking to others he rarely looked directly at them, and, especially when an officer was near, looked down at the ground.

All these were perhaps very close precautions, but he had plenty of leisure and nothing else especially to think about, and he thought that too many precautions were better than too few.

It was when he was so nearly blind that the chances of discovery by one of those with whom he worked, and consequent cross-examination, was greater than the danger of reporting himself to the medical officer and being shut away from the sun, on the twelfth day of the experiment, that he complained to his NCO seriously that he could not see, making some hullabaloo about it. His sight then was too poor to distinguish features clearly six feet away, though by using indirect vision he could see considerably farther. The NCO brought his commanding officer across to the switchboard.

The colonel questioned Edwin for two minutes and sent him instantly to the medical officer.

'Let me know what he says,' he directed him.

To approach a medical officer except in dire emergency at any except the set times laid down in orders is something that one simply could not do in the army; and the lad felt a thrill of satisfaction as he was given a note to take to the medical orderly. For him this was the beginning of the adventure. What had happened before had been mere preparation: from this point on it was his wits against everyone else's, and there was no going back.

He had half an hour to wait before the medical officer was ready to see him. He sat on a bench outside the medical hut looking patiently before him and thinking of nothing. He was normally a nervous person, and this calm was quite out of character. He accepted it and did not attempt to define it. He had only one definite thought in his head: about his symptoms he would tell the precise truth.

'What exactly do you feel is wrong with your sight?' the medical officer asked when they were together.

'I don't know, sir. I just can't see. It is like looking into a thick bright mist.'

The doctor inspected his eyes with the aid of a small torch. Even to the inexperienced young soldier it was obvious that he had no idea of the cause of what he saw.

'When did you first notice this condition?'

'About seven days ago, sir.'

'Then why did you not report it?'

The answer came pat: 'I did, sir, to my NCO, but we thought it might pass off again. It was not really inconvenient until yesterday.'

Very commendable in the army to suffer your disabilities in silence if you can. The medical officer wrote a chit.

'Take this to Major Brown at the hospital in Alexandria. I will ask my orderly to give you a lift in his truck.'

Edwin went outside, and waited again. He asked no questions, said as little as possible. He did as he was told. A small lorry driven by the medical orderly came round the corner five minutes later, and he climbed in. They drove in silence along the twenty-mile road to Alexandria, through the native villages with their populations of bare-footed, white-robed Egyptians, barking dogs, skinny chickens, those villages of dilapidated stinking huts, past the cultivated fields and the vineyards, to the hospital, refreshingly clean and green-lawned in the broiling sun.

'Where is your kit?' the medical orderly asked as they entered the hospital gates.

'Back at the camp. In tent fourteen.'

'Is it packed?'

'No. I was not told to pack it.'

The medical orderly lit a cigarette. 'I'll wait for you,' he said.

He had to wait for a very long time. For three-quarters of an hour Edwin sat in a passage, watching the white-clad young Palestinian nurses hurrying cheerfully to and fro, before Major Brown called him in. Then the eye specialist kept him for half an hour. In a dark corner he studied the boy's eyes with deep interest and concern. He had him look up and down, to either side. He had him roll his eyes, look at coloured lights, gaze through this glass, that glass, another and another. With some glasses the lad could barely perceive the first letter on the sight chart. But not by looking directly at the chart.

'Do your eyes hurt?'

'Very little, sir. Occasionally they smart.'

'Headaches, sickness?'

'Faint headaches now and then.'

Drops were put in his eyes and he had to wait outside for another quarter of an hour. The inspection was gone through all over again.

'I think,' said Major Brown, 'that we had better have you in the hospital.'

'Shall I bring my kit, sir?'

'Yes. Give this note to your medical orderly.'

Outside his door with the note in his hand Edwin realized

that he had overcome the first and probably the most difficult obstacle that he had been called upon to face. Major Brown had suspected nothing of the real cause for the condition in his sight. What he thought was the cause the boy had no idea. He was not really interested. He was interested only in concealing the truth.

Walking down the hospital steps he had to pause and wait for a moment for his sight to accustom itself to the sunlight's renewed glare. The drug that had been put in his eyes had enlarged the pupils, and whereas this gradual enlargement and the effects of it had been only a little noticeable in the sheltered passages and rooms of the hospital, in the fierce sunlight it brought a thick mist, white this time and horribly opaque, rolling with vicious speed down upon him, so that for a moment he was indeed completely blind. He put a hand on a balustrade to steady himself, shading his eyes with his hand, and gradually the blanket in front of him rolled far enough away for him to see to walk. He had to half-guess, half-feel his way to the lorry. A wave of fear overcame him for a moment when he walked blindly into the overhanging branch of a tree in his path, feeling the terrible possibilities lying ahead in consequence of what he had done. Then he recovered himself and walked steadily on.

'Were you told to bring your kit?' the bored medical orderly asked.

'Yes. I have a note for you.'

The other soldier read his note.

'You have to go in tomorrow. Be ready outside your tent at eleven a.m. I'll pick you up there.'

It was only about two o'clock in the afternoon when they returned to the camp, and after having his meal, left out for him in the cook-house, the boy could easily have gone sun-bathing again. He considered it and dismissed it. He spent five minutes behind the native laundry hut, five minutes in the shadow of his tent, pretending to be doing his washing; a quite understandable occupation if anyone were to grow inquisitive, since in that heat his clothes would dry within two hours and be ready in ample time for his entering hospital. Two or three minutes spent loitering outside the telephone exchange waiting to report to his colonel were also occupied in staring at the sun.

Out here in these wide desert spaces, far from any building of size, he experimented again to discover precisely what he could and could not see. In direct vision he was almost blind: he could not read the print in his army pay book, it receded from him on either side in a dancing blur. Indirectly he could see more than he really wanted to. He had told Major Brown that he could see about fifty yards. Actually, he found when he came to measure it, his indirect sight was not far from normal, and he could distinguish the presence of objects a very long distance away. He realized then that to make himself completely blind, as he had intended when beginning on this adventure, he would have required at the least two weeks more.

His commanding officer listened to what he had to say, looked at him with sympathy, shrugged and dismissed him. He saluted and went out.

Walking back across the strip of barren land to the camp he wondered if he had any plans. He searched his mind, but could think of none. He was merely letting things happen to him. He had no idea of what the future may hold, no great hopes and no great fears. Too much must happen before he could know what turn events might take.

He was afraid of being found out; he hoped for his discharge. There was nothing between these two.

To pack his kit took him a very little while, and he went for a walk part of the way to Alexandria and back again before going to bed. At eleven o'clock he got between his blankets under the mosquito net and slept soundly.

The medical orderly brought his little truck around at the time he had promised, to drive him into town to the hospital. Edwin said goodbye to him there. He went into the hospital and was directed to a bed in a ward by a young Palestinian nurse.

'Shall I go to bed now?'

'It is not necessary. In any case, Major Brown will want to see you.'

There were another twenty-odd men in the ward, few of them actually in bed, but almost all with something very obviously wrong with their eyes. Some had only one eye, the other being glass, or perhaps only an empty socket covered with patch or a bandage. Several had a heavy redness around their eyelids. Several merely wore very thick spectacles. He made the acquaintance of two or three of them, as one does, but invited no confidences, and gave none.

Now that he had got so far so easily he had begun to see the possibility of success ahead, and felt his first real attack of nervousness about the risk of being discovered. It was all far too easy. He waited in some trepidation for his next examination by Major Brown.

He need not have troubled. Although the eye specialist spent a long time with him again, asking him to look at coloured lights, at the chart through several different instruments, and put the drops of drug in his eyes again, taking great pains to get at the truth of the symptoms from which his patient was suffering – symptoms which the young soldier was always careful to describe precisely as they were – and, in fact, seemed to come to definite conclusions about them, he obviously had no idea of their real cause. He told the lad nothing about what he had found, and Edwin asked only one question, whether he could be cured, to which he did not get nor expect to get a satisfactory reply. He was told that the condition in his sight was very rare, affecting only one soldier in several hundreds of thousands. He could quite well believe this.

The examination was closed, and he returned to the ward.

His chief worry now that he was safely installed in the hospital was how to keep his sight more or less in the condition it had been in when he entered. Although he had found his sight did not improve rapidly now when he left it alone, he realized that it would probably be a long while before he got so far as to be sent back to England: long enough perhaps for him to recover almost completely. Five years in the army had taught him how long the authorities could spend in dealing with the most straightforward case; and since his was so uncommon he guessed they might spend any amount of time investigating him. He searched his wing of the hospital and the grounds carefully to find a secluded place. Eventually he found two, one amongst a clump of bushes in the grounds, and another a window in the lavatory. He spent ten minutes in the lavatory when Major Jones had finished with him and five minutes in the grounds. No one disturbed him.

He decided to be careful to look at the sun only immediately after he had been examined, not before. For a short while after a period of gazing there was a very noticeable difference in his sight, and he did not wish to draw attention to any very noticeable differences.

The sun had long ago ceased to dazzle him when he first turned his eyes to it. From something impossibly bright at which he had to squint and screw up his eyes and glance at first with this eye and then with that, sneezing and weeping, it had become merely an orange ball, still strong, but capable of being looked at calmly with open eyes. In the hospital on that first day he reached the zenith of the experiment; he saw the sun at its weakest and most impotent. From this time onward he knew that continued staring would cause it to fade and fade, until eventually he would look and see only the bright curtain, he would be able only by looking elsewhere to sense its position in the sky; then he would be to all intents completely blind. He was willing to go so far; but a quarter of an hour a day he knew would not be enough, and he hardly dared risk more. From that moment, although he still gazed at the sun whenever he could, his sight gradually improved, never again to be so poor as it had been then.

His life in the hospital was more satisfactory; he ate better, slept better (bugs, mosquitoes and flies, the curse of desert life, were kept out of the hospital wards) and found everything generally much more in accordance with his nature. Life was pleasant and easy without being dull. Only one thing was absolutely banned to him, and this was a self-imposed restriction: he would not attempt to read. Apart from this, however, the hospital had few restrictions on his freedom. He was not allowed to go out after certain times; he had no wish to go out. To discuss painting with one of the Palestinian nurses who had been to an art school was for him diversion enough. His life in the recent past had been so completely barren incarcerated in the desert, that the slightest normality seemed to him to be interesting.

As he had expected, Major Brown had decided upon a complete overhaul in an attempt to find out all that he could about the mysterious disease from which his patient was supposed to be suffering. He sent him to the throat, nose and ear specialist; to the dentist; he had his urine tested; spent long periods with him personally, while the lad gazed through or into more and more complicated instruments. So a day passed into a week and the one week into two, and Edwin became definitely concerned about the improvement in his sight.

It was when he had been in hospital for two and a half weeks that Major Brown told him he was to be sent away to another eye specialist for a second opinion on his sight. This to Edwin was good news, because he could see that Major Brown was getting to the end of his own examination. Major Green of Cairo, he was told, was one of the foremost eye specialists in the world. If anyone could tell him what was wrong with his sight Green could.

The young soldier hoped most sincerely that he could not.

On the truck going down to Cairo across the long desert road from Alexandria, Edwin found himself accompanied by a medical orderly and a blinded Indian soldier, on the last lap of his journey from Benghazi where an exploding shell had cost him his sight. Apparently Major Brown dealt with diseases of the eye, Major Green usually with war casualties who had become completely blind. He himself had been sent down merely as an interesting case to be inspected and returned the next day. For a little while, meeting the unfortunate Indian, and later, when they reached the hospital and the twenty or so recently-blinded young men in Major Green's ward, the boy experienced a twinge of remorse about what he was doing. But it was a twinge only. He was far too embittered and far too obsessed with the notion of getting his discharge to bother much with his conscience.

He had several hours to wait before Major Green could see him. A nursing sister, telling him to report to her later so that the usual drops could be put in his eyes, allotted him a bed, and left him to himself. He sat and looked at his fingernails.

Major Green arrived back at the hospital three or four hours later (he had apparently been to a hospital on the other side of Cairo) on a bicycle, and examined Edwin immediately. A tall, thin Irishman in a shabby uniform and half-polished shoes, he seemed to be one of those people who have no time for anything but work; yet he found time to tell the boy more about what precisely was wrong with his sight than he had ever been told before. The doctor drew a diagram of the eye, showing exactly where the 'disease' had settled.

'Unfortunately,' he said, 'in the worst possible position. If it had settled anywhere else in the eye it would have had very little effect. You might not have noticed it at all.'

'How will it affect my sight in the future, sir?'

Green looked at his papers and looked at the floor. His voice was deeply sympathetic.

'You won't go completely blind,' he said.

'And is there no cure?'

'I am afraid not. We have found that vitamin B helps.'

He occupied himself with writing for some little while on the papers which Edwin had brought from Major Brown in Alexandria. Then he folded them and returned them to their envelope, handing it back to the young soldier.

'We are sending you back to England and recommending you for your discharge,' he said. 'That is all we can do.'

'Do you think I will be given my discharge, sir?'

The Way We Lived Then

'Oh, that's quite sure. Yes. No one will stand in the way.'

If it had concerned some minor matter the lad would have accepted this assurance and been satisfied with it; but he so passionately wanted what he had been promised that he could not accept the truth of it. He found when he arrived back that everything had been arranged for his leaving. He was to appear before a medical board the following morning and very shortly after that would be sent to Port Said to catch the next ship to England. But even with this exciting news he was suspicious; in fact a little more than usually.

So determined was he to make no slip that he worked himself into a bad state of nerves. The medical board would not stand in his way; yes, but what if he were discovered at the last moment? As he sat in the waiting room with the dozen or fifteen men who had to appear before this board with him he found himself trembling from head to foot. One after another the names of the soldiers with him were called out and they went into the board room, naked, as they were all required to be, with a set expression on their faces; one after another they returned, trying not to grin, a large D – their new medical category, and the symbol of escape – marked in their pay books. One or two had only a C, which meant that they had to remain in Egypt for the time being at least; but they seemed to have expected this. Then his turn came.

He walked into the room. There were five officers there. They stared at him with expressions of surprise and fury.

'What the devil do you think you are doing?'

Edwin stared back, bewildered. Could they be speaking to him? How could they have found out? He looked from one to the other.

'What do you mean by smoking in here? How dare you?'

A sergeant standing at the end of the room looking through some papers caught his attention. Smoking. He must be smoking. He looked from the officers to the sergeant. But they were all staring at him. Suddenly for no reason at all he looked down at his own hand. He had a lighted cigarette between his fingers.

'Go outside instantly and put that thing out!'

Shaking uncontrollably with nerves, in realization of what he had done, the lad hurried outside the door back into the waiting room, dropped his cigarette and trod on it. He turned in the open door and saw one of the officers inside beckoning him.

'I beg your pardon, sir,' he said as he returned. 'I forgot that it was in my hand.'

'That's quite all right.' The man who had shouted at him so angrily before smiled. 'Come here.'

The five looked into his eyes with the aid of a small instrument like a torch. Their attitude now was perfectly friendly. He realized that they understood: he had not meant to smoke.

'What do you do in civilian life?' the one who appeared to be the senior of the officers present asked him.

'I was a labourer, sir.'

'Is that what you mean to do when you leave the army?'

'If I can, sir.'

They were more and more friendly. The senior officer wrote in his pay book. Even upside down he could see that it was a D.

He returned outside and sat down.

I am free, his head shouted. I am free, his insides shouted. I am free I am free I am free I am free. And he looked from face to face of the men who had been in and the men who were waiting to go in, trying not to smile.

He dressed.

At the hospital they accepted it all as a foregone conclusion: a lorry had already been detailed to take himself and two other grade D men from the same hospital to the railway station on the first lap of their journey home. He was elated, but with the emotion repressed deep down inside him. He dared not let it go until he was sure. He could not let it go until he was sure.

Nothing at all impeded him. He caught the train, and travelled in it, with only a short stop overnight in a transit camp, to Port Said. There he embarked on a ship. He was quite positively on his way home.

The journey to England occupied three weeks, three very boring weeks while they ploughed through seas at first blue and then grey, with nothing for the soldiers on board to do except wait; three weeks too, unfortunately, during which his sight improved greatly, since it was impossible now to snatch even a few minutes for sun-gazing. No part of the ship was sufficiently private. His natural glee at being nearer and nearer to his goal was at war therefore with a stronger and stronger doubt that he could continue to hoax the doctors when he arrived there. When he stepped off the gangway at Tilbury at eight o'clock on a damp and foggy September morning on his way back to barracks in Woolwich, he was in a very complex state of mind, and how to obtain his discharge was a serious problem to him.

He had no particular emotions about being in England. He was not in England until he got his discharge.

It was this otherwise insoluble problem of his improved sight which led him to begin to take his first really great risks, once he had settled down and begun the routine of reporting himself to hospitals and medical inspection huts again. When he was asked now about the condition of his sight he lied; and the better it was the more he lied. He had to think quickly. Odd questions, casually asked, became dangerous traps. Doctors he could hoax, but he was afraid of their orderlies: they were nearer to him. How could he see the number of the bus he wanted when he travelled to the hospital – he asked someone else standing in the queue. Was he not afraid of being run over when he crossed the road – he always waited for some- one else to cross and went over at the same time. On the brink of success he realized ever more clearly the cost of failure.

'Has your sight improved at all since you left Egypt?'

'Yes, sir, a little.'

'How much?'

He hesitated. It was a natural hesitation. How could he tell?

'I can see your face now, sir. I would not have been able to in Egypt.'

'You can see the chart now?'

'Yes, but not the letters on it.'

'Not even the first?'

He could read the first three lines: with certain spectacles down to the fifth. But he had never admitted it.

'No. Nothing at all.'

'Try.'

He tried and failed to have any idea. It was a blur to him, he said. It was not an inquisition he was being subjected to, the various doctors and orderlies whom he saw were merely curious; but he schemed and defended himself as if everyone was full bent to trap him.

One last question was left for him to decide: if he would claim a pension. The old soldiers in the barrack room advised him not to do so if he wished to get out: discharges were granted the more easily to those who were willing to forgo their pension. On the other hand, if he did not demand it, who would think the better of his disease? If it were genuine, hadn't he a right to be reimbursed? He put in his claim therefore without hesitation or any concession about the extent of his disability.

He was granted an eighty per cent pension, amounting to thirty-six shillings a week. He was called to the office and asked to sign papers. He did not want any of the medals due to him, he said, for his service overseas. He waited a week. He was given his discharge. With a pack on his back, discharge papers in his pocket, with plenty of money to be going on with and a gratuity due to him, dressed in non-returnable khaki, he left his quarters for the last time and walked across the barrack square to the gate. He passed through, and for a moment stood looking anew at this outside world in which his future lay. Everything he had set out to attain he had attained, his return, his discharge. And he had thirty-six shillings a week to boot.

He hitched his pack more comfortably on his shoulders,

and set out down the road, the road down which he could not see very far. His face expressionless, he saluted an officer on the corner. Then after a few more paces he stopped, turned, and looked after the man; and suddenly, inside him, something began to laugh.

A Fine Room to be Ill In

RAYMOND WILLIAMS

I

The room was surprisingly large for so modest a house. It occupied three-quarters of the space on the ground floor, and its high ceiling, its series of bay and french windows, its large arched fireplace of Spanish walnut, all served to accentuate its size. When Mr Peters first saw it, at the time of the redecoration of the house after six years' service as an army property, it was bare and dusty, the floor unstained, and the one, incongruous, piece of furniture was a full-size enamel bath, which, placed in the mathematical centre of the room, under the oblique dusty sunrays, reminded Mr Peters instantly of a coffin. But it was difficult now to remember the room as it had then been. Mr Peters had paid great attention to the floors – they were rough-scrubbed and splintering, for the house had served as a NAAFI institute and the room had been the service canteen – a circumstance which Mr Peters tried hard to forget. Then the walls had been cream-washed, the formal floral pattern of the plastered ceiling delicately cleaned, the window frames painted, until at last a dignity appropriate to its size had been restored. There were few blemishes; one of the tiles of the firegrate was broken in half, and another was loose, but Mr Peters resettled them with the tips of his long fingers so that from most angles no disturbance could be seen. And there was an unfortunate patch of black paint which some careless workman had spilled near the centre of the room, and which all the efforts of Mr Peters's careful creosoting had failed to remove. The furniture, which was travelling by road, was delayed by an unofficial strike –

an event for which Mr Peters felt every sympathy, for he understood the conditions of the workers, but which was really very trying just at this moment. As a result, Mr Peters had several days, after the redecoration of the room had been completed, in which he could sit in the room, choosing varying points of vantage, and conjure up pictures of how his furniture would look when it was arranged, and finding frequently, as the whole problem settled through his consciousness, that previous patterns of arrangement were not satisfactory, and that rearrangements were necessary in order to accommodate new angles of vision. When the furniture at last arrived, Mr Peters was able to direct the workmen with great accuracy. He knew exactly where each piece should go. Indeed, one of the men remarked to him, 'It's a pleasure, sir, to work with a man as knows his own mind.' When it was all in, and the men had gone, Mr Peters resumed his peripatetic squatting. In general, it was all as he had foreseen. It was true that the carpet looked rather lost. It was a good, large carpet, but really, one could not expect to find a carpet large enough for a room like this outside the private property of a Shah. But it just failed to cover the offensive splash of black paint. Mr Peters moved it back over this, but then it was too far from the fireplace, and it was essential to have a continuity of pattern right up to the grate, so that solitary emphasis was not placed on the tiles. It was a difficult problem. At last Mr Peters took an occasional table, and placing it exactly over the offending patch, he draped on it a fine silk cloth, which on the side nearest the door, and so on the side from which it would be viewed when entering the room, came down to the ground and decently veiled the paint without however drawing too much attention to itself.

The rest of the furniture looked most fitting. There was the fine dark oak cupboard, with its glass doors, behind which could be seen the carefully arranged relics of Mr Peters's travels in Sicily and Mexico. Then the matching bookcase, with its titles arranged according to branches of literature, for as Mr Peters so often said to his students, there is really very little point in a kind of inclusive chronology of literature; it is the development of work in specific media which it is so important to emphasize. So there was drama, from the fine old calf-bound Greek texts, through the red texts of the Romans, on to the green collections of the miracles and moralities, the uniform saffron editions of the Elizabethans, the patterned green covers of Racine and Corneille, the blue omnibus texts of Restoration tragedy and comedy, right down to the cherry collected works of Ibsen, the poison-bottle-green of Strindberg, and the tall black and pastel volumes of the modern verse dramatists. It was the same with novels, with poetry, with essays, with biographies, and with criticism. The size of the bookcase was certainly an advantage. Fronting the bookcase stood the heavy sideboard, also in dark oak, with the rich carvings of the capon and the hare on its doors. Mr Peters was a vegetarian, and at mealtimes he found the sideboard slightly disquieting, but as a rule its solidity, the fine full flanks of the hare, for example, was most pleasing. Then there was the suite, blue-patterned; old, of course, and creaking at times if one sat down on it indelicately, but pleasant; and after all, how could one nowadays replace it, for the sake of some horrid utility rexine?

Mr Peters's occasional woman, who was cleaning for him until his wife and child should arrive from their holiday, seemed to think the room under-furnished. She never actually mentioned it, but Mr Peters was very sensitive to human atmosphere, and apprehended her disapproval. He decided to raise the question openly with her, but she shied away from every direct attempt, and he could only conclude that she was unwilling to discuss the matter since she felt it was likely to reflect on the financial status of her temporary employer. He thought it distressing, and yet at the same time amusing, perhaps even convenient, that everywhere, nowadays, taste should be written down as indigence. He had glimpsed his cleaner's rooms on one occasion when he had visited her; her son-in-law, an unemployed joiner (curious, Mr Peters had thought, how I am always bumping into unemployed building workers in times like these) had just finished decorating them; the walls were ground-washed with eggshell-blue, and over this there was a heavy stippling of yellow and a colour Mr Peters could only describe as puce. Through the bedroom door, which stood open, Mr Peters could see large golden panel frames painted over an offensive biscuit-coloured wall-paper. The bathroom, of which the door was also ajar, was done out in raspberry wash. Mr Peters was glad to get back to the coolness of his own room.

The only subject on which Mrs Austen would ever talk, apart from details of domestic arrangement, was the fine view from the windows of the room. This comprised a stretch of downland, with hollows and terraced level-lines, which ran away to a broad valley through which a river meandered to the sea in great serpentine loops. Gorse and firs were littered over the slopes.

'You should see it in winter, sir,' said Mrs Austen. 'Just like Switzerland it is. And the boys is up there when it's snowing, sliding down all the day. It's lovely.'

'How nice it will be to sit and watch that,' Mr Peters answered, wishing the conversation would not proceed.

'Yes, sir, and in the spring it's the young couples walking up there, and the summer there's families, and children, comes by car. And the schools, all the schools around, different colour caps and costumes they all have. It's a lovely sight. And you've got the very best view of it, all from your room.'

'It is nice,' Mr Peters said, replacing the occasional table over the patch, which she had uncovered in her dusting; 'nice to think if you were stuck to the room you could always see so much life going on outside.'

'I said just the same, sir,' Mrs Austen smiled, gathering her brushes together. 'I said to George the first time I seen your room, there's everything you can see from the window. It'd be a fine room to be ill in.'

'Yes,' Mr Peters said. 'Good morning, Mrs Austen.'

2

The room grew on Mr Peters, and he quickly managed to settle the apparatus of his daily living into its formal pattern. There was the wireless set, for example. Mr Peters was not a devotee of the commercial radio; even the idea of listening to humorous programmes was somehow intolerable to him, for surely there was something indecent in sitting and laughing alone, quite alone, or even with one other person; so that one ended up by being amused inwardly while looking as solemn as if one were in church, and there was something disquieting about that. But still, he liked to keep in touch with the bare facts of the international situation, for although politics was no longer his métier his students kept asking his opinion and he felt he owed it to himself to be able to make reasonable answers. And then there were the sports results and commentaries; Mr Peters did not care to acknowledge his interest in these, for the idea of mechanism in sport was distasteful to him, but he noticed that he always left the wireless on while there were broadcasts of this nature, and that he attached considerable emotional weight to the fortunes of teams and players which had gained his fancy. And yet the sum of it did not warrant a decent radio set. Mr Peters possessed a battered old portable, which he had bought second-hand at the selling out of a bankrupt institute for the blind. It was adequate for his needs, but it was decidedly unlovely. Mr Peters placed it between his favourite armchair and the wall, with the badly battered end hidden. This was all right so long as he did not wish to play it; but he discovered that he only got good reception when the set was rotated to the appropriate angle, and, of all things, the appropriate angle left the broken end exposed to the room and to sight. Reluctantly, Mr Peters moved his armchair so that there was room between it and the wall for the set to rotate completely, and yet remain hidden. His efficiency pleased him. He could let his hand drop over the side of the chair to switch the set on without even having to look at it, and down there in the shadow the jagged end might not have existed.

In the early days of his occupation of the room, Mr Peters found that he could not sit quietly. Whenever he took his favourite place, there would always be some distressing ruck in a chair cover, or the curtains would be hanging badly, or a piece of the newspaper which he had laid under the carpet to protect it from the still-drying creosote would be peeping out, and then he would have to get up to make the necessary adjustment. And yet, so clear and strict was his idea of the pattern of the room, that he found every readjustment demanding new ones. 'The field,' as he put it, in the words his brother-in-law was so fond of quoting, 'is never quiet.' Yet his persistence, his unwearying application, bore fruit. After a fortnight, and just before the arrival of his wife and child, he had imposed a satisfactory order. On the evening before they arrived he was able to sit, for the second time, during two full hours, doing nothing, but just satisfied by the pattern which he had created. Outside, over the downland, the last birds were moving, and a late mist was rising over the cliffs. The loops of the slow river caught the last light.

His wife and child arrived next day in time for tea. He met them at the station with a taxi. When they reached the house he jumped out quickly, anxious to open the doors and to have the room standing ready for their reception. He was so excited by this intention that he forgot to take his normal share of the paraphernalia which the child had accumulated during the journey, and he was called back by his wife just as he was turning the key in the lock. He pushed the door open and went back. As a result, she entered first, and when he arrived with an armful of torn picture books, his wife was already in the room. She put down her parcels on the sideboard, and began looking over the rest of the house. He played with the child, and awaited her return.

'All right, I've made the tea,' she said, re-entering. He had laid everything ready in the nursery.

'How does it all strike you?' he asked.

'Well, darling, I really haven't had time to look.'

'The kitchen's small.'

'Is it? I thought it wasn't bad. But what about this room?'

'It's very large. Larger than I'd expected.'

'Yes, but look at it.'

'Later, dear. Tea's ready now.'

They went out together for tea. The business of unpacking and seeing to the child kept them both fully occupied for some while afterwards. When they got back to the room, it was getting dark, and the child was already in bed.

'Now, dear,' said Mr Peters, as they came through the door. The familiar shape of the room was bathed in the soft light.

'It's nice.'

'Only nice?'

'Well, yes, it's nice, pleasant. What else should I say?'

'Nothing. Have you seen the view?'

His wife crossed to the large bay window, and looked down at the river.

'Extraordinary shape, isn't it?'

'Yes.'

'Glacial.'

His wife moved back across the room.

'Oh Christ, I'm tired,' she said, and flopped into a chair. Mr Peters heard the creak of the springs, and winced. But there was another sound, even more disquieting. He switched on the standard lamp, and saw one of the castors of the chair lying out on the polished floor.

'Well that's that,' he said, stooping to retrieve it.

'I knew it would happen soon. It's been loose for some time.'

'You said you'd get it seen to.'

'I hadn't time. I had so much to see to here.'

'Well, we can get it done. Leave it now.'

'All right.'

Mr Peters sat down in the opposite chair. He let his hand drop down to the wireless. As the music came, his wife said,

'You won't be able to leave those scissors there, darling. The baby will get them.'

'I hadn't thought.'

He took the scissors from the fire seat. They were a pair he had collected in Sicily. His travelling companion had immediately associated them with the mafia. They were extraordinarily long, with fine sharp blades of gleaming steel, and wicked cutting points. They were contained in a sheath of leather for safety. Mr Peters had thought them surgeon's scissors, but his friend had pointed to the elaborate pattern on the handles. 'No surgical scissors would have a pattern like that; it would only collect dirt. Much more probably some sort of torture scissors, that men could carry on their belts.' Mr Peters was fascinated by them.

'Oh, well,' he sighed, 'I'll put them up on the mantelpiece. But they're so useful for slitting open letters.'

His wife was lying back with closed eyes. Mr Peters looked at her, dwelling on every detail of her appearance. Her strong resemblance to himself again surprised him. There was the wiry black hair, of the same jetty shine. Then the prominent temples, the wide-set brown eyes, the firm straight nose, the wide mouth with the pendulous lower lip. Very often, by strangers, they were taken for brother and sister rather than man and wife. His wife was amused by their resemblance.

'Have you ever noticed,' she said once, 'how all this talk about people loving their opposites is quite untrue. You look at any married couple. Usually there's a pretty striking physical resemblance. Clearly contrasted physical types hardly ever marry. We're just one pair of many.'

'That raises lots of interesting questions,' he said.

'Narcissus and Narcissa.'

It was now quite dark outside, but Mr Peters did not add to the low light for fear of waking his wife. He distinguished her breathing through the tiny sounds of the evening.

Suddenly there was a scream from the child, who had woken in its dark bedroom. Instantly his wife was awake.

'I'll go on to bed when I've seen to him,' she said.

'I'll come as well.'

'We'll probably have a night full of screaming. Travel upsets him.'

'Can't be helped,' said Mr Peters. He got up from his chair, and put the scissors, which he had continued to hold, back on the fire seat.

'On the mantelpiece, dear.'

'Sorry, stupid of me. I'm not used to having you both here yet.'

'You're coming?'

'Yes.'

3

There were not many houses in their immediate vicinity. It was what is known as an exclusive neighbourhood. The nearest house on the left was large and grey, with unusually steep gables. It was set in a very large garden, which was delineated by walls of grey stone. Mr Peters knew nothing of its occupants. The only persons he saw moving around it were obviously domestic staff. There were several gardeners, who had a busy time keeping the large lawns tidy, the hedges trimmed, and the little groups of trees free of undergrowth. And Mr Peters had seen at least three indoor servants, and also two cars.

'A pretty prosperous household these days,' he remarked. 'Obviously film stars or crooks. Who else could afford it?'

Mr Peters conceived several plans for discovering the identity of the occupants. Perhaps a neighbourly call; but that could look like mere intrusion. Or he could be a commercial traveller, for a seed firm, perhaps. But then they would almost certainly order, and that would be difficult. He even thought of ringing the bell and saying he was from Mass Observation, but he was reduced to watching and speculation. And then, however closely he watched, looking sideways from the bay window, he was curiously unsuccessful. The only living thing he saw apart from domestic servants was a greyhound. It was a small sign, but ever after he felt convinced, in default of further evidence, that the inhabitants were crooks.

On the left there was a rash of plaster villas, two of them with lurid green tiles. Each of these had a neat garden in front, at which Mr Peters mocked. Sometimes, when he took his morning walk for cigarettes, he would stand and gaze at them. One in particular interested him. It was laid out like a mosaic. There were sharp-edged intersecting concrete paths, and sharp-edged perfectly level lawns, and ribbon beds of flowers. At the moment the display was tulips; there were no other flowers visible. When Mr Peters had first arrived, it had been daffodils. They now lay uprooted and discarded in front of the neat concrete garage. The gaudy tulips stood like the banners of a great procession. All tulip colours, Mr Peters convinced himself, were essentially martial. That comprised their suburban appeal.

'Just think,' he said to his wife when he regained the house, 'of the incredibly corrupt sense of power that man must have. His daffodils parade and blossom. He looks, likes, and passes on. The daffodils are thrown aside. Then he calls up his tulip army, a braver, gaudier, display. He stands under his little concrete porch arch and inspects them. Above him the white arced lambswool rugs – all suburban snuggeries have them – flutter from the bedroom balcony. Flower, my tulips, and fade. Glory and die. Just projecting his will to power on these objects. And why?'

His wife knew the answer and began to serve the lunch. Next morning Mr Peters stopped again to survey the tulips. While he was doing so he became aware of a man advancing towards him down the precise path. He was a short figure, with close-cropped hair and moustache. Rimless spectacles. He wore a belted alpaca jacket, close black breeches, grey stockings and wide-strapped shoes. 'Wells,' droned the immediate response in Mr Peters. 'Not Wells himself, but the Wells scientist type in every book. Obviously the man's a rationalist and an Independent Socialist.'

'Like it?' the man said.

'I'm quite intrigued,' said Mr Peters.

'Nothing much,' said the man. 'Just a bit of stuff I stuck in.'

'It's most impressive,' said Mr Peters. The man waved a loose hand.

'You're the new fellow? Up the end?'

'Yes, just came.'

'Glad to meet you. Pertwee the name. Come in, get to know you.'

Mr Peters found himself following the little man up the path. He looked down at the razor-edges of the beds, and into the full breasts of the tulips. The hall was cool and polished, with plants and a brewer's map of the county.

'My study,' said the little man. 'I'm a sociologist.' Mr Peters took in the details of the room. A large black desk, with an array of rubber stamps; labelled drawers; the walls lined with precisely arranged books.

Mr Peters glanced at the top of a pile of pamphlets which stood on the chair to which the little man had waved him. 'Culture, Religion, and the Social Mechanism' by E. Mortimer Pertwee. He extended a curious hand.

'Little bit of a thing I wrote,' said the man, coming across. 'Let me move the things. Sit down.'

''Course this town's dead,' said Mr Pertwee. 'In a coma. Stiff with prejudice. I wrote last week to the local paper' (he rolled these last words round his mouth); 'told 'em they were all in a coma. Defined it. Always believe in defining my terms. Too many people going around uttering sloppy ideas. Pin 'em down.'

'Is there much political argument in the local press?'

'My letter wasn't political, you know. No time myself for all these practical politics as they call it. Just ignorance. Ignorance of underlying social mechanisms. Get in a lather before they've half understood the situation. Folly. Just personal arrogance.'

Mr Pertwee took a cigarette from a long silver box.

'Smoke?'

'Thanks,' said Mr Peters, stretching out his hand.

'No, no. Not one of these. Too strong. Roll my own, you know. Smoke all the time. Have another. I've got some ordinary ones somewhere about.' He found a Players packet and passed it across. Mr Peters opened it, to find it empty.

'Still, I write about all manner of things to them. Let them know where I stand.'

Mr Peters waved the empty packet gently.

'Oh, none there?' said Mr Pertwee. 'My cat must have had them. Got a cat, great friend. Pity you can't have one of mine.'

'What tobacco d'you use?' asked Mr Peters.

'Tom Long, or something they call it. Get four tins a week.'

'But that's not so strong,' said Mr Peters. 'I often use it in my pipe. I'm quite used to it.'

'You wouldn't enjoy these,' said Mr Pertwee. 'Yes, the local press struggles along. Would you like to see some cuttings of mine?'

'Yes, indeed,' Mr Peters assented, feeling unreasonably irritated by the cigarette episode.

From a drawer at his knee Mr Pertwee took a large black book. He turned its pages and handed it open to Mr Peters.

'There's the last I wrote. About the sewage on the beach. Disgraceful.'

Mr Peters read the clipping dispassionately. 'Very good,' he said. 'Can I look back over the others?'

'Yes, yes, any of it. Carry on. I'll just see if I can find you a cigarette. My maid smokes 'em.'

While the little man was gone Mr Peters glanced quickly over the book. It was a large exercise book, with the title on the fly-leaf in large ink letters – 'Controversy Book, E. Mortimer Pertwee'. Mr Peters quickly realized, with surprise, that only Mr Pertwee's letters were included. There were several headed controversies – 'Nationalization' was one. Mr Peters glanced through it. Letter from E. Mortimer Pertwee – 'Nationalization – Plan or Panacea?' Next, of a fortnight's later date – 'Function, Responsibility, or Irresponsibility'. Obviously letters had appeared criticizing Mr Pertwee. These, however, were not included. Instead appeared a few handwritten lines: 'There followed two replies, from persons I have not heard of. Just the usual stuff. Prejudice. No definition.' And there was a later comment. 'Following my analysis of liberty there appeared a typical piece of sentimental twaddle. I replied as follows.' And so on to the next clipping.

Mr Peters closed the book guiltily as Mr Pertwee re-entered.

'Very interesting,' he said.

'Oh, just a sideline all that,' said Mr Pertwee; 'I couldn't find you any cigarettes.'

'Well, I must be getting on down to buy some,' said Mr Peters, rising.

'Call in again sometime, always here.'

'Thanks, I will.'

They came out into the garden. The sun was warm, and there were vibrations of heat over the brassy tulips. In the next garden a man was working, pouring a powder between the cracks of his crazy paving. Pertwee called to him.

'Hoole, this is Peters. Lives up the end.' Greetings were exchanged.

'Won't shake hands,' said Hoole, a young, bronzed, man. 'Pouring concentrated weedkiller into my crazy paving. Should keep 'em down for a while.'

'Useful stuff,' said Mr Peters. ''Morning.'

4

At his usual shop, there were no cigarettes, and Mr Peters was obliged to go farther into the town. He walked along the sprawl of the coast road in a very critical mood. The monstrous houses, white and bulbous, or boxlike, strongly impressed him. He knew about this place – scene of a famous building-plots scandal; there were no roads, for the plots had been sold from the map, and no community services had land allotted to them. Among the pretentious houses muddy lanes straggled.

Everyone who had bought a building plot thought they would be relatively alone above the sea. When the great mass of houses was begun, those farthest from the coast found that their only chance of seeing the water was to build higher than the man in front. The result could be seen in a varied assortment of scaffoldings, towers and galleries, to which the occupants could climb for their vision of the sea.

Mr Peters came back thoughtfully to his own house. At the gate he paused to look at a lilac tree which was beginning to flower. He plucked a stem and pressed the tiny flowers against his face. Above them, his eyes surveyed the rest of the garden. Mr Peters sought for a word to describe it. He was always particular about precision in language, for he knew very well that the act of choosing words is basically the whole moral choice, the recurring crisis of discrimination in perception. 'Dilapidated?' then 'Neglected?' 'Overgrown?' 'Scruffy?' He found decision difficult. 'Wild?' 'Woolly?' 'Grassy?' 'Natural?' The difficulty of settling on a word disquieted him. He suspected that there was some ambiguity in his attitude to the garden. Well, it was rough, untidy, a wilderness of weeds and brambles. Sometimes he could scarcely bear to look at it. He was glad that from the room one's normal angle of vision passed over it and on to the view beyond. But in the sun his eyes would drop sometimes, and there it would be. He knew that in the hot weather he would want to sit outside, and then there would be no escaping it. Out for a lie in the sun. A *lie* in the sun. What about moral discrimination now?

He went to the hedge and peeped through at Hoole's neat garden. He could see the bronzed figure still stooping over the crazy paving, sprinkling the concentrated weedkiller. He smiled. Well, that at any rate makes things clearer, he thought. His eyes rested on the smooth, green lawn. One day he had seen Hoole going over it with a knife, cutting out the daisies. What could be said for a person who subscribed to this artificial division of flowers which are weeds, and flowers which are flowers. On one side the endless toil to produce flowers which were recognized in the catalogues; and on the other, even greater toil to root out and destroy flowers, often as beautiful, but not 'recognized'. The daisy particularly. The daisy was indeed an abiding pleasure, and if gardening meant rooting out daisies for the sake of toy-soldier tulips, then gardening was not for him.

'The point is,' he said to his wife, 'that these people are really dead. Their daily actions are just like the routine visitations of a ghost. Have you ever tried to deflect a ghost from its haunting path? Trying to shift these people is just as killing. They just clank on regardless, up and down the crazy paving, hoping their tended vegetation will do their living for them.'

'Nonsense,' his wife answered. 'They have their habits and their pleasures, just as you do. They're just not your habits, that's all.'

'They've got no contact with living experience, that's the point,' said Mr Peters.

'Oh, experience. That.'

Continuation of the conversation was made impossible by a scream from the child, who had been sleeping in his pram on the sun loggia, shaded by the branches of an elder tree which had taken root under the walls of the house.

'See to him, darling. Rock him in his pram.' Mr Peters walked over wearily. He took the pram handles and began a steady shaking. The child's cries increased. As the pitch of the screams rose higher, Mr Peters's rocking of the pram increased in violence. Soon it was jumping madly up and down, and the child's continued screaming was punctuated by gasps for breath as it shook around inside. Mr Peters noticed that his teeth were set hard. And then, suddenly, the noise ended. Mr Peters lowered the pram gently and crept away. He joined his wife in the room inside.

He picked up a newspaper which his wife had left open on the hearth, and folded it away under a cushion. He emptied the ashtray into the grate, tipping the cigarette ends, which were always a distasteful sight to him, well away from his view. As he drew the ashtray sharply back, he touched the tiles of the fireplace, and the broken tile fell out and clattered below. Mr Peters replaced it with an oath, and then sat back in one movement in his chair. He had become used to the defective springs of his favourite chair, and normally judged the right place to sit without provoking noise from them. But now he sat too far forward and he heard them creak under him, down to the depths.

He looked casually out at the loggia. The pram was moving slightly. The child was obviously awake, and rocking it with its tiny movements. Mr Peters looked back round the room. On the table the vase of lilacs was set in a cloth of tiny flower droppings. Mr Peters shifted his chair so that his back might be towards this. Again he noticed that his teeth were hard clenched. He relaxed them, consciously, and let the quiet spread through his body.

He watched his wife jump from her chair, and run to the open window on to the loggia. She screamed. Beyond her Mr Peters saw the pram rocking gently towards the open edge of the loggia, towards the drop into the weed-filled garden. Vaguely he realized that he had not secured it in its normal position against the pillar. He watched his wife stretching frantically towards it, and he saw her fingers touch it as it heeled over and fell. Mr Peters closed his eyes.

5

'This is the room I was telling you of,' said the disdainful man.

'Oh, how lovely,' the young woman cried, 'how lovely, Edward.'

'Rather large, isn't it?' said the young man, hanging back at the door.

'Perhaps,' said the disdainful man. 'But I have rarely seen a room with so distinctive an atmosphere. And I, as you know, in the course of my profession see many, many rooms.'

'And think of the delight of planning to furnish it,' the young woman said.

'Can we see the rest of the house?' asked the young man.

'Certainly, certainly. But I would advise you first to examine the prospect from those windows at the end. It is most striking.'

The young woman ran across to the windows. The young man followed uneasily.

'Oh, how delightful, how delightful.'

They looked down the long river valley, tracing the great bends of water which gleamed under the sun. On the downland the gorse was a blaze of yellow.

'Tell me,' said the young man, 'why did the last people leave?'

The other man dropped his eyes. He put a finger to his lips: 'I think they found the garden too much for them,' he said, and in his voice there was no mistaking the disdain.

The Fool and the Princess

———— ✠ ————

STEPHEN SPENDER

TO CHRISTOPHER ISHERWOOD

I

'I was happy.'

The living-room window looked out on to a narrow garden packed full at the end of summer with faded leaves and petals like an opened box of flowers. Between this garden and the road, a low iron balustrading surmounted a narrow base of blackened bricks. On the further side of the road beyond the tarmac was another row of houses, semi-detached, in pairs. Each bistre-coloured house had a peaked gable surmounted by what seemed a dilapidated iron feather.

Mr and Mrs Harry Granville sat on the sofa of their living room in front of the window facing the view. Both had that staring expression which faces have when they look at themselves in a mirror: as with a vague hope of looking beyond the flesh into a mind within, where secrets are laid bare.

Indeed, they might have been looking at the mirror of their own house on the other side of the road, for it was exactly the same. Such a sensation – that he was staring into a mirror at his own image glued in the past at the centre of a picture of his wife and his home had come into Harry Granville's mind since his return from Germany.

His saying, 'I was happy' was the end of five days in which he had said no word about the year he had spent there. He had said nothing and she had noticed his silence. Wasn't it odd that he didn't seem even to notice Home? He behaved in the way which was the opposite of what Kate had expected. She'd thought there'd be too much to say, too much to look at. True, he did play a bit with Gray, but even this he did in a way which seemed odd as though his own boy were a child he'd just met and grown fond of, somehow, not their own child.

Kate was frightened and most of all she was just tired out by Harry's behaviour. If she had spoken to Mrs Wicker, who lived next door, about it, she wouldn't have complained of his being unkind but of something worse; of his being crazy, uncanny, uncomfortable. She was frightened of telling Mrs Wicker: she didn't know what she'd be telling. She had now entered that time when the silence, the evasion had become overpowering, hurtful. Even the most painful truth would hurt less than what she had been through the last few days. As they sat on the sofa, gazing out at the road, in this house they had occupied ever since they were married; this house which would be theirs when they had paid another five instalments on it, there was a whiteness which each noticed in the other, a glassiness, a physical earnestness as of flesh waiting for the knife.

'I suppose you mean that you've never really been happy with me,' said Kate, in the dull, flat, realistic voice of her serious moments. 'I suppose you find me boring. Well, I'm not surprised. But it isn't really fair if we have no happiness to look back on. It isn't fair, Harry, really it isn't. We've never had the chance to give each other a good time, have we, Harry? First of all there was the war, then there was Gray being born, and then you went away and now everything seems finished.'

'But we have been happy, Kate, honestly, we've been happy, as happy as I'd ever been in my life until this happened. Everything isn't over either. We shall be happy again.'

'Then what's the matter?'

'It's just that everything's different. It takes getting used to. Germany gave me a kind of shock.'

'But what's different, Harry? You haven't told me yet what happened.'

'Well, to put it very crudely, and I suppose I can't put it any other way, I met another woman, at the DP camp. It sounds an ordinary thing to happen, but she isn't ordinary and she isn't extraordinary only because she happens to be a princess!'

'Oh, Harry, a princess! You with a princess!'

Suddenly she burst out laughing. She fell off the sofa with laughing, kneeling on the floor, clinging to one leg of the sofa beside him. He gravely watched the top of her head with the hair parted in the middle, coiling in two waves over her ears and drawn into a 'bun' at the back of her head. It was the kind of hair, auburn, frizzy at the edges, which is always a little untidy; the two waves foamed, each with a little spray of disordered ends of hair which caught the light. While she was laughing like this, these two waves of hair made him think of things weeping, drowning: a weeping willow, a picture in the Tate Gallery, which he had seen with Graham Ballard once, of Ophelia floating, drowning on a transparent stream under which were the washed pebbles. And like the water over the pebbles, the vague satisfaction shining from the word CULTURE, of all the knowledge he had acquired during the past year, floated a transparent veil of vanity even over his piteous vision of her distress.

He touched her shoulder. Then he drew a photograph from his wallet. She looked. Within a grey mist-like bubble of light in a muddy pond, drifted the head and shoulders of a young woman. Her black hair framed her oval face. The features were grave and symmetrical with large clear eyes and a chis-elled mouth, which showed black in this photograph. The expression was calm, dignified and intellectual, bizarrely rich and full in this prison photograph, taken in a hard light to emphasize the physical proportions and to ignore what could least accept to be ignored – the human expression.

'Well, your princess is certainly a beauty,' said Kate; she stopped laughing abruptly.

'Do you want me to tell you about her?' he quietly asked.

She said rather drily: 'It's certainly better to know what's coming to you than not know nothing. You do at least know where you are when you know what's coming to you. I can't expect you to tell me everything. I don't think I'd even want to know everything but if you do tell me something, do let it be the truth. Then I can make out the rest for myself. Harry, after the last few days I could bear to hear anything.'

'What's been so special about the last few days?'

'You know it's not been the nice homecoming I expected.'

'You're right. I'm very sorry. I'm really very sorry. I'm ashamed of myself.'

'Go on with what you were going to tell me.'

'Her christian name is Moura. She's got an unpronounce-able other name, but I won't bother you with that. At the camp, they call her the princess, because she's supposed to be descended from Russian nobility or something. She hasn't ever spoken to me about this herself, but she hasn't contra-dicted it to me either. She lives with her mother and her sister in a hut of the DP camp where I worked. Kate, I've never been with her more than a quarter of an hour alone.'

He stopped, flushed, bewildered, conscious (as she was also) of his honesty and his dishonesty. His lips had spoken the literal truth, his eyes knew that what he had just said was true – and yet it was so irrelevant. With an expression of sharpened pain he plunged to a deeper layer of truth: 'Well, I'm just telling you that, though it doesn't make any difference to my feeling for her. She and her mother and her sister were deported by the Germans from their town and made to work in an arms factory near Munich all through the war. Then, later, she acted as interpreter. She knows several languages. She was an interpreter in the camp also.'

'I don't see what all this has to do with *us*, Harry. Was it in connection with translating that you got to meet her, or what?'

'The first time I saw her was the first day I joined the camp. I noticed her at once. I didn't make any attempt to meet her for a long time; it's difficult to explain why, but it was partly just because she made such an impression on me. At that time, before the new commandant – Wingfield, who's there now – arrived, the camp was very rough, in some ways it was a downright brothel, and to ask to meet a woman only meant one thing. So for that reason I didn't ask to meet her. But I think that I always *knew* her, from the very first moment, almost as well as I do now. Sometimes I feel that I knew her before we met. I used to think about her all the time, like one sometimes does think of people. When I was alone, especially in the darkness, I would think of the expression in her eyes, an expression of a soul amid all that misery without a soul. You can see her soul even in the photograph. Thinking about her and imagining being with her became such a joy that it was another reason for not trying to meet her. I felt that I could wait. I wanted to wait. I even felt I knew her better through just waiting.'

'But all the same, you did meet her, Harry.'

'But I never tried to do so. I just met her inevitably. I didn't try perhaps partly also for a bad reason. Because, after all, I was a kind of gaoler. I knew that she couldn't get away from the camp. Still, it wasn't only that. I truly believe that if I had never met her, but just seen her and known that she existed in the world, I would have felt the same as I do now. I would have been completely happy in a way that I never have been before. That is what I have to tell you, Kate. I am trying to be completely honest, Kate. You must realize that it would be just the same if I had never met her and only seen her. When I saw her something happened to me which can't be altered.'

'But in spite of all you say, you did meet her, Harry.'

'Yes. One day I had to interview some of the Russian families to arrange about their being returned to Russia. She accompanied as interpreter. Then, finally, I ended the day with interviewing her mother and sister. So I was with all three of them alone in their little hut. This was just like any other of the little sheds which the families there lived in, except that they had done something to make it seem neater and in better taste. They hadn't got much, but with a few shawls and bits of cloth they had made the place seem civilized somehow. As soon as I got Moura to explain to them what I had come for, the old woman was terrified. She started trying to explain something to me by signs, as though she didn't trust Moura to tell me what it was. She kept on opening her mouth – which looked like a gasping fish, as she hadn't any teeth – and pointing down her throat. It was quite ludicrous really. I thought she wanted me to get her some false teeth, so I kept on saying *Zæhner . . .*'

'What does *Zæhner* mean?'

With a faintly-superior, embarrassed, handsome smile Granville said: 'It's the German for *teeth*. And then I said *Zahnarzt*, which means *dentist*, in a questioning voice. Those are two of the German words I've managed to pick up at the camp. Then Moura said in her almost perfect English: "No, it isn't that she wants. It's something quite different. But don't take any notice. She's being hysterical and absurd." When the old girl saw Moura talking with me, she got still more excited. She started grabbing at Moura's shawl with her hands and wailing. Then she suddenly turned to me and shouted in German *Gift*.'

'What does *Gift* mean?'

'It's the German for *poison*.'

'Why should she want poison?'

'She thought she was going to be sent back to Russia.'

'But why should that make her want poison?'

'Moura explained to me then. You see, they had been sent back to Russia once before, and then they'd escaped back again to us.'

'But why did they have to come back?'

A tired, almost persecuted look came on Granville's face. 'I only know what they told me, but I myself believe it. It's one of a great many similar stories which are about as hard to believe as not to believe. A lot of things happen in Europe today which are as difficult to judge as the kind of stories mediums tell at spiritualist seances. But all the same, when they happen to someone one trusts, one believes them, especially if there seems no reason for their having been invented. Anyway, this is their story. After the victory they were one of a party of Russian families which asked to be repatriated. They thought that after all Russia was their home, and they had loved their work before the war there. At all events Moura had loved teaching. They had many friends in their village. They imagined that there would be some kind of acceptance of them, some kind of welcome, a band, a bundle of clothes perhaps, something, however shabby, as there is for the French prisoners and even the prisoners of the defeated countries when they return home. But there wasn't anything like that. The guards to whom they were handed over treated them like prisoners. They were put into a train guarded by soldiers, also being repatriated, who assaulted them. When they arrived at the frontier, they were sent to a camp where conditions were worse than they had even been in Germany. She said that the whole experience was like being deported to Germany in the first instance, only in reverse. After two days in the camp they managed to bribe the guards with a few things they had saved during all these years. They found that there was quite a traffic in bribery for deportees who wanted to be re-deported. They got to Poland, where they were arrested once more, but again managed to escape. Then they walked half across Europe – these two young women and their mother – back to our camp.'

'But how awful to be threatened with being sent back to Russia after all that. Did you give them the poison?'

'Of course not. It would have been quite impossible.'

'Then will they go back?'

'That is part of what I have to tell you, Kate. I arranged for them not to be sent back to Russia. It all depends, though, on my keeping an eye on their situation.'

'Are you sure, though, that their story is true?'

'I have no evidence for it except their own words. But then we obtained evidence of about twenty families with similar experience in the camp. None of the stories can be proved individually, but, put together, they add up to something. There is no other evidence. All I do know is that they had a genuine desire to return to their country and in fact they did return. Then what they saw frightened them so much that they ran away again. It is difficult to think of any other explanation of their actions than the one they gave.'

There was a silence at the end of which she said: 'All the same, I still don't understand.'

'What don't you understand?'

'I don't understand why it has to make such an enormous difference to us, Harry. I don't blame you for taking an interest in this family at all. If I had been in your place, I hope I would have done the same, honestly I do. But I don't understand why you have taken no notice of me and why you have to treat Gray as though he were a stranger when you get home.'

'I sometimes think that meeting them,' he said, 'was like a meeting on top of a mountain, hidden in a cloud. And then the cloud cleared away and revealed us to each other much more vividly than if there had been never any cloud, cloud of Germany, there before. Now I feel that she has been gathered back away from me into her cloud of misery, cloud of the East.'

'And I suppose you mean that you have gone back also into your cloud of misery.'

'No, I didn't mean that at all: you mustn't put the words into my mouth, Kate, or we'll never understand each other. It's difficult and painful enough to work things out as it is. What I do mean,' he continued with difficulty, pursuing his ungainly metaphor, 'is that I am the only person who has the power to dispel the cloud for them. Yes, that's it, owing to the luck of my situation, I can bring some light into their lives.'

'I suppose you imagine you're a sort of fairy prince who slips the glass slipper or something on the foot of the princess who's a beggar maid.'

He looked at her quickly and then went on: 'And the fact that I can do so for someone else, means that I become much clearer, much lighter, to myself also . . . I hope I'm not hurting you too much, Kate.'

'After all, it hurts me less than when you're shifty or tell me lies or don't take notice of anybody in the house.'

'I think I've told you everything.'

'But – oh, what do you want to do about it, Harry? What do you want me to do with Gray? It's you who has to decide, I suppose.'

'Even if I did want to do anything, it would be useless . . . You see she has to stay at the camp. And I'm here. She can't get away. And in any case, she would never leave her sister and mother.'

'So she won't ever be sent back to Russia?'

He flushed. 'No, I think I fixed that.'

'Now I suppose you're going to tell me that, after all, you'll leave here and take another job at the camp?'

'No, I can't. I've left now and they're cutting down on the staff. I don't mean anything like that, Kate. I'm not thinking of our separating. All I might be able to do would be to go and see her every six months. That would mean, of course, arranging my work here so as to be able to get away.'

'Yes, it does make a difference, Harry. I see, I see.'

He looked straight into her eyes for the first time since his return home. She had the kind of hair which is called auburn and the freckled complexion which goes with it. The eyes were of the colour called 'hazel'. He noticed now that they were red around the edges and that red veins showed in them. His gaze, concentrated mostly on her eyes, occasionally wandered to the rest of her face. He noticed the texture of the skin which had a certain tenderness which went with her kind of complexion, a sensitivity which reminded him of her youth and which yet revealed all the signs of care and age like a photographic plate. There were three lines on her forehead which he noticed particularly. There were occasions (with friends, for example) when the insistent rawness of these lines made him ashamed, but now he felt compassion for them. They were a faintly reddish colour emphasized by exposure and by work. He gently touched one of them now with his finger as though he still might find the power of love which would erase it.

'I hope that I don't make you feel too miserable.'

'I don't mind so much now you've told me the truth. It's

what I imagined that makes me so miserable. When you don't say anything or when you seem to be making excuses the whole time I mind.'

'Everything is better now we both know the truth. It is more wonderful than it has ever been before, Kate. It's as beautiful as . . .'

'Oh, don't say that it is as beautiful as what you told me, Harry. I couldn't bear your saying that.' He thought she was going to cry. But instead she got up calmly, reminding them both that she had to go and look to Gray upstairs. 'Let's always tell the truth in the future, Harry.'

They looked at each other as they seemed never to have looked before. The strangeness, the sense of pallor surrounding everything they saw, which they had felt during the past few days, now included themselves, melted them into each other in its white, pure light. He looked at her and he saw beyond approaching age and nagging care, the girl whom he had courted seven years ago with added to her young beauty the inexplicable miraculous generosity which had loved him, cared for him, forgiven him and borne Gray to him.

2

During the next few weeks he discovered, though, that their relationship had separated, as it were, on two different levels which, after splitting off thus, now ran parallel with each other. One path was their reaffirmed and strengthened trust in each other which, when they were on it, seemed the final truth of their love. The other path was their day-to-day life with each other in the suburban house built during an epoch when all the houses in that part of London seemed of stucco poured into one mould: their life with Gray, now three years old, and brought up according to Kate's standards to be as like as possible to Mrs Wicker's children next door. On this day-to-day level their lack of understanding of each other seemed to increase and the path to lead directly to a place where life together would become intolerable.

The very existence of the deeper level where everything was forgiven, where mind and body were fused, made them the more impatient on the level where everything was wearisome, mechanical and unforgivable. Yet they could not live always on the deeper level, path of dreams, path of tears, path of acceptance and finality, path of a life so strange and unfamiliar that it seemed a postscript to their waking lives, a premature foreshadowing of the union which they might hope for after both their deaths.

A crisis of anger, of tenderness, or of happiness in the course of their everyday life would enable them suddenly to discover themselves once more on that path where the superficial things did not count. They could make these abrupt, violent transitions. What they could not do was keep the new life steadily in contact with the old, transform the new differences which divided them by the steady pressure of the new intensity which brought them together.

Every effort to do so on Harry's part was not only a failure, it had an ambiguousness which made them suspicious and created new divisions. These divisions could only be healed by the catharsis which followed on a violent scene.

One evening, when they had cleared away the supper things and long after Gray had been put to bed, they sat side by side again on the sofa. Kate was knitting and Harry was smoking his pipe. She said: 'It's nice to sit side by side like this again, isn't it, Harry?'

'Why "again"? It isn't so often that I go out.'

'I know you don't go out during the day for a job but you're out often in the evening.'

'Well, I don't need a job, do I? I've saved quite a bit of money. Whatever you may say about me, I've done pretty well for myself if you consider what I was earning before the war. In 1938, I was earning five pounds a week as a clerk, and now I've lately been getting close on £1,000 a year as an official.'

'But you're not earning that now.'

'I prefer to do a bit of freelancing while I wait.'

'I'd like very much to know what you're waiting for.'

'I've told you, haven't I? Need we go into all that again? We've agreed, haven't we? Anyway, I don't know that I ever really want another regular job. I haven't any ambitions so long as I can just get along supporting you and giving Gray the chance of a better education than I had. All I'm waiting for at present is a piano.'

'A piano?'

'Yes, it will be arriving tomorrow, I hope. Graham Ballard is lending it to me.'

'But what will you do with a piano?'

'What does one do with a piano?' He was very good-looking but there were moments when a certain superciliousness went so well with his kind of handsomeness that she wanted to knock his good looks off his face. 'I shall begin by fingering out the easiest Haydn Sonatas.'

'I didn't know you could play.'

'I can't. But I learnt to read a bit of music when I was at the camp.'

'Do you mean to say that you intend to support us by playing the piano, Harry?'

'Why will you keep on about money? We don't want to be millionaires. We just want to be modest and reasonable and a little better off than we were before the war, and I'll look after that. Don't worry. I've promised you, haven't I? It isn't money that brings one happiness but understanding.' He said this last sentence as if it were a quotation.

'Graham Ballard must have told you that.' He did not reply.

'All the same, you aren't often in in the evenings.'

'Well, now that I have broken with Len and the comrades on account of my telling them how those Russian friends of mine were welcomed home to Russia, I don't see anyone. I walk, I like walking. Do you realize that the garden of the old church near here is quite beautiful?'

'It gets me down. I hate graves and graveyards.'

He looked round the room restlessly. 'Couldn't we change those curtains?'

She looked at the curtains which were of a dark orange colour: 'Why?'

'I don't think the colour goes very well with the walls and the carpet . . . And now that I'm on the subject of changing things, I thought if you don't object I'd get a pot of paint and repaint the bathroom. I can't stand that lemon-coloured woodwork with those tiles.'

She put down her knitting and said very quietly: 'You've changed a great deal, Harry, but you don't seem to realize that I haven't changed. I've been here all the time, while you've been away improving yourself.'

'It isn't that I've bettered myself at all,' he said, but with the same irrepressible flare of satisfaction that made the room seem suddenly too small to hold such triumph. 'I'm different, that's all. I can't help being different any more than you can help being the same.'

She looked again at the curtains. They were certainly faded, though she liked their colour. All confidence seemed drained out of her life. Harry and she might just as well never have met as be such strangers to each other as they had become. Yet nothing had happened except that he had said some words.

He had meant to explain that he had had a conversion to an entirely different way of life. There was an ambiguity in this conversation which was real and yet which made him often be false.

'After all, it wasn't just Germany. I know you think everything's due to that. But I'd changed long before I went to Germany.'

She looked hard at him. 'When did you change?'

'It was the war, I suppose. When I joined Civil Defence and when I met Graham Ballard. I suppose you might say I began to educate myself. I started off reading modern books and then I worked backwards through Dickens and Shakespeare. I began to have what you might call cultural values, and to spend my money not on gadgets but on a little library.' He looked across at some bookshelves built into a niche in one corner of the room.

Then he made an effort to shake off once more this deadly self-satisfaction which parodied a change which he felt really an improvement in himself, parodied even his love. 'I realize how you feel, Kate, and I know it's dreadfully hard on you. I know that I'm selfish, that I'm a prig, that I don't make you happy. All the same, I'm not just a materialist. I don't exploit what I've gained intellectually by trying to make more and more money. I want to go on improving myself and I want to live according to better standards and I want Gray to be brought up different from what I was.'

'But I try my best to bring up Gray well, Harry.'

'I know you do, darling. It isn't the way you bring him up that I criticize. It's his being brought up in the same atmosphere as Mrs Wicker's Geoffrey. I'll give you an example of what I mean. This morning I went into the garden with Gray and he was playing round with me when Geoff came out of Mrs Wicker's back door. When Geoff saw Gray he let out a kind of yell, a blood-curdling "Gr-a-a-o-w-y!", threw himself on to the ground in a horrible way and started rolling about, shouting "Gr-a-a-o-w-y!" And Gray became transformed at the same moment into Geoff's utterly base and vulgar world. It wasn't important, but I saw very clearly then what I am afraid of – I am afraid of Gray being sucked down by the world in which we bring him up.'

'Oh, but boys must be boys! Do have some sense, Harry! It's all so unreal,' she went on. 'Graham Ballard can write novels and earn good money from them. He may have taught you to read but he can't teach you to write and be clever like he is. Yet you talk like him and try to play the piano and read. But Graham Ballard won't make you into a Paderewski or a J. B. Priestley. All he can do is teach you not to work. I wish you'd never met him in the first place. And then you meet the princess or whatever she calls herself.'

'It doesn't matter, but according to our information at the

camp, she has the right to be called a princess, though of course that's only a technicality.'

'Well, what does matter is that she's a Displaced Person. It's absurd for a Displaced Person to be a princess. I'm very sorry for her, but the fact is that she's a beggar and she's nothing more. As far as rank goes she's not even as high as I am now. She can't make you a prince but she may make you and all of us beggars.'

'All right. I'll take a job and I'll give up all idea of ever going back to the camp.'

'No. Go back! And don't ever come here again afterwards!'

She burst into tears. There was nothing he could say. He sat watching her, knowing that to touch her or to comfort her would be a lie, a lie beyond a lie. She left the room. He did not follow.

An hour later he made some tea in the kitchen, took it upstairs and knocked timidly at the bedroom door: 'Would you like a cup of tea, Kate?'

She did not reply. He went into the room. She was sitting up in bed, wide-eyed with dark rings under her eyes. He noticed how tired she looked and once more he was grieved by the three lines almost like scars growing across her forehead. The grief at the centre of their life: this was the tangible truth, shown in those scars.

She smiled slowly, timidly, with her smile of the young girl he had met years ago, strangely purified of all the intervening time. 'Harry, come here. I have a little present for you.'

He walked towards her, rather apprehensively. He put the tray with the two teacups on it down on the little table beside the bed. 'What?'

She held a watch in her hand. He recognized the watch but not the wrist-bracelet attached to it. This wrist-bracelet was of small sections, which now that it was not stretched, half-closed over each other in glittering nickel snake scales.

Harry Granville looked down at the watch and said 'Thank you.' He felt suddenly faint.

*

The sight of the watch with its new bracelet overwhelmed him with the memory of a scene in the hut where the princess lived with her mother and sister. This scene was the sequel to the one which he had related to Kate, when Moura's mother had asked him to obtain the poison. The next day he had found Moura alone in the hut. This had been the quarter of an hour in which they were alone. 'Where are the others?' he had said, looking round the little room with the three bunk beds one on top of each other, across which a curtain was half-drawn. 'I managed to get them away,' she said. 'I wanted to talk to you alone. I have something to tell you. I found that mother, in addition to wanting the poison, had got hold of this.' She pulled out from under the mattress of the lowest bunk a revolver. He looked at it. It was small but 'useful'. 'That would certainly be one sure way of getting you sent back – if you were found with that,' he said. 'In fact, really, if I were to do my duty, I should report you.' 'That's why I want to ask you a great favour. Can you hide it?' 'Maybe I can sell it for you. It's a very nice one. I could get quite a lot for it.' 'We don't want anything. If you can just get rid of it, so that I don't ever have to think about it again, you will be doing us a great service.' He put it in his pocket. 'Thank you,' she said. 'It is I who should thank you.' 'For what?' 'For being here. For making me happy when I should be unhappy, for turning a prison into a heaven.' She looked at him without moving. Then she said: 'All I have to thank you for is for being human. After all these years, to meet a human being is better for me than any heaven.' Their recognition was like the burning of light into light. The rough edge of words was dissolved in this great illumination where they were in each other's arms. Even now, thinking of it, he experienced a sense of vertigo. Then her mother and sister came back.

The next day when he visited the hut they were all three there. He drew a watch out of his pocket. 'Look what I've got for you,' he said to Moura. It was a wristwatch with a black face, luminous figures and hands, and a large second hand moving from the centre around the whole face. It had a greasy, worn leather strap.

Moura held it in her hands and looked at it admiringly. When her mother could not see the expression on her face, she said: 'You exchanged the revolver for this?' He nodded. She handed it back to him. 'Will you keep it as a little gift from me? There isn't any opportunity here to give you anything.' He put it back into his pocket and said 'Thank you,' quietly. 'I do not tell my mother,' she went on. 'She would be upset. But it is from all of us.' Her sister, who spoke very little English, turned round at this and said: 'Yes. From my mother and myself also.'

Now he looked at the watch lying on the turned-down sheet of the bed, with the metal wrist-bracelet clasping it on both sides like the wide scales of a flattened snake.

'Do you like it?' Kate asked.

'Yes. Thank you very much, darling.'

'You never told me where you got the watch? You haven't told me much about Germany, you know.'

'Oh, in Germany you can get an awful lot of nice things for a few dozen cigarettes.'

'I didn't know you went in for the Black Market.'

'Well, it wasn't exactly the Black Market. Someone wanted me to get rid of a revolver for him. The best way was to change the revolver for something else. And then . . . he . . . insisted on my keeping this watch as a present.'

She looked steadily at him with wide eyes in which there was an expression which terrified him. It was as though her eyes were fixed on some point where they comprehended all this and then they saw to a point beyond his own comprehension. 'After all, she is not stupid,' he thought.

Her body seemed almost rigid. He was aware of her flesh, waxy and sagging, as one is aware of the flesh of a dying person. Without her knowing what she was doing, her hand crumpled over the watch, picked it up and then dropped it again on to the white sheet. This gesture filled him with a sense of awe and compassion. Then, without saying another word, she got out of bed and left the room.

He heard her walk downstairs feeling her way heavily, with her hand evidently following the line of the banisters. Left alone, he knelt down and laid his head against the sheet and then against the rough texture of the blanket. He groaned. Yet although it seemed to him that he was really suffering, his suffering lacked purity. All the purity was hers, hers moving downstairs, hers moving out into the darkness, hers if perhaps she drowned herself in some river. For himself, by comparison with the grief he caused her, his own agony seemed slightly absurd, unreal. He had to remind himself that his own situation was indeed a real one. Yet even doing so he remained like a sinner, who, conscious that he clings to the fruits of his ill-doing, cannot pray. Like the King in *Hamlet*, he thought, and this thought gave him the faint satisfaction in his recently acquired culture which was an added reason for despising himself, which, while making him more conscious of his situation, at the same time strangely robbed it of authenticity.

She did not come back. At last he stood up and listened in the empty room. There was the silence of the early hours of the morning which filled the town with an emptiness dropped from the furthest distances of the universe. There was the sense of streets outside washed by cold dark winds, of pavements faintly brushed by the reflected lights of the furthest stars. And caged in all the little boxes of the road human beings seemed to fill the whole night with their obscure misshapen passions which could never be moulded into a street or a prison camp. He sighed and his sigh seemed to fill the whole house mingling under the stairs with the tears of his wife.

He walked downstairs to the little kitchen. The light was on but he could not see her. The naked bulb glared with a white fury which shone on the walls of the small room and glittered on saucepans and crockery. On the mantelshelf a clock ticked intolerably.

Then he saw her where she was crouched under the kitchen

sink, her knees drawn up, her head bent over them. She was in a sleep which was a kind of trance. He put his arms round her body and drew her gently towards him. She opened her eyes and smiled faintly at him with a smile which was on the further side of the events which troubled them.

'Come to bed, darling,' he whispered.

She looked at him without understanding. Her mind seemed filled with the ticking of the clock. 'Time,' she said, 'time. The time stitches through me like a needle through a cloth.'

'Sweetheart, you're very tired. Come now to bed.'

At this she understood. She said in the voice – almost a complaining voice – she always put on when she was worried, 'I'm perfectly all right. Leave me here. You worry too much, Harry.' She put out her hand and stroked his face. 'That's what's wrong with you, Harry, you worry too much.'

'Come to bed, darling. I'll look after you.'

Her waking voice merged into her trancelike voice: 'Time . . . the watch, Harry. Your watch, poor darling, your watch like a cross . . .'

'Why like a cross?' he asked. His voice was tired. He knew now that he was absorbed into a centre of his experience, the drama which he did not want, which he had created himself but which now took him completely to its bosom and thrust him beyond mere literary self-dramatization into its own truth, the truth behind their lives of what they were and what they suffered.

'What cross, silly? Why, me and she, the cross on which you're crucified.'

At this point everything might have ended. He would gladly have died with this cross which she had named a dagger against his breast beckoning him to the place where the heart is stripped bare.

But the perception of the truth is not always the end. So he took a sponge, dipped it into some cold water and cooled her forehead with it.

She awoke as the dawn filled the streets with faint milky

light. They were quite alone in this new day and as though they had never known each other. It was as though they had shed themselves, by a painful and wearisome process of everything except their awareness of each other's needs. They did the ordinary things. They put on a kettle and made some tea, then they ate a little bread and jam with it, as though they were picnicking. They were happy. Then they went to bed and slept until the usual morning.

3

'Loot, I suppose,' Graham Ballard said, with a quick glance like a bright-eyed bird's sidelong peck, at Harry Granville's wristwatch.

'No, not exactly,' said Harry, 'but in a way loot, I suppose.' He sincerely did not wish to disappoint Graham's scepticism.

Graham Ballard's eyes took this in. He was a novelist digesting a useful piece of observation. At their meals together, Harry who, like most self-making characters suffered from the desire to please, the desire even to be the character in a book, provided Graham automatically with such scraps of self-revealing information. He paid both their ways, as it were, by being a character in a Graham Ballard novel.

Graham's eyes, now watching Harry over the tablecloth of the Soho restaurant, were certainly amongst the most remarkable in the world of 1945. They held their place in a face of straw by what appeared to be a juggling feat of the watchful, amused mind and will behind them. It seemed as though Graham balanced them and at the same time they balanced him. They gave the impression of movement and stillness of the two flying balls of a revolving mechanical regulator.

Graham Ballard and Harry Granville met every few weeks over lunch. Everything became a routine with Graham. His life was full of arbitrary self-imposed disciplines, habits formed for no apparent reason, except perhaps to convey an impression of discipline and power. In his life his system of habits and beliefs could not be taken seriously by those who knew him; and yet they were taken seriously by many hundreds of readers of his books.

They always took a table on the first floor by the window, and Graham always sat with his back to the light which shone full on to Harry's handsome and self-conscious face. They had started the habit of lunching together in 1940 during the air raids when they had both been wardens at the same post. It had occurred to Ballard almost as soon as he joined the post that Granville was a Ballard character. He seemed a perfect example of the 'card' who is half forced by and who half forces his circumstances; the interest lay in his being at once a social misfit and an obvious product of social forces.

Ballard had not known Granville for many days before he had fully documented him. He came from a lower middle-class, partly working-class family, but he himself had never done manual labour. Before the war he had been in turn an insurance agent, a clerk, a travelling salesman of vacuum cleaners, and for months at a time during the slump he had been unemployed. At the outbreak of the war he had joined the Civil Defence, partly for genuinely patriotic reasons, partly because during his off days in London he could continue to keep several irons in several different fires. In Civil Defence he had immediately shown an ability for organizing entertainments which made life easier for himself and more amusing for his fellow wardens. There had been an amusing 'passage' (Ballard thought of this as of a transition, brilliantly and wittily accomplished, from one theme to another in music) when Granville had almost made the mistake of seeking promotion. However, he quickly realized that this would only lead to a dead-end of routine work and ungrateful responsibilities. The true Granville theme towards which the development, after pursuing a wrong idea for a few bars, moved, now resolved itself firmly around far pleasanter ways of 'getting on'. These were organizing clubs, welfare, theatricals, discussions, and so on. In a war supposedly conducted for the common people by a democracy, 'Welfare', 'Education', 'Discussion', and so on were names which intimidated the authorities into supporting whoever mentioned them.

Granville also had a line in selling American fountain pens and wristwatches obtained through a friend, a transatlantic pilot. There was nothing really inconsistent in all this with the fact that during the air raids he was brave (he even won a medal for rescuing a pretty girl from under a building where she was trapped) yet no one gave him much credit for this, because it seemed inevitable from his whole appearance that he would win a medal, precisely for saving a pretty girl trapped under a building. He showed, indeed, in the time of danger, exactly that quality which lightened even the darker passages of his life: simple good will. After all, welfare, fountain pens and courage all improved the conditions of his fellow-men.

Granville needed to be accepted and approved for what he was, not for what he did. The limited approval which he got for his medal and his welfare work did not satisfy him because it did not answer those self-doubts of which he was most afraid. He wanted to explain to everyone that he was both good and bad, perhaps even rather more bad than good, since he nearly always acted from bad motives, but that he was nevertheless, somehow, in the long run, a force for the good. 'I know that I'm self-interested,' he had the air of explaining to everybody; 'but there is an element of real disinterestedness in all my self-interestedness. I want to confess to you, in order that you'll see that.' It was not just modesty, it was a real passion for clarification which made him explain so often that he really did not deserve the medal. He had demonstratively gone all out for it, and yet, at the last moment, when he was rescuing the girl there had been courage in his action.

The other men in the station could willingly have accepted him as a 'crook' or a 'slicker', one of themselves according to their own opinion of themselves. They could not accept his view of himself as a grey-coloured but nevertheless ultimately salvable spiritual force. He made them feel uncomfortable both for himself and themselves. His probing suggested a metaphysical inquietude. They accepted each other as honest or as crooks; the crooks tolerated those who were honest, the honest those who were crooks. There was a line agreed on by democratic discussion at the post, beyond which one should not be crooked. Crooks and honest agreed alike that during a raid it was not wrong to take such property as would be of personal use to you; but it would be immoral to loot kids' cash boxes. They could not understand that anyone whose activities fell well on the right side of this line should seek to excuse and justify himself. Granville annoyed them when he explained that his welfare schemes, though promoting his own welfare, also promoted theirs. 'You've got your racket, just like we may have ours, if we was to tell you about it. No one's grumbling at you, you're happy, we're happy, cut it out,' was their attitude.

Ballard saw through Granville's dishonesty to his honesty, and then he looked still further and saw another deeper dishonesty underneath. To him, Granville's game was a kind of double bluff by which he first cheated his mates and then tried to obtain their approval so that he might cheat himself. Granville realized that Ballard had this cynical attitude towards him, and he even, to some extent, played up to it. The very fact that Ballard saw through him attracted him. He wanted someone to look through the surface to a level of his existence where he might still be wrong but where at least a genuine struggle was taking place. Then there was the fascination, for him, of Ballard's being a literary artist which gave him in Granville's mind the position of a moral judge. If ever he inspired Ballard to write a book about him there would be written his 'last judgment'.

Ballard despised Granville and yet he had a curious sympathy for him. For the weaknesses and aspirations which he recognized in him and which he despised, he recognized and despised also in himself and in all human nature. He had also the kind of attachment to Granville which the novelist has for the character when he has created. In his way, Granville was a wonderful instrument who responded to Ballard's interpretation of him from moment to moment and from phrase to phrase as an orchestra (to change the metaphor) responds to a conductor. And while he responded in this way, Ballard could notice in the slight movement of the muscles of his face (to change the metaphor once more) a vibration, a reactibility, like that of a quivering needle registering electrical impulses.

And what was this responsiveness except love? And what was Ballard's passion for interpreting himself into Granville's life except love? These were questions which in roving audacious essays of thought Ballard certainly dared put to himself. For if he put a creative impulse into Granville, he also took a lot out of him. In fact, Granville was life, life raw as the bleeding steak he was now eating, which he fed on, from which he derived his own creative life. He fed not only on Granville's life but also on that of his family, for he was soon friendly with Kate who confided greatly in him, openly liked and secretly hated him. Almost automatically he became the godfather when Gray was born.

Yet there was the same arbitrariness about Ballard's relationship with Granville as with, say, the Communist Party, which he had once joined, or the Catholic Church, which he would one day perhaps join. A detached passion was poured into a situation, it entered into every vein, flushed the skin, so that Catholicism became more symbolic, Marxism more historic, and Granville more Fallen Man than ever before, whilst Ballard looked on in staring illuminated delight. But at any moment the whole impulse might be withdrawn, not by weariness or even lack of feeling on Ballard's part, but simply by his having thought up something else. So that although Ballard was the moving force in the relationship, yet Granville was the more dependent on it.

Graham Ballard looked impatiently at the watch on Harry's wrist for some moments, expecting some confession or further explanation. But Harry said nothing.

Slightly annoyed, suspecting a change in Harry, Graham began 'testing out the position', as he would have called his inquisition.

'And do you see anything of our mutual friends of the Party?'

'I'm not on very good terms with them. Karl Marx would doubtless say that the improvement in my own economic circumstances has made me forsake the cause of the working classes and join the bourgeoisie –'

Harry expressed himself clumsily with Graham, docilely exposing his own priggishness.

Graham's eyes were on him again and now the mouth in the lower part of his bright little face with the upper lip hidden under a very fair moustache, revealed itself as an organ almost as vivid as the eyes, which would give a vermilion twinkle. Encouraged, Harry went on: 'But nevertheless, actually, I do have more objective reasons. When I was in the camp I got some of the interpreters to take notes of the stories of some of the prisoners who had returned to Russia since the war and then escaped back to us. I was specially interested in the stories of three of them – three Russian women, a mother and two daughters. I've brought some of the papers to show you – if you aren't bored – as I think they would interest you.' He took some papers, folded, out of his pocket.

'Ah, documents, documents,' sighed Graham. This was the Writer's Role in Society – to be deluged by the Documents: poets who receive truck loads of confessions from schoolgirls, critics on whom wastepaper baskets emptied all their contents for criticism, novelists to whom every fellow-traveller on a railway journey hastened to narrate his (or her) three volume Saga. Harry always showed him documents, like so many proofs of the way in which he led his life. There were the notes about his scheme of reform of welfare in Civil Defence – these actually reached to the Home Secretary – the reports to prove that his education scheme in the Lambeth posts had increased the average intelligence of the personnel and so on, and so on. The effect on Graham of receiving these testimonies was that he felt suddenly professional; distant from Harry whom he now regarded as the case in the waiting room, while he (the specialist) turned over the papers. Whilst

Harry went on talking, Graham glanced lightly at the documents, went on eating and undoubtedly listened and watched closely, all at the same time.

'When I showed these reports to Len and Rex their comment was: "You don't mean to say that you believe this Fascist propaganda."'

'Do you believe what is written here?' asked Graham, idly almost. He seemed hardly to be listening. With knife and fork cutting meat, touching the plate, lifting food to his mouth in mechanical ballet, his eyes followed the lines of the page he was reading.

'As far as I can judge most of it's true. Of course I can prove nothing. The point is, though, that the people who say that they have had these experiences are human beings whom I have met, and who are my friends. One of them is my best friend in the world. Len and Rex aren't interested because they don't really bother even to consider the people who have written these reports as real living flesh and blood. They probably think that they were written by Trotskyist agents living in South America. But, of course, I can prove nothing. I don't pretend to be in a state of knowing things, but I at least know that I am ignorant. Out there one doesn't know things with the same confidence as Party Members here who've read nothing but the *Daily Worker* or *Humanité*. All the same it isn't that I'm against the Party or that I blame Len and Rex. It is that I want to try to learn the truth; whereas they simply regard all evidence unfavourable to their cause as Fascist propaganda.'

'And what did they say when you told them all that?'

He pushed the papers aside, stopped eating and with knife and fork raised in his hands above his plate, awaited Harry's answer.

'Rex said: "I'm fond of you, Harry, but honestly if the Revolution happened now and you was on the other side of the barricades and I had a gun in my hands, I'd shoot you without hesitation."'

Graham laughed. He stared across the restaurant behind Harry and said with great distinctness separating each word and seeming to fling it down like a newly minted coin: 'Yes, they would be delighted to shoot you. With the added pleasure of murdering affection in the name of Authority.'

Harry smiled. For the first time that day he felt that he had won Graham's confidence. He looked across the table at him pleasantly. With the ease of their now reaffirmed friendship, he took a photograph and a letter out of his pocket.

'I seem to be producing even more documents than usual today. But there's something I very much want you to know and understand.'

Graham now pushed aside his plate with the knife and fork laid across it. He did this with a comical, not disagreeable air of resignation. He took up the photograph and the letter. It was written in a clear firm handwriting with slanting letters each of which was sensitively formed.

Dear Harry,

Thank you for your letter. In this cloud which we inhabit it was beautiful to have a sign of light from your world outside.

My mother, my sister and myself are most happy to think of you at your home in London with your wife and child.

Whatever happens to us, you must not think of risking for my sake to break up the happiness which you have in your own house. In a world where so many have been torn away from those they love, you must not allow the misfortunes of those who have lost their families, to draw into the destruction those who are united. So you must consider most closely the feelings of your wife even when she may seem unreasonable. I can understand how she must love you and what she must have felt.

Let me say now that to meet someone who acts like a human being and who greets me as though I were a free and equal human person, creates already for me the idea of an eternal soul beyond this prison. My dear one, if I never see you again, your kindness, your humanity and your beauty are absolute. They are with us for ever.

Moura.

After he had finished reading this letter, Graham looked more intently at the photograph. Then he laid it on the letter and pushed both back across the table.

'It explains the wristwatch. She gave me the wristwatch.'

Graham looked at the watch again and said coldly: 'Very nice. I apologize for the suspicion which had crossed my mind. But one reads such stories.'

'The bracelet doesn't go quite with the watch itself. I'm afraid that Kate chose it for me.'

Graham looked fixedly at the wrist bracelet for some seconds and then he said always with the same freezing politeness: 'Oh, I don't think I have any objection to that. It surely has a certain charm.'

Harry flushed, suffering the torments reserved for the self-educated person when, at one stroke, he is caught out in betraying old loyalties and failing to conform to new standards of taste.

Graham sipped his coffee, holding the cup high over his mouth between the sips and looking at Harry over the rim with shining eyes. He felt suddenly happy. He had this creature where he wanted him, all signs of independence abandoned, returning like a dog with tail between his legs to the master's knees, humbled eyes begging for a sign. Then he said encouragingly: 'From what you say am I to assume that you consider returning to the camp?'

'Well, I'm not going to take a job there, but I intend to pay the camp a visit for a few days every six months. That means I shall have to order my whole life round those few days.'

Still not really concerned, Graham said: 'How serious is this, Harry?'

Harry took a long deep breath: 'She speaks of my letter being a sign of light to her from the world outside. But her letter is just as much a sign of light to me. She lives in her cloud of Eastern Europe, but I also live in my kind of cloud of the confused life I have made for myself . . .' He went on to elaborate this metaphor as he had done to Kate, but in Graham's presence he did not feel quite the same confidence. He stumbled out of literature again to say: 'I owe everything I have to her (apart from a great deal of education which I've received from you, Graham). But before I went to Germany I was divided whether to be a car salesman (you know there will be a tremendous lot in selling cars after the war: and I think you'll agree that I don't flatter myself when I say that I have the appearance of a first-rate salesman); as I say, I was divided between having a shot at selling cars and the idea of getting in on the ground floor of the new education scheme, as a result of my Civil Defence experience which also incidentally gave me plenty of contacts at the Home Office. Perhaps the education scheme was what I would have done. One side of me wanted to do public good and the other wanted to make a lot of money: I think the good would have won, especially as I think there is also a solid future in the education scheme. Now all I want to do is to sit down at the piano you've so kindly lent me and finger out early Haydn Sonatas and perhaps later on a Bach Prelude or two.'

He pronounced 'Bach' in a way which caused Graham slightly to turn away his head. He changed this wince into a sour smile. 'Perhaps I did wrong to lend you the piano.' Suddenly he began to feel very tired. He wondered whether he had eaten too much.

'Of course, I don't imagine that I shall ever become a good pianist,' Harry said earnestly. 'I just want to understand something of music. And if it wasn't music, I'd want to be reading all day. My only wish now is to make myself a civilized person. My Communist friends think I'm a prig and a snob, naturally enough, and I dare say they're right: I *am* a bit of both.'

'Perhaps it's rather more to the point to know what Kathleen thinks.'

Granville hesitated. Then, not answering, he said: 'I've proposed that on my way back from Germany next time she and I meet and have a fortnight in Paris.'

'Do you think it will succeed?'

'I dare say not. But don't you see that either it works or nothing works? Whether or not I see Moura, something final has already happened. I've discovered a new personality in myself just as if I had died and were born again.'

'Oh God,' exclaimed Graham suddenly. 'Oh God, oh God, oh God, my God.'

The idea that Harry had authentic genuine experiences, isolated from those of everyone else, experiences of the universe, of love, of death, sickened him. Quite truthfully he said: 'I felt very sick for a moment, that's all. I'm sorry. Go on.'

Granville looked up at him, timidly, humbly, affectionately. 'Have the things I've been saying sounded very foolish?'

'Oh dear, no, not in the least, Harry,' he answered, meaning that they had and meaning Harry to understand very definitely that he meant they had.

Harry did not reply. Relenting a little, Graham, who had been staring with intense distaste at the coarse fur wrapped like a horse's collar around the neck of a lady just leaving her table, looked at him. Then he looked again, with amazement. For Granville was on the verge of tears. His face was flushed, his eyelids dropped over his eyes to hide the emotion which Graham certainly did not wish to see. With his fork in his right hand he fumbled vaguely at his plate. But in spite of himself Graham saw the emotion: 'Yes, he is at the centre of things. He's out in the night, in the cold, among the wounded multitudes, in the starving huts, and he has found his heart.'

An epigram, every cheap letter of which shone in his mind like a bright newly minted farthing, consoled him for a moment: 'Christ, most malicious of controversialists, knew that no answer is more humiliating than to turn the other cheek.' No sooner was this thought than it disgusted him. The river of self-disgust flowed into the river of disgust and fury with Granville.

Granville began eating again. Ballard noted for the ninth time how revealing his manner of eating was. Granville ate not coarsely but with a self-conscious noisy neatness, snapping his food into his mouth and shutting it as often as possible so as to conceal ungenteel shames taking place at the back of his mouth, between his teeth, within the cavern of his throat.

'But there's no doubt,' Graham thought, 'that he's had an experience, is involved in a world which has snatched him away. Let me be quite clear about this. Nothing reveals his condition more than the tactless innocence with which he tries to please me. It's as though some writer who's been my disciple and whom I thoroughly despise, were suddenly to produce a masterpiece, through no merit of his own but because he had been wrapped into the arms of an experience, an experience of which I myself would never be capable.'

They had now finished their meal. But coffee was still to be served and they could not escape from each other. When the coffee came, Granville broke the silence once more. Looking timidly at Graham he said: 'I am glad that you take Kate's side. Of course, I realize that I am behaving badly to her.'

'Not at all, Harry. If there is a question of sides, I'm sure that Kate does not need defending by me. She is, in her own right, a beautiful woman. Kate is a beautiful woman.'

Harry flushed once more: 'I know.'

They were silent again. But (to revert to the metaphor which had expressed Ballard's feeling so well in the past) the sensitive recording instrument was a needle fluctuating wildly and quite unreliably now inside Harry. Graham had a vague dread of what was coming. Harry looked at him with intolerable irritating innocence and said with grace: 'Oh, I'm so glad you think that. Of course, I've always thought that Kate was very beautiful but I've never dared to say so in front of you.'

Graham was so startled that all he could think of was to say: 'I hadn't noticed that you ever hesitated to say what you wanted to me, Harry.'

Harry looked at him in bewilderment, and: 'You see, owing, I suppose, to my sense of inferiority, I never imagined that you thought anything of us. I have always been very grateful to you for your kindness and for all that I have learned from

you, and I've hoped that perhaps you've got something back
from us, if only in the way of copy for your writing.'

Graham felt in a false, unreal position, as though the whole
relationship with Harry had been exposed as worth only so
much paper on which it might be written down, and he had
an impatient wish to scrap it, brush it aside, be done with it
at once, rid himself of Harry as of any other disturbing phantom
of his imagining. What was unforgivable was that it was Harry
who had revealed this arbitrariness of their friendship, not he
himself in his own good time. But all he said for the moment
was – rather stiffly: 'On the contrary, I admire your wife
greatly and I am devoted to Gray, my godson.' He hoped that
Harry was at least vulnerable enough still to notice that he
had been omitted from his list.

'Perhaps while I'm away, then, you'll occasionally go and
see Kate and Gray,' Harry said timidly, aware that he might
be asking too much. He hesitated, then he added: 'I hope I
haven't offended you by assuming that you weren't interested
in Kate. But (you know what women are) she's always rather
taken the line that you were more interested in me.'

'Waiter, the bill, please,' said Graham.

When he had paid the bill, getting up, he said: 'Perhaps
when you're away I'll have the opportunity of showing
Kathleen that I am interested in her.'

Harry looked inquiringly at him. Then gripping the sides
of the table, and getting up also, he said: 'Tell me truthfully,
Gray, what would you do if you were in my place?'

Graham was now standing up. He left his place and stood
on the other side of the table where his face was in the light.
He stood there in complete silence staring, across the table
he had just left, out of the window. On the other side of the
road was a tall grey concrete building – incongruous for Soho
– which was a hospital. Then Graham turned back into the
room as though to address the whole restaurant. The light
from the window shone on one side of his face, golden on his
moustache, transparent green on one eye; it showed very
clearly the bitter line from nostril to edge of mouth. He was

turning over in his mind a great many ideas as though on his tongue in his mouth which left him with a sour not altogether unpleasing (because his own) taste. There was a malign movement of his mouth, after which he said very quietly and calmly addressing now the whole restaurant: 'I think you should follow your own heart.'

4

Then back. Back to the country whose cities, from above in the centre of the air, appeared as exposed cells in a beehive from which the roof had been torn off, the honey robbed, and the walls of the cells shattered. Back in the country where destruction was an industry and where the inhabitants were sad miners, wandering amongst the slag heaps formed from ruins of their destroyed homes and digging for a little warmth in tunnels and cellars. Back to the country where trees and fields and surviving villages, farms and animals shocked the eye with their pure colours like a reproach insensitive as life in the presence of death, spreading its sights and sounds and foods before the eyes of the living.

Back to the country where the whips had been torn from the hands of the tyrants, where the prisoners had been liberated into camps and sheds into which they were herded like animals; where the tyrants were either hanged or else they mingled indiscriminately with the inhabitants who were slaves; and where the new masters, the occupiers, were embarrassed warders in a hospital for patients afflicted with a fatal disease, warders living a different life on a different diet, yet secretly afraid of the surrounding infection, and furtively playing all the games of corruption which they knew to be symptoms of the disease itself. Back to the country where the most valued pleasure was to fill the lungs with a few breaths of tobacco smoke, and where ten minutes of this pleasure, in its little paper wrapping, became the basis of currency with which everything could be bought or sold – office, love, drink, property.

Granville had his moment in the aeroplane when, above a pavement of white cloud, in the stone-cold air where the sun lay like a stone of fire, revolving and shooting arrows of gold upon the serene flat wings of the aeroplane, and below upon the sparkling pavement; he had his moment – lying calmly on steel wings – in this upper air of peace, when he seemed at the apex of his own life as at the apex of a triangle, and he looked down each side of this triangle where one great line reached back to London and the other forward to the camp where the princess lived in a small hut.

The difference was revealed, laid bare now as with a knife. There, in London, Kate stood in the kitchen, sitting room and garden (all mingled into one in his vision) with the flame-like auburn hair and the little veins of fire spread through all her body. The house where they lived became more than ever what it was – one of a hundred such of the same pattern on an out-of-date building estate – and yet now it was rich and dear and warm, lived in and breathed over, like one orange in a heap of oranges in a small shop window. And his wife was a bird in her nest and the nest was lined with warm feathers and there was a sense of young life all round her, of Gray and of other children to be born. His eyes, looking down from the centre of the empyrean (pressing all round him with dense blue packed with crystals of light) his eyes hovered round the pillar of her neck, chose their resting place in the nape just beneath where the hair begins and falls down over the shoulders. His mind, suddenly eloquent, as though his whole chest swarmed with words, broke forth into a warm flow of language like words heard in a dream, serene elucidations, passionate explanations, renewed declarations. Yet when he woke for an instant from this trance and tried to shape these words into sentences which he might put into a letter, he could not remember what they were.

At the foot of the other earthwards-dropping line of the triangle was Moura in her hut amongst the ruins. Oh, the difference was that his whole being flew in and out of hers, that she understood the burden of his knowledge, that he laid down a great sack of unutterable realization of terrible things at her door, that there in her misery and holiness, in his misery and holiness, he rested.

In the first picture, everything was thick, external, impenetrable, opaque. Work was done, children were born, there was a great richness and a great price had to be paid for this richness. Home and happiness and indifference to everyone else were the gods which Kate worshipped, and this was right and healthy and natural in a way. But could he accept it? Could he offer the presents and the whole-hearted devotion and the oblivion of everything except a bright warm hearth, at this shrine? Could he undertake the greatest sacrifice of all, the sacrifice which health and nature and sanity and happiness required – but what was this sacrifice? What was the ultimate reality demanded of him? It was at this point always that his mind shied, but now in the aeroplane in the great white-suffused blue dome of light, the truth, the truth – or what was from here the illusion of the truth – brushed him with its wing. The greatest sacrifice required of him – yes, this is it – was that he should deny what he had seen, that he should turn his back on the ruins, the suffering, that he should sacrifice his own sympathy for the suffering of others, that he should be selfish, forget the anguish, that he should forever reholster and repair the dilapidated furniture of worn happiness of two people living for their family and shutting out the world.

But with Moura everything was transparent. The terrible reality corroding the world was received into her heart like the seven swords in the heart of the Virgin Mary, this reality was her, and there at the very hub of the world's anguish (situated geographically a few miles from Frankfurt) it was transformed into their love. Nothing was required of him except the acceptance of their truth at the pure, vacant, motionless centre – a prison – the centre . . .

And now the pictures disappeared and like a knife a thought, only a thought, was left: the realization that in life, human relationships, in relations between men and women, there are no simple solutions of black and white. What is selfish may have an aspect where it is unselfish and unselfishness may be selfish. The sacrifice which Kate required of him was natural and inevitable, and from this point of view it was selfish of him to refuse to be selfish. The unselfishness of his knowledge of the agony of the world was a form of selfishness in his life ... But words like 'selfish', 'duty', and so on, dispersed the vision and filled his mind with generalizing thoughts and ideas.

He wondered vaguely now whether, all over the world, there were people who shared his thoughts. Thousands of people, apparently happy and satisfied, doing their work and their duties as citizens and members of their families, who had a hollow in the centre of their lives, a cave in which those who starved many miles away from them, starved in the centre of their consciousness, in which those who were unjustly condemned cried out for justice, a mass grave in which mutilated bodies unrecognizably shoved away and mangled and buried, nevertheless stank and cried out.

But perhaps this way of thinking was wrong. You walked down a street of a town and you did not suffer because in one basement a man was beating his wife, on the first floor of one house a scoundrel was raping a girl of fifteen, and in an attic a woman was dying of cancer. And what was the difference between walking down a London street where such things might be going on, and flying above the Europe of camps and prisons, of wars and mass graves and of a thousand injustices?

An hour later, as he stood outside the door of the Camp Commandant's office, his thoughts had become far more practical. They were that he mustn't let the Commandant know his one obsessive wish to see Moura.

The Camp Commandant was a tall American, a New Englander, with a deal of greying hair, an aquiline nose and the kind, strong, intense eyes of an English Victorian statesman. When Granville entered his office he was standing over his table-desk with hands leaning slightly on it. His head was drooped, he was a little round-shouldered, and he had the appearance of a great grey eagle who had descended amongst these ruins, having seen all things, in order to be kind and stern.

He had a slow, sententious way of talking, more English in accent than that of the English. 'Glad to see you, Harry,' he said. 'We've all missed you here. I'm sorry you're not staying longer. It's a damned nuisance, in fact, that we aren't in a position to persuade you to take a job here. We need people like you.'

Harry sighed.

Then the telephone bell rang. Wingfield took up the receiver and Granville heard a conversation about a concert which was to be held at the camp that evening. So at all events he would see Moura then. 'There's a concert this evening in the great barn,' said Wingfield, putting down the receiver. 'All the staff hope that you'll be coming to it.'

'I'd like to very much. But meanwhile, can I do anything this afternoon to help?'

'There's nothing much that you can do. Things are pretty well organized just at present. But if it interests you to do so, you can come along with me to Wiesbaden. I have a parcel to give to someone there.' He walked across to a cupboard from which he took a parcel. 'Recently I've been having these things posted out to me from the States and I've been distributing them amongst some of the worst cases here.' As they left the hut and walked across a muddy yard of flattened mud to the car, he went on: 'At first, I couldn't make up my mind whether to distribute my parcels amongst a great many people, giving them only one or two each, or whether to concentrate on a few people and try really to improve their conditions efficaciously.'

'And what did you decide?'

'I decided to be unjust, and favour a few. I find that social inequality always produces a certain number of results, whereas if there is complete justice everyone almost starves. I dare say that is why I'm not a Communist,' he said slowly with a curious sententiousness which underlined both his seriousness and his humour.

They drove through the haggard remnants of Frankfurt or rather the remnants of an anonymous, expressionless large town. For everything which made Frankfurt Frankfurt and gave it a unique personal character had disappeared and all that was left were just remains of buildings and a few buildings without character which now had acquired prominence simply by survival. There were many streets turned into discarded shattered boxes with a few beams, columns and girders standing like gallows. Harry was familiar with all this, as one knows a story which has been told again and again. He had never understood the destruction. The thoughts and the lives of the people living among these ruins were a mystery to him; and yet they were a mystery which he knew very well, a mystery at the back of his mind always, whether he was awake or asleep. There was a moment now when these streets of broken houses seemed realer to him than the memory of the bright, complacent street where he lived at home with its dismal yet cocky houses all apparently pressed from the same stucco mould. He seemed to press his eyes into this scene, as though the shattered town were part of his own flesh, as a hand caresses secretly a disfiguring scar.

They came to the crossroads where there was a wide space beyond them as all the buildings had been destroyed. There were only very low, jagged, tooth-edges of wall, heaps of rubble, blowing dust in the hard white photographic sunlight. Men and women, drably but neatly dressed, with flesh and in clothes which seemed to have no colour, were threading their ways along paths amongst the ruins. They trickled from ruined block to ruined block over the crossroads, completely absorbed in their journeyings, taking no notice of the traffic, as though they belonged to a different world from that of the requisitioned cars and the jeeps, an insect world, an ant-world, occupied in carrying small bits of wood from place to place.

From their car, Wingfield and Granville watched these

people as though they were removed from them by a great distance. When they nearly ran a man over and he stood a yard from the windscreen, it still seemed as though his proximity were an illusion produced perhaps by looking at him from a mile away through a telescope. Without seeming to notice them, he just managed to move across their vision without being thrust under their wheels.

'The Jerries have no traffic sense,' said Granville.

He made this remark as one might say: 'It's a fine day.' It was a safe, banal observation of the Occupation Forces which a hundred officers made to each other every day when driving through their particular Zone, just as in Nuremberg, the Occupying Forces greet each other with the question: 'How many people have you executed today?'

'I wonder why that is?'

'I don't know.'

'I have an idea it might be because they don't care a damn whether they're run over or not,' said Wingfield drily.

Now they left the town and drove through poignant green countryside where trees insistently were undamaged trees and grass was grass. There were villages where fruit trees with over-arching laden boughs, wistaria and roses, seemed to hang over and between the over-sweet houses, filtering the sunlight with their nets. The cream-coloured houses were intensely intact. The very old beams and the gabled roofs shocked Granville as though with a vulgar newness in comparison with the destroyed town of Frankfurt which, in a few seconds, had been transformed into a place infinitely ancient, receding into abysses, flying backwards through time to join the craters of the moon.

Granville was very tired after the journey. His mind seemed driven along parallel lines of thought, as the car drove along the parallels of the road. 'They could all be knocked down with a feather,' he thought, looking at the houses. 'I have to keep them up with my will.' Paris would fall, London would fall, his home in London with Kate and Gray would be destroyed if he did not sustain them with his will, as Wingfield with his wakeful, watchful mind kept the car from running off the road.

Why had he come to Germany? To see Moura, of course. But this reason now seemed an abstraction, a formula. It was a transparent, vague blur unfocused a hundred yards beyond the windscreen and never getting nearer.

Wiesbaden still retained its characteristics of a town where there were thermal springs, with large gardens, wide streets, a pleasantly dull restfulness, a broad green holiday indulgence and the second-rate. They drove to a narrow street on the outskirts of the town and stopped at a house. 'The parcel is for Dr Grosche who lives here,' said Wingfield. 'Would you like to wait here, or would you care to come in? I warn you it's not very pleasant.'

'I'd like to come in with you.'

Directly they went inside the entrance of the stairway of the house, they were oppressed by a sweet, sickly smell of decay, damp, bugs and illness. As they climbed up the stair-case, Harry noticed that all its walls were severely cracked. Damp spread through the cracks, and in places the walls were stained with patches of green fungus. On each floor there was a little window which looked out on to a garden filled with fruit trees. They climbed up to the fourth floor, where Wingfield knocked at a narrow door. There was no reply. He knocked again and waited. There was still no reply. Wingfield said: 'There must be someone in, because I know Dr Grosche isn't fit to go out.'

Five minutes later, they heard a shuffling in the corridor of the flat. Then the door was opened by a man wearing a long white nightdress and nightcap. In this garb he looked as though he did not belong to this century at all, but to another time, an age of eighteenth-century prints of the decrepit husband in nightshirt and with candle in hand stumbling into the bedroom where the young wife lies sprawling on the bed with a satin-attired young beau. He was very thin and his stomach protruded from out this long slab-like thinness so that it jutted like a ledge, making his nightdress protrude abruptly. His face was pale and lined with long, mostly vertical lines which fixed it in one final expression from which it did not trouble now to alter.

He said in a voice which showed not the slightest interest in them, 'My mother is out. That is why I did not answer. I have been sleeping.'

He made a deprecatory gesture, pointing with his arm like a signpost into the flat: 'You may come in if you like but you see there is only my mother's room and my room here, and my mother has been out all day trying to get one or two things, and she has not had time to tidy my room, I cannot do so myself either, so it is all in a terrible mess.'

'We should like to come in for a few minutes only, Dr Grosche. We certainly don't want to bother you in any way,' said Wingfield, 'but we would like to see how you are.'

Dr Grosche led them into a small room where there was no furniture except a bed, a table, two chairs and a wicker contraption in front of the window, devised to hold a flower pot containing a plant. He walked over to the bed and half-reclined on it. They sat on the two chairs. His face seemed almost the same soiled texture as the sheets. The room was filled with an asphyxiating odour, the mixture of sweet sickliness as had penetrated even to the front door of the house, but here it was much stronger.

'Won't you lie down properly, Dr Grosche?' Wingfield asked. 'I'm sure you can't be comfortable lying that way.'

Without saying anything, Dr Grosche pushed back the sheets and got into the bed.

Wingfield put the parcel which he held in his hands on the table, and said: 'A few things for you, Herr Doktor.'

Dr Grosche looked across the room at the table with the parcel. His face did not change its expression, he made not the slightest sign of acknowledgment.

Nor did Wingfield seem to expect any thanks. 'Do you get insulin?' he asked.

'I get some, but it is only 30 per cent of what I require for my condition. The Occupying Forces explain that they do not have insulin for the use of German civilians.'

'And what about food?'

'We get our rations, but of course it isn't possible to get the kind of bread required for *diabetiker*, or any of the other foods which are specially required.'

Dr Grosche answered all these questions in a flat, tired, expressionless voice. There was not the slightest note of criticism or irony in his remarks about the Occupying Forces, there was not the least self-pity either. If his tone of voice suggested anything it was that the situation was as he described it, he knew quite well that nothing whatever could be done, and he would rather not tire himself with providing unnecessary information.

After ten minutes, Wingfield got up and they left the flat. On their way downstairs, he mentioned that Dr Grosche had once been a brilliant lawyer, that he had never been a member of the Nazi Party and that there was nothing against him. As they descended the stairs the odour of the flat became less penetrating, and then at last they were in the bright sunlit street again, with the fruit trees showing in the gardens and the birds singing.

On the pavement, Wingfield stood still for a moment breathing in the air. His fine profile showed against the background of the street, his eyes looked away, into the distance. In this small posture, he looked like a very beautiful photograph of a very distinguished citizen.

'Well,' he said, 'we might just have a cup of tea at the local Officers' Mess and then we should be getting back, or we shall be late for the concert.'

Tea was excellent. There was butter and cakes and fruit salad with cream. At the next table some officers were agreeing very loudly that despite all the disadvantages of being in Germany you could make more for yourself on the European Black Market than at home.

It was getting dark as they drove back along the wide motor road to Frankfurt. Wingfield drove steadily, altering his speed little between thirty-five and forty kilometres an hour, registered on the dial of their requisitioned German Opal. Apart from the road billowing up like dirty snow in their headlights nothing showed except large signs posted every hundred yards or so along the side of the road stating that the speed limit was not to be exceeded. These brusque announcements alternated with a terse, one-line poem squeezed out of the soul of American civilization:

DRIVE SLOWLY DEATH IS SO PERMANENT

A few miles farther along the road, Granville heard the roar of a jeep behind them. Dazzling lights reflected on their windscreen through the window at the back of their Opal. Then there were bursts of noise like backfiring. Suddenly the jeep passed them, crossed in front of them and stopped dead. Wingfield drew up just in time to avoid running into this jeep. Two American police jumped out of the jeep and advanced, covering them with their revolvers. One of these men was pasty-faced and very round, like a ball, the other was pasty-faced and very thin, as if cut out of cardboard.

'Hi, you, stop!' said the round one.

'What the hell do you think you're doing?' asked the cardboard one.

'We opened both our guns on to you. Didn't you hear us?' asked the round one.

'The damned things are empty, both of them. Why didn't you stop?' asked the cardboard one.

'I didn't hear anything,' said Wingfield. 'Did you?' he asked Granville.

Granville said: 'I saw their lights, and I thought I heard backfiring. I'm not used to being fired at.'

'I'm commandant of the DP camp ten miles along the road,' said Wingfield.

'We don't care who you are,' said the round MP.

The other one said in his thin, mean, nasal voice: 'We took you for bloody krauts. Anyway, you was speeding.'

'And you're coming along with us,' said the round one.

185

The round one got into Wingfield's car, the cardboard one took Granville into the jeep. He started up the motor and then stopped it again, getting into gear five times before he managed to move away. Every time the jeep stopped with a jerk the thin MP seemed to think he was making himself ridiculous and he cursed Granville violently in order to re-assert himself. Granville said nothing, but munched some chocolate of which he had a bar in his pocket. 'That's torn it,' he thought. 'I shan't see her tonight. We'll spend tonight in jug.'

At last the jeep got away with a jerk and they arrived at great speed at a police camp. This was a large compound surrounded by high wire railings. It consisted of a system of low concrete buildings connecting with each other by corridors. Wingfield and his round MP were waiting for them in a bare room with concrete walls, one naked electric bulb hanging down from the ceiling, a trestle table, a stove and half a dozen chairs. There were several other MPs standing in the room. They said nothing but loudly munched sausages or chewed gum.

As they came in, the cardboard MP who accompanied Granville called across to the round one, who was waiting there with Wingfield, a dramatic appeal to the good sense of all the other MPs in the room: 'See, we emptied both our guns at them, didn't we?' and with a dramatic gesture he flung his gun down on the trestle table, removed the cartridge container from it and passed this round the room. With grunts and expressions of amazement each MP handled it, shook it, turned it over, as though he had never seen such a thing as an empty container before. Then the last one threw it on the table beside the gun, without a word. Impressed by this success, the round MP now produced his empty container and the same thing happened.

In a corner of the room, seated on a stool, a young German woman accompanied by a little boy about three years old was silently weeping. Granville looked at her, understood that she must wait for a very long time for some very slow process of justice. And suddenly he felt reassured. He was English, accompanied by an American officer, and he would not have to wait as long as she.

Meanwhile the round MP and the cardboard one had gone out of the room to find someone whom they referred to as 'the captain'. After a few minutes they returned with a pink-faced, pale-eyed officer.

'Who are you, sir?' he asked Wingfield.

Wingfield explained who he was.

'Wasn't you speeding? Wasn't you going more than forty-five?' the round MP called across the room to him, where he was standing in front of the table, behind which the police officer had stationed himself.

'As an American officer, speaking to another American officer, I don't think it would be in order for me to answer the interruptions of your men,' said Wingfield.

'Quite right. You hold off,' said the captain to the round MP. 'Now, sir, please tell me what you have to say,' to Wingfield.

'We were not going more than forty. Our *requisitioned Opal car* isn't capable of going more than forty. You can try it out yourself.'

There was a silence produced by the emphasis with which Wingfield had said, '*requisitioned Opal car*'.

'When we passed them wasn't we going at least fifty-five?' the round MP called across to the cardboard one.

'I should say we was. Say, captain, if what he says is true, I'll bite my arse,' said the cardboard one in his nasal, fluty voice.

'You mind your language, my man,' said the captain.

'We emptied both our guns on them,' said the round one.

'That reminds me,' said Wingfield, stooping tall-ly over the table. 'I wish, as an officer, to lodge a complaint at being fired on by your men.'

The officer, who had been gazing abstractedly at the ceiling in order to avoid the necessity of having to rebuke his men for their interruptions, now suddenly appeared to wake up: 'You wish to lodge a complaint, do you? All right, here's some paper.'

Wingfield wrote out his complaint and handed it to the officer. The whole room had become silent.

The captain now became very dignified. He took the paper and made a little speech, as though he were responding to a toast he had received: 'Gentlemen, as far as I'm concerned, I'm sorry this ever happened. I'd like to draw your attention to the fact' – looking at the paper – 'that you admit you were exceeding the speed limit. Now we have to be very careful. This is an extremely dangerous bit of road and there have been too many deaths on it. There are plenty of signs on the way telling you not to speed. I hope that this is the last that we shall hear of this incident, gentlemen, goodnight.'

They went back to the car. Wingfield drove on in silence at exactly the same speed as before. He did not speak for twenty minutes and then all he said was: 'I suppose I'll have to get those markings painted up if I want to avoid trouble.'

'What do you mean?'

'Well, I don't think those boys would have bothered to stop us when we were going forty if they hadn't thought we were Germans travelling in a German automobile. I guess they were pretty surprised when they found out who we were and they just put the best face they could on the situation.'

'But what would have happened if we'd been German?'

'They'd have taken the car, that's all.'

'And what would have happened to us?'

Wingfield did not answer at once. Then he said: 'Well, they'd emptied both their guns on us, hadn't they? Perhaps that would have been a little awkward for them. But I dare say they still had some ammunition.' A moment later he added: 'It seems to me that the Germans won't miss the SS while they've got those thugs hanging around.'

Granville was not listening. For the first time that day he really felt sure that he was going to see Moura. Now she was no longer an unresolved blur in his mind, forever remaining a hundred yards removed from the headlights. He could visualize her, he could hear her voice. He felt sure that he would see her that evening.

When they returned, Wingfield took him to his own lodgings which were in a workman's house at the edge of the camp. There were two barely furnished bedrooms, a bathroom with a geyser, and a sitting room with a chocolate-coloured carpet, a leather-covered sofa, a leather-covered armchair, two tables and a bookcase. It was like the study of an unmarried school-master. In the bookcase were a few books belonging to Wingfield mixed with sentimental literature left by the German family from whom the house had been requisitioned: books on flowers, on youth, on womanhood, on mountains and on the New Germany.

Wingfield, with his grave, formal politeness, welcomed Granville once more. He said: 'You don't realize how good it is to see you, in circumstances in which we can talk. The most difficult part of the life here is that there is no one to talk to.'

'But the princess?' asked Granville. 'Can't you talk to the princess?'

Wingfield looked at him without a flicker and then he said slowly: 'She is a remarkable woman, an excellent interpreter, and devoted to her mother and sister. Whether she is a princess is another matter. I don't know whether it interests you, and I don't want to disillusion you, but you have to realize that when people are deprived of every motive for existing, sometimes they cling to the picture of a past which is at least partly only fantasy.'

'I don't care a damn whether or not she's a princess. The fact that you think well of her is worth much more to me. I only used the name because it's the one by which she's known at the camp. When shall I see her?'

'After the concert.'

'She won't be at the concert then?'

'No. Her mother is ill in the hospital ward. I thought that you might like to see Moura, so I arranged that she should visit her mother this afternoon during the concert and that her sister should do so later tonight.'

'Do you mind then if I don't sleep here tonight?'

Wingfield smiled his grey, kind smile, the smile of a puritan who has lost faith in puritanism. 'I think I can trust you.'

'What does that mean?'

'Well, I should say it means that as far as she's concerned I think you can do no wrong.'

'And what is wrong?'

'I mean that between her and you nothing which you did would be wrong.'

Granville's eyes filled with tears. The sensation, which he had had so often recently, was now clearer and stronger than ever, the sensation that he had come a very long journey to a place where all previous values of his life were transformed. He could not tell whether this was a place of happiness or of unhappiness: perhaps it was of both. Sometimes (as just now) he felt a light-headedness which made him wonder whether he was ill. It even occurred to him that now he could choose willingly to die. After all, recently many thousands of people had died prematurely, and perhaps some of them had had a sense of choice before death, as he was having now. A strangeness had come not just into his life but, he felt, into all life, which he was not yet accustomed to. On this great height where he now seemed to live he felt there were other people as isolated as he – and yet together in isolation. And now, looking at Wingfield, he wondered whether he might not be one of these.

All through the concert a sense of joy grew stronger in him. The concert was held in a bare empty barn, containing a few benches on the floor which was simply the earth, a rough stage, and an empty space behind, where those of the audience who could not find places on the benches stood. When Granville came in with Wingfield, members of the staff who recognized him came and shook him warmly by the hand. Some of the DPs whom he knew made a vague movement of response towards him, as animals respond with a movement of their bodies and an expression in their eyes, to a person they know. But the audience was far more interested in the 'show' which they awaited with a tense, electric impatience as for a spectacle of pure magic, instead of an improvised concert arranged by themselves. The curtain at last went up and a series of short performances followed on each other in quick succession. First of all, an opening chorus of girls who sang with the metallic harshness of music sung through combs; then a knock-about play in which a clown with a large red nose and torn, baggy trousers was the obscene hero; then a duet caricaturing in ballad form the progress of Hitler's generals through Europe; then a tall languid lady in sweeping ballroom dress danced a Viennese solo; she was followed by six male Russian dancers who kicked and squatted out their peasant dances with crude conviction; and the concert ended with a hymn to Stalin. The whole performance was rough and threadbare, and yet at the end it made a single impression. This ragged caravanserai of lost people acted out here on the stage their passion, their humour, their hatred, their romantic dreams of luxury, their yearning for freedom, their love. At the end, when the curtain fell, the whole grim, desolate place had reaffirmed its life, and there at its centre Granville was ready to reaffirm his love.

5

He opened the door of the hut, and without either of them saying a word, he held her in his arms. The bones of his body, clothed in flesh and moulding of muscles, was a strong frame which held her and she was the masterpiece of which it was the assured, golden, humble, fitting setting.

Everything was right. This miraculous feeling of rightness triumphed like the masterpiece on the canvas, like the sound on an instrument played with such skill that it expressed the whole of a mind. The wretched hut, enclosed in the wire-surrounded, soldier-guarded camp, amongst the hacked and mudded early autumn fields, was violin, paper or canvas, on which the life was written which reaches outside life, outside every dwelling.

They could say nothing. Their fears were fused with their laughter, their moment justified itself before eternity, their innocence pleaded to their past and their future and was acquitted, they locked within their arms the joy to which all the freedoms and comforts and riches, fought for by the poor and pampering the spoiled, and which they lacked, can only lead or amount to nothing. There was no betrayal or dishonour, they took nothing from anyone because they required nothing but this moment, and within this moment, in which they knew each other and said nothing, they could love others.

When at last they let each other go, they still said nothing. They looked at each other through eyes blinded with tears at eyes blinded with tears, beyond each other's features and the discoloration of each other's eyes into what seemed the very pure sources of their feeling for each other. It was as though they had the power to look beyond each other's features and then beyond even the situation of their lives, beyond every dramatization of their moment, to a place where they needed and found each other ceaselessly and with completeness.

'I have found you again,' he said at last. 'It has been a very long journey, and in some ways today has been the longest day of all.'

She looked steadily at him. He saw her looking with her rather light eyes in the pale oval face surrounded by the very black hair. 'I have been waiting for you.'

'I have missed you. Have you missed me?'

'Yes. Though I never felt I was without you.'

She laid her arms on his shoulders so that her hands held the back of his head. The stillness, the woodenness of his rather insipidly handsome features touched her profoundly. And now a vibrating sensibility quivered on his eyes and his mouth as he turned his head in her arms. It was as though this head, head of a salesman, a shop-walker, a clerk, an air raid warden, an unemployed, a literary card, a petty arriviste, was filled with one predominating thought which emitted wonderful flashes stirring in the eyes and transforming the features, rays which spread out into the darkness.

'I can't explain it,' he said.

'You cannot explain what?'

'I can't explain why there are no barriers between us. With everyone else I feel a kind of obligation to do something, to offer something, to act, to say something, to be something that I'm not, to respond, to make myself acceptable. With you I feel absolute peace. I simply have to rest and wait. What we are we are as one person with one mind and one body. Yet this mind and this body don't have the shabbiness, the disgrace, of my own separate mind and body. It was as though I were transformed within a new mind and body through you and that then I became for the first time really and wholly my own self.'

'It has always been like that, from the very first moment, has it not?'

She didn't speak English inaccurately but she introduced little shades of emphasis and question into it which were not exactly English. Her voice showed now that she had indeed shared his peace.

'Yes,' he said, 'but I wondered whether it would happen again. I was afraid to come into this room – especially after this afternoon.'

'What happened this afternoon?'

'Nothing. I went in the car with Wingfield and we went to visit a man dying of diabetes. By the way he told me that your mother was ill. How is she?'

'It is nothing. She will soon be better.'

He moved about the little hut in which there were the three **bunks** one on top of the other, a table, an electric light, and a few bundles of clothes. Involuntarily he pressed his right hand – he had washed his hands twice at Wingfield's – to his face and he smelled again that smell of sickly-sweet urine.

He began talking once more. 'Everything seemed bound to obstruct and divide us. Or if not to obstruct us exactly, at any rate to make us feel so insignificant that even our love might seem of no importance in relation to the tremendous, awful outside things. Here you are in this camp, in this country, where everything is so full of horror that I could easily imagine this afternoon being terrified by each other's flesh and even by the idea that we were human beings. This afternoon everything human seemed horrible.'

She looked at him and said: 'It is more difficult for you.'

'Why more difficult for me?'

'Well,' she spoke rather slowly, 'because you see things. I'm shut up here and I have only my thoughts and my sister and mother to love. After all it's a very simple life in which I can devote myself to an idea.'

'What is the idea?'

'That nothing can divide us.'

He leaned back against the bunks. She had been standing beside the little window of the hut. Now she came over to him until they were quite close to each other. The thought crossed his mind unpleasantly that in a sense it was indeed easier for her than for him to be single-minded. She looked into his eyes again but did not touch him when she repeated again: 'You see, nothing can divide us.'

He put his arms round her again and hid once more in the light and darkness and silence of their physical embrace. After a few seconds he moved restlessly about the shed again. Then he said, rather guiltily: 'All the same there is my family, there is the fact that I no longer have a job here, there are all the problems and difficulties of getting here, which may still get more difficult, and even when we are both in the same place, there is the difficulty that we can hardly ever even meet in a room alone. Excuse my going on about these practical things, but they are important.'

She put her arms on his shoulders and held the back of his head again: 'Dear friend, it is more difficult for you to have faith than for me. Nothing can divide us.'

'Oh, no, it's you who have a bloody time, you who are a prisoner, not me!'

The crudeness of his words carried him away. He felt alone, faithless, misunderstanding her already, after only these few minutes.

'I'm here all the time, dear Harry. What do you imagine I think about when you're not here?'

'I don't imagine. I'm sure,' he said with a sudden return of their vision. 'When I'm alone away from you at night, I only have to shut my eyes, to find my whole mind flooded with your voice. And my voice seems to mingle with yours. It is like a river of our two voices flowing through the night. And it's impossible for me to believe that you aren't really part of those thoughts. It's all somehow connected with the fact that when we are together there are no barriers, no explanations, no difficulties.'

'It isn't exactly that there are no difficulties,' she said gently. 'But our difficulties belong to both of us. Don't you see that all your difficulties are mine? Don't you see that our being separated is something which I carry about with me here and that you carry about with you over there? How can I explain? But don't you see that it's so much the burden of both of us, shared by both of us, within a life that belongs to both of us, that we can't ever be divided?'

She appeared to him with a strength which almost frightened him. She was on the verge of shouting, trying to make herself understood in the difficult medium of the foreign language. 'Don't you see that our being separated is something which unites us? What would divide us would be the fear of either that the other didn't care.'

'It seems to me,' he answered, 'that if we're inseparable we ought to be together. I'll do whatever's possible, however difficult it is. I'll take some kind of job in Germany – it doesn't matter what – I'll obtain a divorce and I'll follow you wherever you are until we can get married somewhere, somehow. After all, if you and your mother and your sister could get all the way from Russia back to here, I can also make my way to be where you are. If we wait and be patient, finally all this inhuman system of things will break down, and we'll be able to get married.'

'I think the way you talk is very English, very American, very much what is called capitalist and democratic,' she said. The slightest accent of scorn in her voice gave him a sudden feeling of fear, a realization that she was a separate person, foreign to him, having a completely different outlook. 'You seem to think,' she went on, 'that every problem can be solved by paying some money.' She paused. 'I have come to realize that there is only one solution, acceptance.'

'But what way is there of our not being divided?'

She looked at him again for a few seconds in silence. Then she smiled. 'All I meant was that separation cannot divide us,' she repeated.

'But explain again what you mean. I don't understand.' He sat down, bent at last with tiredness, with a feeling that all the effort of the last weeks had at this moment crystallized into one single word: separation.

'I meant that we experienced something that can't leave either of us. To me that is very clear. Meeting you was like touching a friendly and human hand in a night of endless fear and darkness. It's difficult, perhaps, for you to see that as clearly as I do, because you are hardly ever alone, and then you are so kind and friendly,' she said with a slight tremor in her voice, 'no doubt you give a great deal to a great many people and they also give something to you. But I have had time to think.'

He looked at her again, with new eyes, gradually accustoming himself to the realization of her as a separate person, gradually ceasing to be awed by it and beginning to gain strength from it. He noticed the foreignness of her features, with the high cheekbones, the rather narrow chin and the very clear way in which the eyes were cut in the face. He noticed the blouse she was wearing, a white smock-like blouse with long sleeves tied around the wrists, embroidered round the collar and tucked at the waist into her skirt. He felt a sense of doom in the presence of her passion and her devotion. As he went on listening, her voice seemed full of the richness and the hard poverty of a vast populous life unknown to him.

'When we went back to Russia which we had thought we loved so much, our motherland where we were received not with a homecoming but with insults, I realized that I would never have a home, or rather, that my home would be this camp and perhaps other camps, the life which I made for myself with my dear mother and my dear sister. It's true when I met you first – you were so different from anyone else I met in all these years – I couldn't bear the thought of our being separated. I dreamed of a home with you and of a different kind of life in your wonderful country and in a world where people are allowed to respect each other's humanity.

'But when you had gone away, I realized already from your letters that you had also your own home just as much as I had mine. For us to live together would only be spreading the disease of separation from which everyone in this camp suffers, from me to you. It would be just like giving you the cholera of which we have had cases here or like giving your little son the scabies that all these children have. I would be taking you away from your family where you can and must be happy, where you have created something, to make exiles of both of us. And I would be betraying my mother and my sister. It's very difficult for you, my dearest friend, but if you'd lived through those weeks in which we went in the train to Russia, and if you'd experienced that terrible homecoming, and if you'd escaped and wandered with them through that herd of human beings turning all the time into something worse than animals, and if you'd tried to keep alive the little flame of love which burned between us three, you'd realize that one can't just take a train and earn a lot of money and buy a new house and build something new and beautiful on everything old and ugly and difficult which one's betrayed.'

Granville put his head in his hands as he had done three hours before in Wingfield's room.

He realized that she had decided everything without him. He was depressed by a sudden disillusionment. Everything seemed at an end.

She continued gently, brightening: 'And you know now that we can never be separated.'

'But everything you say is to prove that we can and must be separated,' he wailed, childishly almost.

She caressed his bowed head. 'I know it's difficult for you, coming from your world of what you call and what is in some ways freedom, because you don't quite realize how single, how solitary, how unique, how absolute –'

Once more she could not express herself. She tried to put it in another way. 'Perhaps if we lived in another kind of world where we had many friends, many relationships, lots of money, we could afford this destruction of your faith and my faith, to make something new for each other. But don't you see, my darling, we have so very little, so very very little. What we have we can never lose. For us three there will never be another human being who can take your place.'

'*For us three!*' he repeated bitterly. 'You talk as if you were all three in love with me. But it's you I love, and only you.'

She smiled: 'But I feel that in you I love three people.'

'What three people?'

'Yourself, your wife and your little son, Gray isn't he called? I think often of him, of you, of them, of all of you. And I think you love me partly because you know I think like that. I am true to your decision, and you also, in your heart, are true to mine.'

'But tonight we have each other.' He suddenly caught hold of her, laid his head against her, covered her eyes, her forehead, her mouth with kisses, rapaciously, again like a child, a child who wants to eat his mother. He shut out his sight of everything distant with the close view of her features, he buried his mind in the scent of her hair.

Then exhausted, almost sobbing, he sat down again in the same position with his head in his hands which smelt still of the odour of the diabetic.

'Darling,' she said, 'I want to ask you a question. Please do not be angry with me for asking it. Please.'

'What is it?'

'You must answer me truthfully. I want to know. Do you love your wife and your little son less because you love me?'

He looked up, wonderingly. This question occurred to him for the first time, and he frowned trying to answer it. Then he said slowly: 'Our life is much more difficult, but I love them more. Much more, even.'

'Can you tell me why?'

'It seems a funny reason to offer, but I suppose in the first place it is because I couldn't find a reason not to love Kate. The result of my relationship with you was that I hunted about in my mind for reasons to criticize her. I tried to use you as that reason. You provided me with little reasons, of course –'

'What reasons?'

'For example, this one –'

He held up his hand and showed the watch attached to his wrist with the nickel bracelet.

'– this bracelet which she bought for the watch you gave me. It seems to me to be in rather bad taste, or perhaps I only imagine that because the watch was your present. Most of my reasons for criticizing her were her lack of taste, her middle-class attitude towards things such as Gray's upbringing, certain things in which I compared her with you. Of course, when I made such comparisons you always gained. You are educated, generous, quite apart from the fact that your origin is aristocratic –'

He looked up at her as he said this.

'Go on,' she said.

'But then I found that these criticisms were really rather superficial. The outside things for which I criticized her led always on to something else, something touching, something piteous, something loving, something pure, something really and entirely hers, which was not vulgar at all. The criticism simply rebounded and became a criticism of myself. It was I who was vulgar and mean to criticize her for the way her actions expressed themselves and not for the motives behind the actions. For that motive was not vulgar at all.'

He looked again at the shining nickel wrist-bracelet laid around the skin of his wrist.

'What was the motive then?'

'The same as the one which, without any vulgarity or indirectness, you have shown to me. Love, I suppose you would call it. But when I looked for an excuse to get away from her, I found in her the same quality as I find in you.'

There was a long silence.

'Tell me some more,' she said.

'Of course, there were scenes, there was jealousy on her side. And on my side there was not just my love for you – which might really never had led to any misunderstanding – but there was guilt and snobbery. Sometimes I feel that if no element of these had entered in, nothing about us would ever have worried her. The motive in her which was hidden under her upbringing could accept us. In fact, in spite of all the difficulties, there was one side of her and me which did begin to lead a life in which we accepted everything and developed a new and deep tenderness towards each other.'

'Then you understand when I say we can never be separated?'

'But there is also the side where everything is different. The side where there is loneliness and desperation and jealousy and awful scenes.'

'Yes,' she said. 'I know that it is difficult for you and she who are out there in the world. Here we live a life like nuns in a cell. So long as I have my mother and my sister to live for, and my love for you, I am not unhappy.'

He looked at her with the acceptance at last dawning within him. He said wonderingly: 'Sometimes I think that the difference between her and us, perhaps also between your mother and sister and us, is that you and I are much older: though, that is strange as I am so childish in some ways. I mean that we have been a very long journey beyond everyone else, and met alone.'

She said in a voice of dreams: 'It is because our knowledge of each other is timeless. It is outside all these considerations which cause what you call "the awful scenes". Don't you see that we must keep it outside, invisible?'

'Yes.'

'There is one thing – it is really not very important,' she said rather rapidly, 'which I ought to explain to you. I am not a princess. All that was wrong.'

'Oh!'

'You see, when we were children, my mother always told us that we were descended from one of the families entitled to a royal name. My sister and I, we used to laugh at her, but secretly we believed it and perhaps we were rather pleased. As we got older, when I became a teacher and a translator, of course, all that had no importance and we never thought about it. But just quite recently, when we lost everything, our position and our home, and we were sent to Germany to work for the Nazis, our name became important. It is extraordinary how if one has nothing one invents or exaggerates something, in order to cling just to a memory, a past, a name. Besides which, I had always accepted what my mother said as true. Formerly, I would have thought it mad for my mother to invent a title which to me was so unimportant. But later on, for the first time in my life I was happy to have some rumour attached to me which gave me some distinction. Then, after our return to Russia, when we had been liberated, as it is called, the distinction became more important than ever before. I had a moment of bitterness when I was glad to feel myself different from those soldiers, those officials . . . Then, when you came, I was glad to have something to offer you.'

'It doesn't matter at all! Please don't talk about this!' he cried out violently.

'Well, now, during my mother's illness she has told us that it was all a lie. You know she is an old woman, a person whose life was before the revolution, when she was a governess in a princely family. So she has never accepted the new order of things. She invented this myth that she was related to the family with whom she lived and worked. They are all dead except her, and it was easy to invent a lie. But it is all a lie. It is all a lie.'

'For me you will always be the princess.'

She looked at him steadily, and said quietly: 'You are good.'

'Oh, no, I am not good,' he exclaimed with the same violence. 'I am not good at all. Who am I but an adventurer, a snob, an arriviste?'

'You are good,' she said.

'Then it's very easy to be good,' he went on bitterly. 'A little decency, a little humanity, a little kindness, a refusal to exploit other people's misery, and today one is an angel in Europe. But if I was really good –'

'If you were really good?'

'I don't know what would happen. I don't know at all!'

They waited a moment, then he went on: 'I'll tell you something quite absurd, which I couldn't tell anyone else. You know I read a great deal nowadays? Well, one day I read that a priest said to the author of a book I was reading that very few people, he believed, were sent to Hell, because at the very moment before dying almost everyone repented completely of his past and in that second chose the good and not the bad. Well – I know it sounds absurd – but when I read that it seemed to me that in that moment I would almost certainly be damned – I don't know why – but I felt sure of it. So, you see, I don't think I'm good.'

She looked at him with a flooding of her eyes in which everything they had said and felt was summed up: 'You are good,' she said again, softly.

She stood up and came towards him. She held out her arms as in a great cross. And this cross they joyfully accepted.

6

Harry Granville watched particularly Kate's hair which now, since she had come to Paris, she did in quite a different way. The bun was gone. Instead, the hair was combed down from the top of her head and drawn back behind the ears, where it fell in stiff, moulded curls over the nape of her neck and almost to the shoulders. As she moved along the Quai against a background of Notre Dame and the Louvre in the distance, with the leaves of the trees planted in the ditch along the side of the river polished to the autumnal colours of half a dozen different metals in the middle distance, he thought pleasurably that this style of hair set against such a background looked like the photographs of girls in fashion magazines.

There was something absurd, stilted and endearing about this coiffeur with its stylized imitation of carelessness. Her head moved through the air like a flower-pot overflowing with curling ferns.

Harry had been delayed for some days in Frankfurt by new regulations and formalities introduced for leaving the American Zone of Germany. In order to make as little change as possible in Kate's plans (which involved sending Gray on a month's visit to Kate's mother in Kent), Graham Ballard offered to take her to Paris.

So that when Harry arrived, Kate had already been a week in Paris. She had a room in a small hotel in the Rue de l'Université, one of these roads lying between the Quai Voltaire along the banks of the Seine and the Boulevard Saint Germain running parallel with it. It was a street containing many such little hotels, some of them cheap and almost squalid, others more expensive and occupied chiefly by foreigners. All these hotels, cheap or dear, had an air of being run by concierges who sat behind indoor glass windows in the hotel halls, in their little wallpapered rooms full of velvet, sofas, and armchairs. In addition to all the hotels in the Rue Jacob, there were the *laiteries, épiceries, fruitiers*, one or two restaurants and a bar. The rows of houses on either side of the street were tall and all in the same style, built in stone. All the streets between the river and the Boulevard running parallel to them had the same predominating characteristics: hotels and food shops; whereas the streets running transversely, down to the river from the Boulevard, were characterized predominantly by art shops, book shops, antique dealers and small jewellers.

This little stretch of Paris is not the most beautiful part of the city, but perhaps it is the most seductive. The streets are sufficiently narrow for one scarcely to be able to see the houses from a distance where one can judge them as architecture. Yet more than any other part of Paris this has an atmosphere which crowds in and floods one from every side. The shops, with everything they contain, have an air of permanence, as though nothing were ever sold, ever removed from their windows, and yet everything has a freshness which prevents it from becoming oppressive. The prints and paintings in the windows seem always the same Daumiers, the same anonymous 'Old Masters', the books in the *librairies* always the same editions, and even the *artichauts* in the windows of the *fruitiers* seem always to have gleamed with the same shiny olive colour in the shadow beyond the glass. And the little parcel of narrow streets between the river and the Boulevard is saved from dullness and monotony, by the presence below of the great gleaming pewter brooch of the Seine, above by the parallel of the broad sweeping Boulevard.

The miracle for Harry was the extent to which Kate took all this in. She liked walking about the *quartier*, she remarked even that the sky was like a roof over the Rue de l'Université, where it pressed over the grey-gold stone. She liked going into the cafés; she walked along the Seine. A new world had been partly opened to her, a world which was not just the tourist's view of Paris, but also a conversion from a narrow point of view which distinguishes between things clean and dirty, sensible and silly, useful and useless, to a wider enjoyment.

This change was largely due to the influence of Graham. During the past week, he had made Kate 'do' everything. They had been to the Louvre, up the Eiffel Tower, on top of the Arc de Triomphe, to the Champs Élysées, to Napoleon's Tomb, to Nôtre Dame, to the Sainte Chapelle and to Versailles. They had taken coffee at Weber's and the Café de la Paix (Ballard avoided going with Kate to the Flore) and they had eaten meals at restaurants where Kate had become a little tipsy on red wine.

To Harry who (although he did not realize it) was essentially as incapable of acquiring 'culture' as Kate, the transformation of his wife was a mystery which he explained to himself in general terms of, the influence of Graham Ballard, beauty, 'getting away from home' and 'taking herself out of herself'. In his way, he participated when he was with her, in indefinable moments of vision. For instance he went with her on top of the Arc de Triomphe (even though Kate had 'done' this once with Graham already); and from there they perceived how a great city can be thought of as a series of spokes emanating from a hub. The city lay all around them like a wheel with the houses blocked in like crystals along the wide spokes which were the avenues, and with the great sky drawing spires into its ceiling and dropping flakes of light along the avenues and between the roofs. For Harry and Kate such moments of liberation, when their eyes as it were entered into the design of the city were few, compared with the hours of eye-and-foot-aching weariness in the galleries and the churches. Yet even when they understood little or nothing, they were brought together in humility, respect and wonder.

For him, most of the wonder was not Paris at all, but Kate. He attributed this also not to Paris but to Graham. The pleasure of seeing her happy was so great that he felt no jealousy. He even encouraged her to leave him and continue to see things with Graham, saying that he would 'do' the things that they had 'done' already, by himself.

Their gradual approach to each other helped them both. Visibly she was becoming cured of the misery of the past months, and he was being cured in a different way by watching her learning and to appreciate her from a distance, from outside. Moreover he wished to be alone for an eccentric reason which seemed impossible to explain. He wished to walk along the streets and then to touch the buildings. He would run his fingers along the line of a wall, to feel that it was there. Not only walls, either; but also a hoarding along one of the broader streets leading down to the Seine from the Boulevard Saint Germain needed, as it seemed, to be touched

by his hand. All those images of bottles, underclothes, per-
fumes, naked girls, announcements of theatres, photographs
of Maurice Thorez and of General de Gaulle, political mani-
festos, carried on a hoarding, appeared so unreal to him
that he needed to touch them to make sure that they were
there.

He had come from a world where he had seen things back
to front and inside out: the entrails of houses poured into
streets; tubing, pipes, central heating systems torn out of great
buildings like the intestines of a horse gored by a bull; the
gilded woodwork and metalwork of altars and crucifixes torn
from its back and frame and showing an inside-out of dirty
putty. Now the persistent existence of things swimming as it
seemed against the destructive stream of time, the outsideness
of things held in place and not showing their seaminess of
splinters and rough edges and rubble, amazed him and filled
him with a nervous foreboding. It seemed more remarkable
to him now that a city could remain a city than that it could
become a heap of ruins. All these countless tons of stone and
girders and wood and concrete, could be reduced as he knew
to a core of rubble within a few seconds, and it was fallacious
to assume that because they had gone on enduring for centuries that they would continue to exist. In our day the mountains
of rubble have become symbols of a truth, for they are an
opened centre, an opened wound, around which millions of
lives move. Destruction has become a faith, a philosophy, a
system which criticizes, by the palpable fact of its feasibility,
a world still standing wrapped in the massive centennial sham
of the illusion that because it exists and has existed it can go
on existing.

These thoughts were only felt vaguely by him, but nevertheless they explained his mood. Kate, like Paris, and with and
in Paris, had her 'outsideness', for example, her hair done in
its new style. And just as he wanted tenderly to touch the
walls of the city, so he wanted tenderly to touch her and simply
to know that she was there. And why was he not jealous? he
went on wondering, as they walked along the bank of the

Seine. Because Kate's happiness was his cure. It was more important to him that she should be happy than that she should be his: perhaps that was it. But another explanation immediately occurred to him: that it was impossible to be jealous of Graham.

Now they stood still, looking over the parapet of the Quai to the lower pavement at the edge of the river, where the fishers eternally stood fishing as they had done through the centuries, like minor poets in a long tradition of minor poets content to write poems about the smaller flowers, minor fishermen content for ever to catch the smallest fish and to pass the centuries in this way.

But he was not thinking about the fishermen when he said: 'Once you told me that Graham took more interest in me than in you. But now it seems to be the other way round.'

'You're like those fishermen, fishing for compliments, Harry,' she answered, looking at the fishermen, one of whom had now caught a minnow. She moved her eyes from the fishermen to the mudgreen water for ever weaving and un-weaving the reflection of the grey bridge. 'You know quite well, Harry, that Graham isn't in the least interested in me. He only likes to have me round when he's with Jules.'

'Who is Jules?'

She flushed. Indeed, she always went red very easily, he thought. 'Haven't I spoken to you about Jules Sanet?'

'Not that I noticed.'

She flushed a still deeper colour when she said: 'Well, you'll meet him tonight when we eat at that little restaurant which Graham likes so much.'

'But tell me who he is.'

'He's a medical student who's doing some kind of research into the throat, nose and mouth. He's extremely clever and he's very poor. He comes of a working-class family and was discovered by one of the professors here who has paid for his training.'

'And now he's been discovered by Graham, I suppose,' laughed Harry.

'He's very nice. He's very nice indeed. And he doesn't let Graham get away with things. He quarrels with him the whole time about Communism. He's a Communist, only not a bit like your friends, Len and Rex.'

'You seem to know him very well.'

'Yes, it's funny, isn't it, how you get to know people when you're abroad.'

'Does he speak English?'

'That's what's so queer, Harry, he doesn't speak a word.' She started laughing infectiously, in a way that touched him profoundly, making him feel closer to her than before in Paris. 'What will make you laugh, though, is that I speak quite a bit of French. You know, not much, but I can make myself understood. I can really make anyone understand anything I want them to.'

Harry started laughing also. 'How on earth did you learn?'

'You'll tease me, but when you were away, I did a bit of studying from an Easy French Course, and then I listened to conversation lessons on the wireless. I can assure you I worked very hard when you were away. Oh Harry, I did work hard.'

Harry put his arm round her waist.

They had crossed the bridge and they were looking at the shop windows in the Rue de Rivoli. She went into one of the shops and he waited for her outside. He waited among the crowd of shop-gazers and passersby for half an hour and then went into the shop to look for her. She was not there. He realized that she must have left the shop by a door different from the one by which she had entered it and then lost him in the crowd.

He went back to the hotel bedroom and lay down on the bed, waiting for her to return. In that half hour, he quietly began to feel the chill, the fear, the solitude, the darkness, which would be his life without her. The shade of the room made him see, as through a dark glass, the light on her dress, on her hair, on her face when she flushed.

She came quickly into the room and stood looking at him. She was out of breath.

'Oh, I thought I had lost you!' she exclaimed.

'Oh, I thought I had lost *you*, Kate!'

She came over to him, and whilst he was still lying on the bed, he put his arms round her and drew her down to him.

'I have found you,' he said.

She kissed his forehead: 'And I have found you.'

Two hours later they got up and went to the restaurant. It was in a little square just off the Boulevard Saint Germain. There was a monument and plane trees in the middle of the square, seeming almost to fill it, it was so small. The restaurant had a door opening directly on to the street, a low ceiling, and two dining rooms, one leading into the other. At the side of the room which the restaurant door opened into, there was a long table on which dishes were laid. In the farther room there was a hatch leading into the kitchen. The younger brother of the chef, who worked as his assistant, seemed always to be leaning on his elbow looking into the restaurant through this hatch. He wore a white chef's cap and had a sallow, almost ivory skin. On shelves around both rooms there were bottles of wine and of liqueurs. The half-dozen or so tables in each room were rough as tables in a workers' restaurant and covered with sheets of paper instead of table-cloths.

Kate did not understand why Graham liked this restaurant so much, though she had got so she could say she 'didn't mind' the food.

Kate and Harry walked through the first room of the restaurant to the second room where they saw firstly the chef's brother leaning through his hatch and wearing his white cap, and then Graham seated at a table almost opposite him, with a young man. Jules Sanet had thick, fair, wavy hair combed back, a long but not over-thin face with a forehead prematurely lined, and with a nose whose point was drawn down over his upper lip. It was a face too full of character and experience to be called good-looking, and yet the combination of such emphatic lines and features with an air of extreme youthfulness was oddly attractive. The expression had that combination of cleverness, irony and softness which is dramatic in some Italian faces. But he was too fair for an Italian. Physically he was strong and well-built and yet there was something mournful and tired which one noticed at once in his way of holding his body. He was a young man who carried the load of the years of war.

They walked over to this table, and Jules gave a quick glance at Kate with a narrowing of his eyes which was an intimate smile of recognition. Graham was looking remarkably at ease. Speaking French, knowing Madame, the proprietress, ordering the right wine and food, arguing with Jules, he bristled and purred with content. He translated the menu to Kate, then consulted with Jules about the meal. 'Our friend here,' he said, alluding to Jules, 'doesn't approve of this restaurant, but he agrees that since we are here the best way to help the Revolution is to produce a crisis by eating as much as possible.' The meal he ordered was not really enterprising, but it was good. He ordered firstly ham, to be followed by chicken, Camembert cheese and a cake – a kind of *mille feuilles* with coffee cream – which was the speciality of Madame. They drank a red *vin ordinaire*.

Graham was in a strong position. Being the only intermediary between Kate and Harry and Jules, he could direct the whole conversation. He started off by explaining Harry to Jules:

'Jules, my friend Harry Granville has just come from the American Zone of Germany. Doubtless he can provide you with information about the condition of the German workers.'

Jules' attentive, smiling face, held a little on one side, seemed weighted down with an uneven burden of irony which emphasized the lines on the left side of his forehead.

'Oh, *les Allemands*,' he said. 'How you English love the Germans.'

'But as an internationalist, aren't you interested in the

German workers?' asked Harry, who so far was able to under-stand the conversation.

Jules laughed, and what he next said had to be translated: 'You English are always discussing the problems and the welfare of Germany. You send food to the poor German miners in the Ruhr, while the poor French workers almost starve.'

Harry became nervous and officious, falling into the role which he vaguely felt Graham required of him. 'I think that the reason for our concern with Germany is that we happen to be an Occupying Power, so we have large numbers of people there concerned with administering it, which they try to do well. If we occupied France, we would doubtless send food to the French miners.'

Translating this according to his Anglo-French, Graham found in it a cleverness which Harry certainly hadn't intended: '*Mon ami dit que si les Français veuillent que nous, les Anglais, nous interessions dans les conditions françaises autant que les conditions allemandes, il faut que nous occupions la France.*'

Jules laughed and shrugged his shoulders. '*Quand même,*' he said, '*quand même . . .*'

'He says that our preoccupation with Germany is nonetheless a trifle exaggerated, and he suspects that our motives are imperialist, capitalist, and far from disinterested,' Graham interpreted happily.

'Why does he think we aren't disinterested?'

Jules shrugged again, and Graham translated: 'Our interests are in German coal, German industry, and the enlistment of the German population in the Western Zone, in order to conduct an imperialist and capitalist war against Russia. I think that is your nuance, isn't it?' he asked Jules and repeated the reply which he had invented for him in French.

Jules laughed again: 'Thou hast said.'

Harry said warmly: 'I'm not more sympathetic to Germans than to other people; in fact less so. It is simply a matter of what I feel when I am in the presence of human beings who are miserable. The fact that they are Germans doesn't stop them from being human beings.'

'Doesn't it?' said Jules. 'When the Germans occupied our country and other countries they didn't treat us as human beings. They didn't even claim that they themselves were human. They said that they were super-human and that the rest of us were sub-human. Now that they are suffering I still have more sympathy for the suffering of the French and of the other peoples who were occupied by Germany.'

'But when one has seen a case such as this –' Harry began, and he told the story of his visit to the diabetic Dr Grosche. Ballard translated the story with only a few emendations. Jules listened attentively. Then he said: 'Of course, as the story is told to me, it doesn't mean very much. Doubtless if I'd been there, I would have been rather upset, but all the same, on principle, I am indifferent.'

'Then you really mean to say, Jules,' Graham said with amusement, 'that this story of the poor Boche dying of a disease, which could be cured by a few kind foreigners with a little insulin, doesn't stir feelings of sympathy in you?'

'It might if I had been there,' said Jules. 'But even so I could tell you worse stories of the miners in France in the mines where I worked. And they were suffering from conditions not provided just by an occupying power, but by the long tradition of their own fellow-countrymen, French capitalists. But of course capitalism is the same in every country.'

This gave Graham his opening. Leaning forward eagerly, he said: 'You mean to say that you believe things like this only happen in the capitalist countries? If that is really what you think, it is high time that you met Harry. Harry has been working in a camp for Displaced Persons, and there he has had a certain experience of the treatment given to Russians by Russians. I want Harry to tell you some of his experiences.'

Jules looked up from the chicken which they were now eating and then looked at Harry with a hesitant expression.

All were aware of the incongruousness of making dinner-time conversation about people who were desperate and starving, and yet they went on enjoying their meal, because there was no reason not to do so. Harry accepted this situation unhappily, Jules ironically. Kate objected to the conversation which she saw was being arranged by Graham for his own reasons, and she took no part in it. Ballard, on principle, was fundamentally indifferent to the suffering which was being discussed. Indeed he regarded the agony of Europe with the same kind of distaste as he did an over-publicized sentimental book. He justified this refusal to sympathize with enormous quantities of human misery by a quotation from Rilke – a writer whose sensitivity is beyond dispute. Rilke said in one of his letters that 'the whole possibility of human suffering has already been, and is being, experienced'. Graham deduced from this that sensitive people like Rilke and himself had their nerves sufficiently jarred by the troubles that came their way for them to ignore large and vulgar appeals from starving populations and murdered soldiers for their sympathy. Rilke and Ballard knew all about human suffering anyway.

Harry said to Jules: 'I ought to explain that my evidence is based on statements made by the Displaced Persons themselves. Of course, it is very difficult, impossible even, to corroborate this evidence. But I know personally the people who have made these statements and I have confidence in them.'

'Tell Jules in particular the story about the princess which you told me,' Graham said, looking at Kate, who remained silent.

Harry told the story of the princess. Then he told two other stories about Displaced Persons, also based on statements made to him at the Camp.

'How do you think this tenderness of the Russians to their compatriots compares with our crude capitalist methods?' Graham asked Jules.

'When your forces invaded the continent, didn't they find themselves opposed by armies which included in their ranks not only Germans, but also Russians, Poles, and even, alas, Frenchmen?'

Harry interrupted: 'But I must say that I don't believe for one moment that any of these DPs whose story I have told were collaborators or Fascists.'

'Who knows?' said Jules. He spread out his hands, and his voice acquired a note of richness, of charity, of profound acceptance. 'Who knows? No one says that a poor wretch who is forced by the Germans into fighting for them is a Fascist, but all the same, if he's found out, he's bound to be shot. That is necessary. It is an act of history.'

'But these people didn't fight for the Fascists, I tell you.'

'No, most certainly they didn't. And you know quite well that Harry would never have spoken to them if they had,' said Kate angrily.

For a moment Jules turned to her and looked into her eyes.

'You see!' accused Graham.

Jules gave a laugh, followed by a sigh. His face seemed to fold around the sorrowful lines which had not, as it were, been brought into play that evening. He had entered the familiar night of suffering for his Party. They were all opposed to him. And Harry suddenly felt a profound sympathy for him. The arguments which Ballard used and the ignorance of Kate seemed to him flippant, or if not in themselves flippant, at least made so by the circumstances of the conversation.

'Well, they may not have fought,' Jules said, 'but they may have worked in some ways for the Germans or they may, indeed, even have been misjudged. I'm not criticizing them personally. On the contrary, I'm the last person to reproach a poor devil of a Pole or a Russian for being forced into becoming a slave worker. They are the victims of a human tragedy, that is all. But all the same, it isn't their personal tragedy that counts. From what you yourself report about their attitude, it seems as though when your friend, the princess, got back, she didn't understand the situation in Russia any longer. She didn't understand that her compatriots had to take extraordinary measures to protect themselves against the infiltration of Nazi sympathizers, returning into the country among the army of slave workers. Perhaps, since she was an aristocrat, her failure was very understandable; but it is nevertheless dangerous to the Revolution.

'Here in France we are more kind, it is true, but the result is that while we make an example of a few outstanding collaborators and perhaps also a few little ones, we are infested by a great many who succeed in escaping through the meshes of the net which is laid for them. Who else but they have enormous quantities of French money printed by the Germans which is now causing inflation? Who else but they organize the Black Market?' Smiling, he put one hand on the table and moved the fingers so that they crawled across it, rat-like. 'Perhaps we in France were right to spare all these rats sooner than risk punishing a few people unjustly. But who can say that it wouldn't have been better for our country to tolerate a few isolated injustices than to tolerate these people being free to do us so much harm?'

'If you think it's right to condemn one innocent person in order that nine guilty ones may be punished, I disagree with you,' Graham said.

'It depends on the circumstances in which a society finds itself,' said Jules.

'Well, I must say, my dear Jules, that if there's one principle I really would die for, it is that it's better for a hundred guilty people to escape justice than for an innocent one to be punished unjustly,' Graham said in a strained, petulant voice.

They fell silent, and Granville looked at Jules Sanet and then at Ballard. Just then Jules turned to him and smiled with a resignation which seemed to say: 'I did not want to be drawn into this argument, but now that it has begun I must say what I believe.' At the same time he felt irritated with the look on Ballard's face which had changed from malicious amusement to pompousness.

The chicken was taken away and the coffee gateau was brought on. This was a kind of *mille feuilles*, made of the thinnest slices with coffee cream spread between them. Granville took up his fork and lifted the first layer of the cake carefully away from the rest. Then he said, before he had eaten any of the cake: 'I see what Jules means. As a matter of fact, the Russian DP of whom I spoke did interpret for the Germans.'

'You mean the princess?' asked Graham.

'Yes. And in fact she wasn't a princess really, either.'

'Oh, but how can you say that, Harry!' exclaimed Kate. 'You know that she was extremely honourable.'

'Yes, I do know that she was honourable, and also I regard her as a friend. But for the time being I was trying to put aside my personal feelings and to see how, from Jules' point of view, even with a person one completely trusts . . .' he did not finish the sentence.

Jules looked happier. He said to Harry in a friendly voice: 'What we are discussing are, as far as I'm concerned, hypothetical cases. But let us admit by all means the possibility of an occasional injustice. All I say is that one has to see the whole situation. It's no use looking at the injustice to one, or to two, or to three, or to a hundred innocent persons, without relating this to the danger within a given social situation of letting the guilty go unpunished. When one considers –'

'I don't agree at all,' said Kate, red and stupid with anger. 'You are just making excuses for things you know to be wrong, unjust, untrue.'

Jules said nothing.

'You talk in a vague, general way about conditions, Jules,' said Graham, 'as though you admit that under certain hypothetical conditions, injustices might happen, though you don't really believe this. But you must know quite well that there are facts. And the facts are concentration camps, Siberia, thousands of people condemned without trial.'

'Facts,' said Jules. 'Yes, of course there are facts, though I don't know enough either to agree with or dispute what you say. We live in a world in which more facts have been released upon us than in any other period of history. That is part of the difficulty. And I admit that it is this sense of an enormous number of facts, none of which can be considered in isolation, which so impresses me; and perhaps that makes me rather too indifferent to the separate facts which seem so important to you. But I also have in my mind a great many facts –'

'What facts?' asked Kate.

Jules looked at her again with, on his face, that strange expression of striving and compassion. 'What facts? Russia's fight, Russia's losses, Russia's enemies in the capitalist world, Russia's enormous task of recovery from the devastation caused by war. One has to count in all these facts. And even then it isn't just the accumulation of facts that matters, but the way in which one understands them and interprets them into action. It isn't your experience of individual injustice or individual suffering which matters but your ability to relate them to the whole experience of history, and then, beyond that, your ability to change history.'

When this had been translated to him, Harry said slowly: 'I admit that a situation might arise in which we have to accept suffering and misery as inevitable.'

Following up his advantage, Jules became more rhetorical: 'In established social conditions as in England and America, the suffering and misery which have produced the social order remain buried in the foundations and the structure of the system. Very few people bother to tell about the prison camps of a so-called respectable society: those prison camps are slums, conditions in the mines, the armies of unemployed, not to mention the whole past history, now buried deep in the foundations, of women used to drag trucks in factories, child labour, and so on.'

'Oh, but they do bother,' said Graham, 'they are always protesting about social conditions.'

'Well, then, yes, protests are allowed to the extent to which the society feels that it can afford there to be protests. But nevertheless human suffering is built thick as the bricks in a wall within the whole structure of capitalist societies. It is so solidly built in, that one hardly notices it. It's only when the bricks are flying about, as the result of destruction such as the present destruction in Europe, or when the walls are being built, that one notices that each brick is the life of a human being. So that these societies whose foundations are deeply buried and whose walls are so thick that you scarcely hear the voices stifled within them, can afford to scream with indignation at the societies where everything is either going up or being torn to pieces. And I'm afraid that when a revolution is taking place, we have to deafen our ears to some extent to the voices of individuals who are victims of the structure which is being put up, and we have to judge the society by the architecture of that structure itself. Judged in this way, the Communist architects seem to me to be building a juster and more beautiful city of life than the capitalist and imperialist architects did.'

While Jules spoke, Harry, with the crumbling delicate taste and texture of *mille-feuilles* in his mouth, saw Moura buried alive, submerged under statistics, crushed under the massive architecture of a great and ruthless future. He saw, if there were question of her being tried, that she was condemned without question by the mere facts of being where she was and in the situation in which she was. And he understood that she herself, in her Russian way, somehow recognized and accepted this, that, if accused, she would plead guilty.

Suddenly Jules looked tired. His face became a mask on whose forehead lines of sorrow were twisted with lines of irony, like the hemp of a rope.

Now they were drinking coffee. Jules took his cup and drank the whole of it before he spoke again. Then he said: 'Do you imagine that I'm a Communist because I don't feel any concern for the life of individuals? On the contrary, it's because I feel deeply about the lives of the workers. During the war, I myself was forced, under Vichy, to work in the mines. There I saw the conditions in which the miners worked and lived. They can be unemployed for years, they can suffer from illnesses and be uncared for, they can live meaningless lives in slums. I saw how they lived and I saw how the employers collaborated with the Germans. That is why I am a Communist.' He paused, and then he added: 'There is also another reason. During the war, as I say, I worked in the mines. The fact that I did so, should show you that I have every reason to sympathize with those poor slave labourers who are now being punished in other countries because they worked for the Germans. But I think that even if I had to suffer the punishment they suffered, I would be able to understand. It wasn't till the last months of the war that I joined a group of the Resistance. The idea haunts me now that I didn't do enough during the Occupation.'

'So you want to prove to yourself that you are brave by dying on the barricades?' asked Graham.

'I do not want to be too late again.' Then he said sadly: 'But I hate talking about politics. Why do we always do so? It always ends with the same arguments, a circle in which we go round and round.'

'I don't know how the discussion began,' lied Graham, 'but it ends by you accepting a doctrine which would make it impossible for me to publish my books.'

'*Mais* –' said Jules. '*Mais* –' And then they started an argument as to whether the writer should be free to write exactly as he chose.

When Kate and Harry left the restaurant, the argument was still going round in their heads, like shouts and paper bags in the bodies of children who have played too long and stayed up too late at a children's party.

They walked along the Boulevard Saint Germain in silence for some minutes. Then Kate said: 'I get furious with Jules when he talks like that.'

'Why?'

'Fancy you asking "why", Harry! He thinks that it is necessary to deceive and dictate to the people in their own interests. What does he know more about the people than we do?'

'He has worked in the mines, and he thinks they need defending.'

'Graham has been an air raid warden all through the war, and he knows as much about the people as Jules does. We are the people ourselves, and we are quite happy without being defended by Jules.'

Harry said nothing. At last Kate asked: 'What are you thinking?'

'I think it isn't just a question of knowing, but of caring. Graham knows a lot, he understands people, he writes about them, but he doesn't care. The whole of the conversation this evening for him was just an argument which he wanted to win.'

'Then you mean to say that you agree with Jules?'

'Oh, no. I agree with Graham.'

'Then why do you defend Jules' point of view?'

'I don't. But I think that Jules cares. For me there are two kinds of people – those who care and those who don't. I may disagree with those who care, but that isn't the point.'

'What is the point then?'

'Just that they care. When people who care talk, they are talking about people who live in slums, in camps, in factories, in mines under the ground. I think Jules may be wrong, but he knows about those people, and he wants them to be happier. The others, like Graham, are just talking about themselves. Everything that we were talking about this evening was for him a conversational game of chess of which he had put down the pieces on the board, and which he wanted to win.'

'Oh – you are a fool. I haven't any patience with either of you.'

'With Graham and me, you mean?'

'No, with you and Jules.'

They walked on in silence till they reached that corner of the Boulevard where the tower of the Church of Saint Germain des Près rose like a tall and broad dark gate of stone opening into a darker night of stars and religions and past centuries. Here they turned down the road to the right towards the Seine. As they were passing the doors of the church, she said: 'May we go home now, Harry?'

'We're going back now, darling.'

'I mean, to London.'

'Why, I thought you were so happy here. You are getting

so much from it. You seem years younger. You are wonderful in Paris, Kate. I had meant to tell you that before.'

He put his arm round her waist.

'I have been very happy but after that conversation tonight I want to go home.'

'But what was said to upset you?'

'Can't you see that Graham was trying to upset us both? Anyway, I want to see Gray.'

'All right then. We can leave tomorrow. In any case, I shall have to be looking for a proper job.'

A few paces further on, he asked: 'But won't you say goodbye to Jules?'

'Yes. I shall see Jules before we leave.'

'Oh.'

They arrived now at the hotel and went through the entrance hall, where there was the window on to the concierge's room. They went upstairs to their room.

An hour later, Kate was lying in bed, the head of which was drawn up against the inside wall. Only the light over the bed was lit, and Harry stood half in darkness on the opposite side of the room to the bed, looking out of the window. He had a view of the other side of the road and of crowded roofs beyond it. Very few lamps, like holes cut through dark metal into a box filled with light, shone from the street and from windows. The shadow of war had still blotted out most of the lights of Europe. Over the street, through a vague brown veil, the night with all its freedom from the mistakes of time, pressed down against the notoriously female city.

As he looked, that thing happened which had happened on the road leading back from the police camp outside Frankfurt to the camp for Displaced Persons. Suddenly the memory grew defined, he could visualize Moura, and his mind was filled with a swarm of words. Words which were communicated and which yet were not arranged consciously into sentences. It was as though their two minds were a common hive of passionate living words, flying out of each into each. And as iron filings tend towards a shape which is the field of attraction from a magnet, so these words clustered round certain impulses. The strongest impulse of all was the over-whelming sense of an experience completely stated and completely shared, the sense of inseparability sealed by the acceptance of separation. First the words, and then the face, and then the eyes, and then the expression in the eyes, the welcoming smile and the farewell of equally welcoming tears, all this was hers, all this was his, it created a shape like two images superimposed, with their wide dimensions in which he moved from his own thoughts into her thoughts, from her thoughts back into his own.

Everything was understood, everything was theirs, nothing could ever be betrayed or misconceived. The great sacrifice, the great acceptance, was an island on which they met, was eternity in which they met. With the full knowledge of this in his mind, like an overflowing silver grail held in his hands, he turned away from the window where was her East, her prison, her suffering, her loyalty, her love, to this still rich, fruitful, self-sufficient, complacent West lying there on the bed, selfish and yet unselfish also.

As he turned he caught sight of the watch on his wrist, where the wrist-bracelet clutched to its sides. The shadow of sadness, which comes when we remember little signs against which we have futilely complained, passed across his mind.

'Kate, I have something to tell you.'

'What, Harry?' she asked sleepily.

'It was true when I said tonight that Moura wasn't a princess.'

'What was she then?'

'Her mother had told her she was a princess. But she found out later that she wasn't. I thought I should tell you that.'

Suddenly Kate sat up in bed and stared at him. He noticed how strange her eyes were in the bright light against the rings of flesh around them in the eye sockets. For a moment he had an impression of madness.

'How dare you tell me that!'

'Tell you what? What have I said wrong?'